... Telegraph

'Assured, well-paced and ambitious ... an exceptional achievement' *Guardian*

'The current king of the hot young writers is Richard Mason' *The Times*

'Gripping, psychological drama' *Elle*

'An amazing novel ... how Mason could have so much wisdom and insight is baffling ... a literary gem'
San Francisco Examiner

'As a study of the awesome power of first love, it dazzles'
Birmingham Post

'Redolent of early Evelyn Waugh ... Mason displays narrative drive, verbal skill and technical mastery' *Express*

'*The Drowning People* is this summer's *The Secret History* and author Richard Mason is the publishing world's latest Donna Tartt' *Newsday*

'Compelling – nodding to Fitzgerald in both its Gatsby-esque world of beautiful people smoking elegantly and luminous women' *GQ*

'Remarkably assured ... a romantic novel in the du Maurier tradition reproducing the portentous, elegiac tone and slowly revealed secrets of this seductive genre'
Publishers Weekly

Richard Mason was born in South Africa in 1978 to activist parents who settled in England when he was ten. Brought up and educated in Britain he wrote his first novel, *The Drowning People*, before going to Oxford. In the intervening years, Richard finished his degree, then set up an educational charity in memory of his sister Kay. The Kay Mason Foundation provides scholarships to disadvantaged South African children.

www.richard-mason.org
www.kaymasonfoundation.org

By Richard Mason

The Drowning People
The Lighted Rooms
History of a Pleasure Seeker

The Drowning People

Tenth Anniversary Edition

RICHARD MASON

PHOENIX

A PHOENIX PAPERBACK

First published in Great Britain in 1999
by Michael Joseph, Penguin
This paperback edition published in 2011
by Phoenix,
an imprint of Orion Books Ltd,
Orion House, 5 Upper St Martin's Lane,
London WC2H 9EA

An Hachette UK company

1 3 5 7 9 10 8 6 4 2

A CIP catalogue record for this book
is available from the British Library.

ISBN 978-0-7538-2841-0

Typeset by Input Data Services Ltd, Bridgwater, Somerset

Printed and bound in the UK by CPI Mackays, Chatham ME5 8TD

The Orion Publishing Group's policy is to use papers
that are natural, renewable and recyclable products and
made from wood grown in sustainable forests. The logging
and manufacturing processes are expected to conform to
the environmental regulations of the country of origin.

FT
Pbk

www.orionbooks.co.uk

For my parents, Jane and Tony

Foreword

to the Tenth Anniversary Edition

I was eight years old when I started writing my first novel – in Johannesburg, South Africa, in 1986. The country was tearing itself apart. I knew something of this because my parents were involved in anti-Apartheid politics, but life at my school went on in a state of colonial calm. We wore blazers and caps and socks with garters. We learned about England, in English, and read Enid Blyton. In the book I wrote, which was seven pages long, there was no mention of the rioting townships. It was about mice, set in Elizabethan England.

Two years later, my parents emigrated to Britain. In London I found a freedom I hadn't known before. I was able to go to a shop by myself and walk on the streets alone. This was unthinkable for a white child in Johannesburg at the height of Apartheid. I saw buildings that were hundreds of years old – castles and churches in which human dramas had been playing out for centuries. Over the next five years I wrote hundreds of stories and began to read some of the great English novelists: E.M. Forster, Evelyn Waugh, Vita Sackville-West, Virginia Woolf. I was fascinated by the rituals and manners of English life.

As an outsider, I set myself the task of decoding them.

When I got a scholarship at Eton, I found myself in the rarified world that some of my favourite characters had grown up in (Sebastian Flyte, the dissolute hero of *Brideshead Revisited*, is an Old Etonian).

I was sixteen when I decided to write another book and finish it this time. The prospect was daunting but it was also thrilling. I had always known I would be a writer. I felt an urgent need to *start*, to develop the discipline I would need to make enduring books. I wanted to understand how the authors I loved had cast their spells, and the only way to understand magic is to attempt it yourself. I took to getting up an hour earlier than my friends and writing 500 words every morning before chapel.

That summer, I fell in hopeless love with a girl who was six years older than me – a mesmerizing American beauty. We exchanged rapturous letters. Her stepfather was an English aristocrat and I was intrigued by the dissonance between her free spirit and the stuffy world of Earls and Dukes. The experience gave me my material: the dizzying feeling that another person has the power to make you do anything.

Life for an Eton schoolboy in the 1990s had much in common with the atmosphere of the 1890s. We wore tailcoats and stiff, detachable white collars. We doffed imaginary top hats to teachers. We had a school language, impenetrable to outsiders, that had been centuries in the making. On the rare occasions girls were allowed in this hallowed world, they were usually in ball gowns. I was fascinated as only an outsider can be.

I left school with files of manuscript. I got a job updating a two-hundred-year-old travel journal and went to live in Prague. There I found a city whose bars were thronged with Americans writing poetry and film scripts. Life was cheap. People encouraged one another. I took a very deep breath and began.

I had written 2,000-word essays at school. I could imagine writing something of that length. So I wrote 2,000 words every day for 50 days. Sometimes it took two hours. Sometimes it took eighteen. I didn't let myself go to sleep until it was done. The result? A 99,999 word manuscript full of repetitions and digressions and wildly over-coloured language. I knew it was terrible, but I also knew I had done something decisive: I had proved to myself that I had what it took to sit at a desk day after day, turning words into a story.

The summer before I went to Oxford, I sat down to rewrite the entire thing. By now the characters I had created had lives of their own; they were independent of me. Simply by writing thousands of sentences, I had got better at making prose. I borrowed a cottage from some friends and lived by myself in the English countryside, completely consumed in my work. I wanted to have finished something coherent before I went to university. Often I wrote 5,000 words a day. In the process, I learned one of the most important lessons of life: how to be alone.

The night I finished the first readable draft of *The Drowning People*, I made a list of all that the experience had given me. It was a long one. I felt calmer in myself. I was a better writer than I had been the year before (though I still thought I was much better than I really was). I had lived in a European city and written something that looked very much like a novel. I had got over the mesmerizing American beauty.

I decided that night that even if no one else ever read it, I was glad to have written it.

What happened then is that a *lot* of people read it. Within eighteen months I had learned what it's like to win a literary prize voted for by thousands of readers across Europe. I had been savaged by some critics and lauded by others. I had seen my name on the spine of a book and signed thousands of copies on tours and at festivals, in many different languages.

The experience began as a blast but turned brutal. I wanted to write another book but instead my days were filled with TV chat shows and airports. Once the first excitement subsided, I began to dread all the talking I had to do. The stress of growing up creatively in public almost killed my love of writing. That made me want to kill myself and I very nearly did so when I was 25.

But the book also made wonderful things happen. With some of the money I sent four disadvantaged kids in South Africa to some of the country's best schools. A decade later, the Kay Mason Foundation and the readers who support it are helping dozens of children get the educations they deserve. Our scholars now attend the schools once reserved for the white élite, though the garters and caps have gone. All of this was made possible through the generosity of people who have read this book, and the many editors around the world who published it with such passion.

Each time I regretted writing *The Drowning People*, I thought of a family whose lives it had changed for ever. That helped me cope when a certain journalist said

I should have killed myself rather than write it.

Over the years, I came to agree with a lot of the negative criticism. I regretted having started my career so young and chosen a learning curve so steep. I was genuinely surprised by the numbers of people who wrote to me saying it was a book they would remember all their lives. That these letters are still arriving ten years later seems unbelievable, and I am grateful for them.

In my youthful determination to write something as long as the books on my shelf, I repeated myself endlessly in the first edition of *The Drowning People*. I tried out many different ways of saying the same thing and kept every one I liked. This tenth anniversary edition has given me the chance to revisit the text and to make some improvements. My 2,000 words-a-day strategy had left me with far too many words. I cut over 20,000 of them. I also set the remembered events in the 1930s: an idea I had when I was sixteen but didn't attempt because I knew nothing of historical research.

I no longer write a set number of words a day. I don't think that's the best way to make books. But it's the way this book was made – the only way I knew how, then. I hope that those who loved it as it was will forgive the liberties I've taken with it.

Richard Mason,
New York, October 2010

'I leaped headlong into the Sea, and thereby have become better acquainted with the Soundings, the quicksand, & the rocks, than if I had stayed upon the green shore, and piped a silly pipe, and took tea and comfortable advice'

John Keats,
from a letter to J.A. Hessey, 8 October 1818

Prologue

My wife of more than fifty years shot herself yesterday afternoon.

At least that is what the police assume, and I am playing the part of grieving widower with enthusiasm and success. Life with Sarah has schooled me in self-deception, which I find – as she did – to be an excellent training in the deceiving of others.

Of course I know she did nothing of the kind. My wife was far too sane, far too rooted in the present to think of harming herself. In my opinion she never gave a thought to what she had done. She was incapable of guilt.

It was I who killed her.

And my reasons were not those you might expect. We were not unhappily married. Sarah was, until yesterday, an excellent and loving wife. She was conscientious, in some respects, to her core. It's funny, that – how completely contrasting standards can coexist in a person without seeming to trouble them. My wife was, at least outwardly, never anything but dutiful, correct. 'She gave of herself tirelessly in the service of this island and its people' – that's what the chaplain will say of her when the time comes, and he will be right.

Sarah had many virtues, chief amongst which was an

unflinching sense of duty made graceful by serene execution. That is what she will be remembered for. And her serenity was not only for herself: she had a way of making the lives of those around her serene also. It was serenity on her terms, of course, but I would have welcomed it on anybody's terms when I married her, and that has held true over fifty-seven years.

If you knew me, you wouldn't think me at all the murdering type. Indeed, I don't consider myself a violent man and I don't suppose that my having killed Sarah will change that. I have learned my faults over eighty-two years on this earth, and violence – physical, at least – is not amongst them. I killed my wife because justice demanded it, and by killing her I have seen a sort of justice done.

Or have I? Doubts trouble me. My obsession with sin and punishment, laid to rest so imperfectly so long ago, is returning. I find myself wondering what right I had to judge Sarah, and how much more harshly I will be judged for having judged her.

It might not have come to this. I might never have known. But Sarah's inexorable sense of wifely duty exposed her. She was organizing a surprise party for my birthday, not that anything remains a secret for long on this island. I've known something was afoot for a month or more. And I was touched. But I'm particular about parties. I don't like the tenants invited, and I don't like some of Sarah's more fawningly agreeable friends. So it was only natural that I should want to consult a guest list so that by hinting at least I could have made my wishes known.

I chose yesterday to search her desk because my wife was out, supervising the extension to the ticket office. And quite by chance I found the drawer she has kept it in all these years.

Even now, with her dead and nearly buried, the arrogance of it chills me.

I

I am in the little sitting room (in days gone by a dressing room) that connects my bedroom to Sarah's. It is the warmest room in this icy house because it is the smallest.

Very little of the world's clutter bothers me here. This is precisely as I wish it. I don't approve of technology – all those little gadgets, each one more fragile than the last. Constantly breaking. I refuse to have a mobile telephone. With both doors closed and a fire blazing and the radiators on under its pointed Gothic windows, this room is like the world as it once was – before everyone communicated endlessly. It is almost cosy.

There is no desk in here, only a sofa, two chairs, and a small table covered with books. Their inscriptions have long since faded; their givers are dead. They have sat on that table for more than forty years, I should think: a bible, calf-bound, from my mother; my grandfather's *Fowler's*; Donne's love poetry, an old edition of Ella's borrowed long ago. There is a music stand in the corner too, a graduation gift from my parents. From where I sit I can see my initials engraved on its base:

For J. H. F. June 1934.

June 1934; almost sixty years ago. That stand was mine before I ever knew her.

It is important to me that I should have explained myself to myself by the time everyone arrives. The coroner's inquest is set for tomorrow. Then there'll be the funeral and the interment, and the house will be full of people. From this evening there'll be no peace for weeks. If ever I am to put the events of my life in some sort of order I must begin the sifting now.

It is curious, my lack of compunction; not complete, perhaps, but almost. Now that Sarah is gone and I know the truth, I feel very little. Hardly any outright regret. Just a curious, empty, almost eerie, calm: a numbness that shows me, perhaps, quite how much I have learned from her. It strikes me that in some ways I should be glad, though I am not; that the absence of gladness is a striking one, for years ago this knowledge would have freed me. It would have given me what some call a new lease of life. I might have gone back. So it is odd that I should feel nothing now, or at most next to nothing.

The events of those weeks long ago, in which the seeds of it all were sown, have a playlike quality. They belong to a lost time before the war. I know the plot and can empathize with the characters; but the young man of twenty-two who plays such a central part is a stranger to me. He bears little relation (beyond a slight, decreasing, physical similarity) to the image that confronts me as I pass the looking-glass by the fireplace, as I stare at the books, at the music stand, at the waves and the gun-grey sky.

My life seems to have slowed. The present takes up so much time. I see myself as I was at twenty-two. Very young, certain physical gangliness characterizing my movements (I was tall, with long legs). My mouth is thin-lipped, my

6

eyes a pale brown. All are set in a regular oval face with small ears and a slightly pointed chin. Hardly handsome.

I suppose my family life and upbringing must go some way to explaining why my adult life has turned out as it has. My father was a man of deliberate gesture and unshakeable self-belief, a quality I don't think he succeeded in passing on to me. What he did give me is stubbornness. It has sustained me when all else has failed, when arrogance and self-belief have deserted me.

What did my parents want for me? What were they like? It is so difficult to know. We were not rich. We knew rich people, and I suppose that my parents, like any parents, hoped that their son would go far in the world. In *their* world, I should say. They did not look outwards. They never ventured beyond the narrow range of their own ambition. They read *The Times* and voted Conservative and held unchanging and predictable views on the events of the day. Because they were kind they insisted on planning my future on their own terms, with all the tenacity of challenged sincerity.

My own private plan of becoming a concert violinist, flatly and sullenly expressed in my last year at Oxford, met with no favour. My late adolescence was marked by the slow build-up of family tension, its explosive release and subsequent subsidence over long days of icy politeness.

It is ironic that I should end my life in a house like this one, with a titled wife whose family history is as weighty as any to which her parents-in-law could ever have aspired. It is ironic too that, having made so much of following my own lights, I have succeeded ultimately in achieving only what my parents wished for me all along. My musical

7

career died gradually as my marriage progressed. Sarah could not hope to fuel it as Ella had done, nor did she try to; and my reserves of emotion have dwindled unavoidably over time. My talent lay in translating private passion into public performance. As the private passion stopped flowing, dried, and finally turned to a dust so fine that the slightest wind scattered it to nothingness, there was no longer anything to be translated. Technically I remained pre-eminent, for I have always been diligent; but I stopped playing when I could hope for nothing more than mechanical brilliance.

My education was unremarkable. I was clever enough to go to Oxford, which was a great relief to my parents; and until the age of nineteen I made a creditable enough return on their investment in my private education. But at university I was encouraged, by those I knew and the books I read, to cultivate a certain detachment from home life and its aspirations for me, a detachment which made me critical during term-time and superior in the holidays. It was then I turned with real determination to my secret love, the violin. And it was then, comparatively late but in time enough, that I had the leisure and the teaching to discover that I might be really good: good enough to matter. Good enough, certainly, to use my music as the basis for my first serious confrontation with my parents, which raged the whole of the summer of 1934 and centred around my stubborn insistence that I was destined to be a musician.

But I digress. I remember what I looked like at twenty-two; I see the boy's half-smile and his rosy cheeks and the hair tumbling over his forehead into his eyes. But I don't know him at all. I have no empathy with his tastes and only a little with his enthusiasms, surprisingly few of which have remained.

I struggle to remember the people with whom he filled his life, the friendships he made. He was curiously intense, for he was a young man of extremes, inclined to manic sociability and profound gloom by turns. Of course a few stand distinct from the tableau. People like Camilla Boardman, the girl my mother always hoped I would marry: pretty, confident and well connected. More substantial than she liked to seem. But I was insular at twenty-two. Indiscriminately friendly, I shared myself intimately with great discrimination. I still do. Perhaps I had little to share. Life was as it was and I accepted it on its own terms, much in the way I would later accept my marriage to Sarah: with a dogged determination I would not admit to myself.

Unthinking, unseeing, unknowing, I drifted through life until I met Ella. It was she who threw me into the sea of life. And she did it quite unthinkingly, little caring how much good or how much harm she might do. It was in her nature, that wild abandonment, that driving need for experience and explanation. It was she who made me swim, she who pushed me from the safety of the shallows. It was she with whom I floundered, out of my depth. It is to her, and to my memories of her, that I must turn now in seeking to explain what I have done.

In memory she is a small, slight girl, my age, with tousled blonde hair and green eyes that sparkle back at me complicitly, even now. She is in a London park, Hyde Park. It is an early morning in mid-June. Birds sing. Keepers in green overalls are setting up deckchairs. The air is sweet with the scent of newly mown grass. I can hear myself panting.

9

I had been running, up early and out of the house to escape the frost that had settled since my acceptance to the Guildhall. My father had strict views on the desirability of merchant banking. My mother, usually a useful ally, sided with him, saying that no grandchildren of hers would grow up in Hounslow because their father was an impoverished musician. I had begun by reminding them that many musicians make a living. Later more violent things were said. The atmosphere at home had not yet recovered from the latest scene, staged two days previously, and I had no wish for another meal of silent recrimination.

So I went running in the park. I can feel the pulse of the blood beating in my head, see what I wore: a white singlet; school rugby shorts; the socks of my College Boat Club. I can see what Ella wore, too, because I noticed her long before she saw me. She was sitting on a bench, in a black dress that pulled tight against her slender hips. Her eyes were dazed from wakefulness. A pearl necklace (which I have since, on another's neck, come to know well) was in her closed hand. She was a dramatic figure in the half-light of the early morning. I ran past her twice before she noticed me, each time shortening the route by which I doubled back unseen and passed her again. The third time I passed, she looked up at me and her eyes focused. She smiled.

I stopped, panting, a little distance from the bench, regretting my last circuit of the carriage track. When I turned to look at her she was still smiling.

'I'm sure I know those socks,' she said. 'They're College socks, aren't they? There are so many kinds of sock in England.'

'They're the socks of my College Boat Club,' I said with adolescent pride.

Remembering it now, I find it curious to think that the course of my whole life hung on something as inconsequential as my choice of footwear that morning. Ella would not have noticed different socks. Without her remarking on them as she did, I would probably never have known her, because I'd never have found a way of talking to her on my own. In that case I would not be the person I am today; I would not have killed my wife yesterday afternoon; I would not be in this smoky room, trying to keep warm, listening to the waves of the Atlantic crash on the rocks beneath my windows.

I watch myself saunter over to the bench where she is sitting, a question on my lips. Ella remains absolutely motionless, the fine bones of her neck and shoulders showing clearly through her pale skin. She is a little hunched, which contributes to the effect of her fragility. She would look innocent but for the cut of her dress and the stylish parting of her short hair, which a hand pushes back from her eyes occasionally and ineffectually. Getting close, I see that pronounced cheekbones make her face almost gaunt, as do pale blue rings which undercircle her eyes. But the eyes themselves are bright: sharp and green, they move swiftly up and down me.

'Oriel, Oxford, aren't they?' she says.

'How do you know?' I ask, smiling.

There is a pause while the smile on her lips fades and she looks serious once more. Her fingers become conscious of the string of pearls in her left hand, which she puts into a small square bag at her feet with an unconscious gesture of protection.

'I know someone who has them.' 'Who?'

'You wouldn't have known him, unless you're older than you look.'

Since she doesn't seem disposed to say anything further, I question her more closely, telling her that one never knows.

'His name's Charles Stanhope,' she says, uttering a name I do not recognize. I say this and she looks up at me and smiles.

'I'm sorry to have interrupted your run. But I've been sitting out here on this bench for so long I think I'd've stayed here for ever if someone hadn't disturbed me and broken the spell.'

'What spell?'

'The spell of wakeful hours.'

She looks up at me, eyes twinkling. I see her fumble absently in her bag for a cigarette case, watch her light one and follow silver-grey smoke circles upwards to a pale blue sky.

The park is noticeably warmer now. People are trickling in, and as they pass they cannot help but look at us, an odd pair under the trees. I can smell the faint odour of sweet perfume and soap and stale cigarette smoke that surrounds her; hear the click of her lighter flint as she makes a flame; see, as she holds her cigarette, that one of her nails is bitten to the quick.

'Have you been out here all night?'

She nods, with a tightening of pale lips. 'Oh yes. This bench and I are old friends. It's heard more of my secrets than it cares to remember.'

'Has it offered good advice?'

'That's just where benches have the advantage over people. They don't offer advice. They merely sit, listening, reminding you by their immovability that nothing in life is that earth-shattering.' She looks up at me. 'I suppose you think me very melodramatic.'

'Not at all.'

I'm itching to ask her more but am constrained by ... what? By twenty-two years of being told that it is rude to pry. By a fear she is troubled by love for another, whom I instinctively hate.

'You are very polite,' she says eventually, in a tone that sours the compliment.

I nod, and as I do so her words sound in my ears like an accusation. I feel that something is required of me, but what it is I do not know, and as I am not experienced in talking to pretty women I say nothing.

'I wonder if that is your personality or your education,' she goes on. 'This admirable respect you seem to have for my privacy. In your place I'd be curious to know what prompts a fully grown woman to sit up all night in a lonely park and grow garrulous with the larks.'

'Would you tell me if I did ask?' I say quietly.

'Five minutes ago I might have done.' She closes the clasp of her bag with a click. 'But you've cheered me up too much for confidences. And of course this old bench is still just where it was last night, a fine example to us all.' She smiles and pats the worn wood of its seat. 'I feel better now, and less inclined to bore you with my troubles.'

'They wouldn't bore me at all.'

'I'm glad to know you have *some* human curiosity.'

We both laugh again.

'Could I ask your name, at least?'

I'm braver now that I sense she is about to go.

'You could. A name is the least private thing about a person.'

She gets up and leans over to stub out her cigarette on the ground. I see she isn't wearing any shoes and watch her pick up a black silk pair that have been collecting dew under the bench. There is a pause.

'Well, then, what *is* your name?'

'I'm Ella Harcourt,' she says, standing, and offers me her hand.

I shake it.

'And you are?'

'I'm James Farrell.'

'Well, Mr Farrell ...'

There is a slight awkwardness between us, born of an intimacy almost attempted and just missed.

'It was a pleasure,' she says at last. 'Enjoy the rest of your run.'

And she turns to go, barefooted, her shoes in one hand. I see the redness on her heels where the pumps have been chafing her. She walks delicately, but purposefully and quickly. She does not look back. I sense that she knows I am watching her. It is a long time before she is gone completely from my view, because the carriage track is straight and almost empty.

I look after her shrinking form, hearing the thud of my pulse once more, aware of tiny sounds usually lost: the scratch of squirrels' claws on bark; an indignant magpie.

2

At twenty-two one labours under the delusion that one knows everything; at eighty-two, I find to my regret how little I hold certain.

My memory, long disused, is imperfect: that I freely admit. Yet particular images remain with one always. Ella sitting in the park that first morning is one such image; it has returned to me as complete and perfect as if I had observed her yesterday. And it has brought with it a host of others: the sights, sounds and smells that surrounded our second meeting; the weight of the people crushing in on every side; the tinkle of their purposeful laughter; the sweet taste of brandy in champagne.

Rising above it all I hear the cadences of Camilla's voice, the shrill, rapid emphases of her speech, the fantastic elongation of her vowels. 'Daahling!'

For the scene that now flickers into life is Camilla Boardman's twenty-first birthday party. I see Camilla, auburn curls framing her face, leaning on the present table, smiling at no one in particular and fingering the silk bow of a large striped gift. The 'intimate dinner' for 'a few of her closest friends' is over, a dinner to which I have not been invited, and I am arriving with a horde of others to join the crush.

I am tired. I have spent seven long hours practising in a cramped, airless room at the top of my parents' house. An endless trill from a Beethoven violin sonata drums in my head and my fingers twitch involuntarily at the stimulus. A difficult passage of pizzicato, frequently repeated, which joins the trill as I say my first hellos, has made the tips of the fingers on my right hand ache. I want nothing more than to go to bed, to dream of my music in peace, but Fate and my mother have decreed otherwise and sent me, bathed, brushed and faintly bemused, to the birthday party of a highly eligible girl who scares me a little but whom I like and who my parents think is someone 'one should know if one can'.

My fellow guests and I are under the high ceilings of the Boardman drawing room in Cadogan Square. Bewigged, darkly painted gentlemen stare down from the walls.

In remembering the friends of my early twenties Camilla Boardman stands pre-eminent. Her curls were curlier, her dresses tighter, her breasts rounder, her vowels longer, her use of the exclamation mark in conversation more indiscriminate than anybody's I had ever met.

My mother was delighted I knew her and harboured secret hopes of just such a daughter-in-law. I was thoroughly in awe of the great auburn-haired beauty who flung her arms around me on the slightest provocation (a compliment she paid to all the men she knew) and who, that evening, took her present from me with a squeal of delight and dragged me into the centre of the room to 'mingle'.

Hastily, for streams of guests were arriving, Camilla performed introductions.

The faces of the people to whom she introduced me are faded now. Their names have collided, blurred and finally commingled with the names of countless other guests with whom I have spoken for ten minutes and then never seen again. I remember colourful dresses and gleaming white shirt fronts; curls; hopeful sideburns; occasional laborious attempts at dishevelled bohemian chic; monogrammed cufflinks. These were the people my parents had educated me to know and whom it pleased me privately to despise.

I have said that my mind at this age was beginning to take its first tentative steps towards independent thought. These steps, naturally enough, were leading me away from the received ideas on which I had been brought up. I was conscious of looking much like my fellow guests and of making conversation much like theirs, in accents just like their own. This made me wonder, as the trill continued its endless tattoo in my head, if perhaps they were judging me as I was judging them. Perhaps this was a charade for us all.

In my superiority I was not overly hopeful.

I little knew, as I stood at Camilla's party that evening, how soon my eyes were to be opened to an infinitely more varied and correspondingly more dangerous range of moral possibility than that to which I had hitherto been exposed. My mind was too obsessed by its habitual worries about how other people saw me, and I saw them, to see beyond the confines of its own social rebellion, which (because it was only ever stated privately or, very occasionally, in the ugliest of the scenes with my parents) was hardly rebellion at all.

That evening I was preoccupied by the possibility that some amongst my fellow guests might despise me for the same reasons I despised them; might think that I, too, talked only of holidays in the South of France, or of weekends in the country, or of parties in London that I had been to or pretended to have been to. And all the while I talked animatedly of someone's villa in Biarritz, lacking the means, the courage, and perhaps even the inclination to give my criticism voice.

I had, in those days, an ability to think and not to think; to convince myself that I was living when I was not.

I smiled, I drank the cocktails, I discovered that I had been at school with someone's brother and told an amusing (and not altogether kind) anecdote about his time there.

Occasionally the high notes of Camilla's conversation drifted towards me: the string of superlatives with which she greeted the arrival of each guest and gift. Hasty introductions; loud exclamations over dresses. I was nearing the end of anything useful I could say about villas in Biarritz when I felt her nudge my arm and push into the centre of the group a lean, rather pale young man, tall, with floppy blond hair and small hands which belied his great height.

'James, darling,' she said, 'this is an old friend of yours.'

I had never seen the man before in my life. But the complete assurance with which Camilla made this pronouncement encouraged me to think I must have done and I racked my brains for his name.

'Hello,' I said, shaking his hand warmly. It was moist.

'Hello,' he said, a searching look in his eyes too.

It occurred to me that neither of us knew the other. I said so to Camilla.

'But you must, darling. You were at Oxford together. At the same college. Charlie's also an Oriel man.'

'I don't think we were there at the same time.'

'Well then, I'll have to introduce you.' Our hostess groaned, as though the weight of the world had been placed on her shoulders while Atlas went to find himself a champagne cocktail.

'James Farrell, Charlie Stanhope. Charlie Stanhope, James Farrell.'

This was said very quickly, with much waving of her manicured hands. The rest of the group seemed to know Stanhope well, and I had plenty of time to examine him while he submitted to the kisses of the women and the handshakes of the men.

A week had passed since my meeting with Ella Harcourt in the park and I had resigned myself to the fact that I would never see her again. Yet here, unexpectedly, was a link which might take me to her. She had recognized my socks because they were the socks that Charlie Stanhope wore, so she must know him; and if she knew him, he must know her and might, if prevailed upon, introduce me to her. Watching Stanhope's small hands grasping the shoulders of the women he bent to kiss, I felt a rush of barely containable excitement.

When he was completely upright once more, I saw how very tall he was. Taller than I and, if possible, even more gangly, with hair the colour and consistency of straw and pale, watery blue eyes. A large, aquiline nose sat awkwardly on his gentle face. I could tell by the strangled movements of his Adam's apple that his collar was too tight.

I considered my options methodically, delighted by this unexpected opportunity but cautious of it too. I decided to establish the groundwork of acquaintance before probing him for details of his friends; so I did not renew my conversation about French villas but turned instead to Stanhope and began the conversation Camilla had intended us to have.

'How did you find Oxford?'

In an understood progression we moved from college to general university life, his elegant narrative punctuated by well-mannered promptings from me. Stanhope's anecdotes belied their smooth delivery and were, I noticed with relief, unremarkable.

Charlie Stanhope had done all the things expected of an undergraduate enjoying the best days of his life. Conscientiously he had jumped into the river on May Morning and come away with an Upper Second and a Rowing blue. Conscientiously, with the faintly bored good manners of someone overused to such conversations, he described each incident to me. Now he was working at the family bank and living in Fulham. He played tennis at the Hurlingham Club; he went to Ascot on Ladies' Day with his grandmother; he had recently become engaged. He nodded his thanks at my congratulations.

'A wonderful girl,' he said absently. 'But don't say a word. We haven't announced it yet.'

I warmed to Charlie Stanhope as he spoke, with the warmth that comes from dissipated hostility. If Ella Harcourt's troubles involved another man, they did not involve him. Though I knew nothing of her beyond what she had said in the park, and though I had no way of knowing whether I would ever see her again, I knew enough to know that someone as blandly unobjectionable as Charlie Stanhope could have no hold over her. He was not a potential rival and I began to warm towards the innocuous, obviously bored young man who spoke with such practised ease at my side.

With dismissive nonchalance I asked him, once the topics of university and career were exhausted, whether he happened to know anyone by the name of Ella Harcourt.

'I know her well,' he said, looking down at me through white, almost invisible lashes. And since he did not seem disposed to say anything else, I asked him how long he had known her.

'Oh, years.'

'You wouldn't happen to know how I could reach her?'

He raised a quizzical eyebrow at me.

I felt myself about to lie, without quite knowing why.

'I have something of hers. She left it at a party we were at together last week. A bag. I wanted to return it.'

'That's good of you,' he said. 'But why don't you return it now?'

And I followed his glance to the door, through which Ella was just entering.

I can see her quite clearly: standing under the heavy gaze of a patrician Boardman ancestor, smiling at Camilla but not looking at her. She is wearing the dress I first saw her in; or no, it can't be quite the same one, because I can see her shoulders. It is, at any rate, black. It makes her look pale though her cheeks are glowing.

She is shorter than Camilla and not as immediately

21

pretty. I wonder suddenly what the hollow under her collarbone would feel like to touch.

I can see Camilla taking her present and deliberating for a moment over where to put it on the table already over-heaped with gifts. She elects the uppermost summit, where Ella's package balances because it is so small. Its wrapping paper is brown; it is tied with a gold, gauzy bow; I wonder what it is.

'I'll tell her about it, if you like.'

Stanhope's voice, insistent in a way I had not yet heard it, broke through the chill of my excitement. Already he was moving through the crowd in Ella's direction.

'The bag, I mean,' he called out as he disappeared.

Through the crush of people I walked slowly towards Ella, brushing against elbows and shoulders, smiling my apologies. I watched Stanhope tap her on the back and saw her turn, smile and kiss him. I watched them both move out of the flow of arriving guests and altered my course accordingly.

'Good evening, Miss Harcourt,' I said when I was finally standing behind her.

Hearing her name she turned and, seeing me, smiled. It was an awkward smile, its awkwardness expertly concealed.

'Mr Farrell. How unexpected.'

For a moment we looked at each other, she trying to remember precisely what she had said to the stranger she had never thought to see again, I taking in every detail of her delicately boned face: the straight parting of her short, rather boyish blonde hair; the blue rings still under her eyes; the glow of her cheeks; the vividness of her green eyes. It was she who remembered her manners first.

'You remember we talked of Charles Stanhope.'

I nodded, enjoying Stanhope's mystified look. He was standing slightly behind her as she faced me.

'Well, here he is.'

She turned half round to him so that she was standing between us.

'Charlie, I want you to meet a friend of mine, Mr Farrell. He was at Oriel, too, though a little after your time, I think.'

Stanhope smiled at me. 'We know each other already. We've been talking for the last hour, while Your Ladyship has been frizzing her hair.' He gave Ella's shoulders an affectionate tweak. 'Farrell here has one of your possessions to return to you. A bag, which that pretty little head of yours left somewhere last week.'

I met the look of her unflinching eyes, trying not to blush. I saw her expression change from surprise to comprehension, from comprehension to – I thought – a slight mischievousness.

'Yes,' she said eventually, eyes sparkling, 'how silly of me. But you know how forgetful I can be.'

'Don't I just.'

'Would you be a dear and get me some champagne? No brandy in it, please.'

Stanhope nodded and disappeared obligingly. Together we followed his blond head bobbing through the crowds, a good half-foot over everyone else's.

'So, Mr Farrell. We meet again.'

I nodded. 'Thank you for sparing me just then.'

'That's all right. I'm rather flattered, as a matter of fact.

23

And I'm glad to see that you have more audacity than you showed the first time we met.'

'Is lying so audacious?'

'Lying to Charlie Stanhope for information about me is. I applaud you.'

We smiled at each other.

'How are you?'

'Oh, much the same as when I saw you last.'

'Your problem remains'

'You are forthright tonight, aren't you?'

But before I could answer, Stanhope had returned with a glass of champagne for Ella. Beaming, he surveyed the room and we heard a voice begin to sing 'Happy Birthday'. Soon everyone had joined in a spirited chorus and the lights dimmed as a large, white birthday cake with twenty-one candles was rolled in on a trolley.

Camilla, in the middle of the room, blushed becomingly.

'Isn't she miraculous?' whispered Ella in my ear.

3

The arrival and distribution of the birthday cake caused a rumpus and when it had subsided Ella had disappeared. Stanhope I could see in the distance, actively procuring a slice of creamy sponge cake. I found myself talking once more to the girl with the villa in Biarritz, whom I suspected of toying with me in the hope that I would make a play for an invitation. I took a perverse pleasure in doing nothing of the kind.

It was not until I had a slice of birthday cake in my hand and was telling Camilla what a lovely party it was that I saw Ella, standing alone, looking out over the sea of bodies. At whom? For whom? For me, perhaps. It was small encouragement, but it was enough.

I disengaged myself and made my way to the small recess in which she was standing. It was lined with books, never read. In another room, music had started. We stood together for a moment, watching people move off in search of the band. 'I would give a lot to know what's going on in all those minds out there,' Ella said suddenly, not facing me but continuing to stare out at the room, dense with dinner jackets. 'If, of course, there are any. A possibility which the behaviour of their owners makes me doubt.'

This so closely mirrored the spirit of my own thoughts

that I was taken aback. It also confirmed what I had spent this and other evenings worrying about: that I was not alone in my criticism of this world of heavy social ritual and display; that I was not immune from my private censure of others. It was not a comforting thought.

'Everyone has a mind,' I said. 'It's a question of whether they choose to use it or not.'

'I suppose I owe you some sort of explanation for such a piece of arrogance,' she said quietly.

'Only if you care to give it.' Relief at my apparent exclusion from her judgement made me magnanimous.

'Oh, I'm happy to explain myself. God knows, I've had enough practice over the years. You see Mr Farrell, my problem is not the absence of a mind, though sometimes I wish it were. My problem . . .' She paused.

I waited.

'My problem . . .'

'Yes?'

Ella hesitated; and as she did so she seemed to think better of her intended confidence.

'My problem is that I talk too much,' she said at last. 'I shouldn't be telling you any of this. We hardly know each other. I'd better go and find Charlie.' She leaned down to pick up her bag.

'No, don't,' I said quietly; and the unintended urgency in my tone made her stop. 'Don't go. Tell me.'

'You can't honestly be interested in the ramblings of a girl you hardly know.'

'I am. Tell me.'

There was silence.

'Well,' she said at last, looking out of the alcove at the

26

streams of guests beyond it, 'my problem is that I have a mind but choose to use it so infrequently. I'm only ever goaded into self-control when events have long since over-taken me. That's my trouble. I'm rude about the people out there because, I suppose, I want the comfort of knowing I'm not alone in my world of fools.'

'You have at least one fellow citizen in me, if that's any consolation.'

'You're very charming.'

She fumbled in her bag, the same one I had seen a week before. Again I heard the click-click of its clasp; again I watched her take out a cigarette case followed the first silver rings of smoke upwards, though this time they rose to a white ceiling and not to a blue sky streaked with rosy dawn.

'I find myself hoping against hope it's not my fault I've washed up where I have. The currents of people's expectations are strong. Who am I to try to swim against them?'

'You forget I have no idea what your particular island looks like.'

'No you haven't, have you?' Her tone was almost tender. She took another long drag on her cigarette. 'And I won't bore you with its geography. But you'll agree Society is like an ocean?'

'I'm not sure.'

'Look at all the people at this party. All swimming dutifully with the current. They don't need to plan their direction. I wonder how many of them do. I wonder if any of them try to swim by themselves for long.' Another drag on the cigarette. 'People move in schools, like fish. It's safest that way.'

I listened, fascinated by the holistic insouciance with which Ella could express what I could not.

'But does it make them happy?' I asked.

'What?'

'This moving in schools.'

'It must do. If they've never known anything else, they can't want much more than what they have. Ignorance is bliss, sometimes. For some people.'

'And for you?' Secluded in the alcove, I was only half surprised by my boldness.

'Unfortunately I possess just the wrong amount of knowledge. Enough to know how little freedom I have; not quite enough to know what to do about it. I think I should've swum harder, because in the past I've intended to swim for myself. It's just so . . . tiring.' She stubbed out her cigarette with an air of finality.

'Well it's not too late now, whatever you've done. You have your entire life ahead of you.'

'Don't say that. The prospect isn't a particularly appealing one. And in any case . . .'

Her words were drowned by the arrival of Charlie Stanhope. He put his arm around Ella's waist and apologized to me for stealing her.

'Let's dance,' he said.

To my surprise, I saw that Ella allowed herself to be led away without protest.

I stayed where I was, content in the afterglow of her frank green eyes. Languidly, leaning against the books, I watched her retreating form with Stanhope's arm draped awkwardly over her shoulders. Further and further from me she swayed, but through the crowds my eyes remained on the back of her small blonde head, fixed there, for I felt the moment ripe for a sign.

Sure enough, when she reached the far end of the room I was rewarded for my pains with a brief backward glance. But far from wearing the smile I had expected, the face she turned to me was drawn and pale, and it woke me from my reverie and called to mind the glazed, wakeful eyes I had seen in the park.

Before I could move she had been led through the door and was lost in the crush of people who lined the passage beyond it. I heard the music once more and pictured the grace of her swaying body; and as I did so I caught a faint sweet whiff of lemon soap, cigarette smoke and expensive perfume.

I remember how I felt then. Even now, in my armchair by the window, the mere recollection of the speed, the grace, the infinite possibility of that moment is enough to make my breath quicken. It was like the first kick of a powerful drug, inexpertly and incompletely administered; it broke the boundaries of previous sensation and made me determined for more.

Naturally enough, my immediate impulse was to follow her; but I waited, wondering how to effect her recapture more subtly, anxious not to anger her. How was I to know she would welcome my intrusion? I wondered whether she might feel she had overstepped some sort of mark; and I thought delightedly that our conversation had hardly been the talk of strangers, though strangers we were. I wanted to tell her this, to share my excitement; but I lacked a pretext to seek her out and I knew that I must wait for her to find me.

It was then that I saw her bag on the floor at my feet. I leaned down to pick it up, hoping against hope that she had left it on purpose, my thoughts running to all kinds of wild implications. As I straightened with it in my hand I put it quickly, almost furtively, on the shelf by my side in case anyone else should see and rescue it. Deliberately I waited: five minutes, ten, fifteen; relishing the intrigue of it. Then I reached for my prize and, threading my way through the thinning throng, I went to find her.

A quick tour of the room I was in convinced me that she was not in it. Nor was she in the passage. Nor in the room set aside for dancing.

As I heard Camilla laughing, it occurred to me that Ella might have left without saying goodbye and a pang hit me in the throat. Steadying myself, I went again into the passage, now emptying, and checked once more, wading through the first flurries of goodbyes and thanks. She was nowhere to be seen.

With irrational tears pricking my eyes, I looked towards the staircase and began to climb it, for if she had gone without saying goodbye, if all my excitement had been founded on nothing, if that was how she spoke to all the men she knew, I wanted a small dark space in which to be alone. Camilla Boardman was not someone to be faced in any but the most expansive of moods.

So I climbed the wide slope of the Boardman stairs up to a dark landing and up again, past another landing and another, the broad sweep of the staircase getting narrower with each flight.

By now my ascent was slow, cautious, in a dark so black that I had stood on Ella's hand before I even noticed she was there. She was sitting on a step, her back to the banisters. Her cry was sharp and her alarm real.

'Who is it?'

She spoke shrilly, aware for the first time, perhaps, how it might look to be discovered, so high above the party, by one of the Boardman guests.

'Just me,' I whispered.

'You, Mr Farrell? What on earth are you doing here?'

'James, please. I could ask you the same question.'

'James. You could, but you won't. You'll wait for me to tell you, all bound up in that English reserve of yours. But I won't.' This last was almost petulant. 'I don't see what business you have following me around this godforsaken party. It's enough having to bear Charlie—'

I cut her off by pressing her bag into her hand. 'I came to find you and give you this. You left it by the bookcase.'

There was a pause. I heard a click and the rummaging of fingers; then a flame flared up and cast an orange glow briefly over us as the cigarette was lit. I saw, in the short life of its glare, that Ella had been crying.

She saw that I had seen.

'Girls,' she said as the flame went out, by way of explanation. 'Don't take any notice. We all enjoy a few tears. Me more than most.'

There was a pause, as I settled myself two steps below her, my back to the wall. When our eyes grew accustomed to the dark I wanted to be facing her.

'I'm sorry for snapping at you,' she said at last. 'I suppose this is one of those nights. Thank you for bringing this.' She rattled the contents of her bag. 'Don't take any notice of me.'

31

'That's the second time you've said that.'

'Then you should pay attention.' She took a long drag on her cigarette but was careful to blow the smoke away from me. 'I tend to mean what I say.'

'I can imagine.'

'Why are you doing this?'

'What?'

'Why are you still here? Why haven't you gone down-stairs? Isn't it obvious I want to be alone? Thank you again for bringing the bag. In my very weak way I need cigarettes now more than a world of conversation.'

'So you would have me rejoin the fish?'

She leaned towards me. I could make out the dim line of her nose in the darkness.

'No,' she said in a different tone, 'I wouldn't have you rejoin the fish. I'm not sure that a life of swimming with the current would altogether suit you.'

I glowed with pride. There was silence again.

'I agreed with what you said,' I ventured at last.

'With what? My little monologue on oceans and currents?'

'Yes.'

'I'm apt to let my metaphors run away with me a little. Particularly when I'm trying to explain my actions to myself. It was kind of you to have listened.'

'We share many opinions.'

'Do we?'

'Yes.' I waited, sensing that something more was required of me. 'I've spent the whole evening despising myself for being so like all the other fish.'

'I'm sure you're not.'

32

'I hope I'm not. But I dress like them; I speak like them; perhaps I even think like them. My convictions aren't very strong or well formed, at least not by comparison with yours.'

'A lot of good my convictions are doing me *now*,' she said drily.

And through the darkness I could sense that she was smiling.

'The thing is, Mr Farrell. I mean, James. One just has to accept a certain amount of social pressure. The danger comes when you feel yourself giving way to it, when you feel it pulling you under. Control over our own lives should rest with us but in practice it doesn't. We think as your friends do; as our family does. How many people do you know who act outside the boundaries of their own little set? Very few, I think. And even fewer in the school we happen to swim in.'

'Which school is that?'

'You have to ask me? After spending an evening with those people downstairs, you have to ask me?' She was indignant now. 'Money should give you liberty; education should free you. But they don't. Privilege is a chain which binds us to the world of our great-grandparents in a way in which other fish in other schools *aren't* bound. You've no idea,' she finished wryly, 'how high family expectations run if an ancestress happened to seduce Charles II and get a title out of it for her disgruntled husband.'

'Did one of yours?'

'Oh yes. You may think I'm American because I sound it. But that's education. I'm English to the core. Family tradition is so tangled up with who I am that sometimes

33

I wonder how much of me is real. How much of me can I really claim as my own?' She took a last draw on her cigarette. 'Sometimes I think that most of my psyche belongs to the generations who have gone before me. They're the ones who control my life.'

She finished this speech with her cigarette, and I heard the rustle of cardboard as she put the butt in an empty box.

'Filthy habit,' I remarked.

'Isn't it?'

We sat in silence.

'Do you think me very odd, James?' she said at last.

'I think you remarkable.' I almost felt for her hand, but I hesitated too long and the moment passed. 'What does your island look like?'

'My island?'

'The one the tide's washed you up on. Tell me what it looks like. So far you've only said it's uninteresting, though it hardly seems so.'

There was a pause. I could now see the faint outline of Ella's nose and jaw opposite me. When she opened her mouth to speak I saw a tiny flash of white teeth.

'Forget islands,' she said. 'I've done something I shouldn't have done, something I certainly shouldn't be telling you about.'

'Go on.'

'I've allowed events to overtake me and I don't know what to do about it.' She waited, lulled by the darkness, and then moved abruptly. 'I should be going down now,' she said quietly and I heard the rustle of her dress as she got up to leave.

34

'Aren't you going to tell me what you've done?'

'If you really want to know, you haven't long to wait.'

I heard the creak of the banister as she felt for it and began her slow descent of the narrow staircase.

I didn't hold her back. Instead I sat in the dark listening to her cautious retreating footsteps. I heard the door of a bathroom two flights down open and close and open again after a few moments; and I imagined her, radiant once more, walking down the final broad sweep of the staircase into the Boardmans' hall, tranquil above the chaos of dancing and farewells.

I myself was not tranquil. The incomplete feeling of unsatisfied curiosity burned in me. But I waited, as I had waited earlier in the alcove; I waited until I was certain that she had had time to lose herself in the crush of guests. Then I got up and made my way gingerly downwards.

Remembering it now, I see myself on some kind of vantage point, presumably the stairs. In front of me is a narrow hall, black-and-white marble, highly polished. Through a set of double doors, jammed open, I can see the drawing room and the groups of tired, laughing people ranged on its chairs. It is past two. The door to the dancing room is closed but the music is clearly audible nevertheless. It dies suddenly and I hear a raised voice I recognize, cheerful, excited, asking everyone if they wouldn't mind moving into the drawing room, for it has an important announcement to make.

The closed doors open soon after this and I watch a stream of people, flushed with exertion, flood the hall and then the drawing room. Amongst them I see Ella, with

35

Charlie Stanhope still in attendance. Excited ripples of exclamation spread outwards from Camilla Boardman. She is beaming. The party is going fabulously. It is past two and almost nobody who matters has left. She is delighted by the forthcoming announcement: delighted because she has been told all it is to contain in advance. She looks forward tomorrow to telling everyone that she could barely control herself last night but that she knows when a secret is a secret.

I read all these thoughts clearly in her unwrinkled brow and in the victorious gleam of her brown eyes. I see the girl with the villa in Biarritz smiling vacantly, a little drunk, her champagne cocktail in one hand, the other anxiously touching the back of her hair to make sure that a vital clip is still in place. She sees someone she knows, forgets the hair, and throws an arm around him.

It is only when I hear the same loud, excited voice that spoke before, asking everyone for a moment's attention, that I realize that it belongs to Charlie Stanhope. It surprises me momentarily that he should have something to say, but then I remember his engagement and instead of going into the drawing room I stay where I am on the stairs to get a good view of the proceedings. I scan the women near him as I hear him tell the crowd that as a collection of his greatest friends he wants them to be the first to share his happy news.

It is only when I see his hand in Ella's that I know the worst, and even then I struggle to believe it. The proof is conclusive, however, when I see Stanhope lean down and kiss her and I watch her return his kiss as everyone's glasses rise in a heartfelt toast and someone starts singing 'For

They're Two Jolly Good Fellows'. Both pull apart, flushing with happiness; and Ella looks up, smiling her thanks, and sees me on the stairs.

Our eyes meet, I think.

4

The details of how I left that over-large house are blurred. What I remember after all these years is the clarity I took away with me that night.

Now I knew what Ella's island looked like: the security of a loveless but socially acceptable marriage. Barren indeed. I could see the current that had washed her up on it and picture the subtle stages by which she had succumbed to the tides dragging at her feet. I remembered her talk of ancestors and tradition with the fascination of the uninitiated. My own family might know families who had such things, but we had no direct experience of them ourselves, however much might be implied to the contrary.

I could speculate about the intimate conversations Ella had endured with her mother, the number of times she had been asked whom she liked best of the young men she knew. Her family would have pounced on so blandly well-bred a suitor as Charles Stanhope. To please them she would have begun to see more of him; would have allowed him, perhaps, to imagine that she felt more than she did.

And then events, as she had told me herself, had overtaken her in a spectacular fashion and before she knew what was happening she was being subjected to the congratulations of her friends and the rejoicings of her family.

It was a romantic dilemma and one which held for me the romantic role of Ella's saviour. I clung to it in the weeks after Camilla's party and nursed plans of private rescue like the schoolboy I was.

Had I had any idea quite how far wide of the mark my conclusions had fallen, my feelings would have been very different. As it was, I threw myself into my daydreams with a vigour that carried over into the rest of my life and surprised my parents, for I was no longer a sulky companion at the breakfast table. Instead of warring with my family, I focused my attention on a more immediate goal: the liberation of Ella from the clutches of convention.

Had I had any opportunity to execute my designs I might have embarrassed myself seriously. Even now, as I look back on that time, I shudder with embarrassment. But I also chuckle at my own naivety. I cannot bring myself entirely to pity the earnest figure I was, with the shuffling gait and furrowed brow. I envy that lost self his passion, for he was in love, and in hopeless love at that. It is not an unpleasant sensation.

It was not a sensation which persisted long either, at least not in its initial form. For six weeks my mind was filled with daring plans but little action. My one concrete success was in obtaining Ella's telephone number from Camilla Boardman on the pretext that I had had no opportunity to congratulate her friend on her engagement.

But the gruff voice that answered the telephone at the Harcourt house in Chester Square regretted to say, on each of the weekly occasions on which I scraped together the courage to call, that Ella was not at home. Thus thwarted, I considered writing and rejected it; considered waiting

39

and accosting her on her pavement and rejected that too, at least as an initial measure; considered flowers; a dramatically phrased telegram; an engagement gift with a meaningful card; and rejected them all. For days I was in the sweetest of black despairs as I imagined the date of Ella's wedding drawing ever nearer, with me helpless to do anything about it.

I was brought down to earth one afternoon by seeing the object of these dreams, her nose in a book, sitting under a wide-brimmed straw hat on a deckchair across the water from me.

I was in Hyde Park once more, having walked from my own home and made the long detour via Chester Square in the hopes of seeing her. I had settled myself by the Serpentine to enjoy the sun and indulge in idle contemplation of how things might have been.

Confronted so unexpectedly by the reality of my musings, I was taken aback. Then I thought I must have been mistaken and looked again, my pulse quickening. Over the water sat the girl on whom my thoughts had focused exclusively for more than a month, which at that age is an eternity. There was no mistaking the delicate oval of that face, the slightly upturned tilt of that small nose. For a damsel in such distress, she looked irritatingly healthy.

Slowly I got up and made my way around the lake and through the crowds on the bridge, wondering what she would say when she saw me. As I approached I saw her reach into a large basket at her feet and extract a cigarette case and a small silver lighter. I paused and watched her fingers as she attempted to light the long, thin roll of tobacco in her hand.

When I was sufficiently close but still behind her and so out of her view, I stopped, coughed and called her name. The pale blue of the eyes that turned to face me warned me, though no other feature did, of my mistake. They were eyes I did not know then, but which I have come to know intimately since.

'I'm afraid that I'm Sarah Harcourt, not Ella,' the girl said, turning towards me and taking off her sun hat, shaking out a wave of dark-brown hair. 'There's no need to be embarrassed.' She smiled at me, sensing my awkwardness. 'We were often mistaken for each other as children. We both look like our American grandmother.'

Sarah's accent, very English, betrayed no trace of Ella's transatlantic lilt.

As she spoke I looked closely at her and saw that she was not quite as like Ella as I had at first thought. Her hair, which fell in a neat shiny sheet to the middle of her back, was the most obvious point of difference between them. But Sarah's face was different too: it was longer; her lips were thinner and more set than Ella's; the bridge of her nose was more severe. She belonged, I thought, to a different generation; and although I took her to be about my own age, I felt instinctively deferential towards her without quite knowing why. Sarah Harcourt, it seemed to me (and in this I was correct), was not a person with whom liberties could be taken lightly.

'Can I do anything for you, or will only Ella do?'

I hesitated.

'I'll tell you where you can find her if you'll buy me an ice cream. I'm completely out of change,' she went on, looking up at me from the striped canvas of her deckchair.

The note of command in her voice, though faint, was unmistakable. I complied. To make conversation as we walked towards the kiosk on the bridge, I asked her how she came to have an American grandmother.

'It's a long story but I'll tell it to you, if you like.'

'I'd like that very much.'

She looked at me searchingly, assessing my sincerity. I must have passed her test for once we were re-established by the Serpentine, ice creams in hand, she began.

As she talked she convinced me, as perhaps no one else could have done, that Ella Harcourt was unlike anyone I had ever met. If, in my daydreams, I thought I might have magnified her beauty, her image taught me I was wrong. But Ella's charm went deeper than that. A certain similarity in gesture and manner between the cousins served only to emphasize the superiority of one in subtle respects I tried to define as I listened to the other. The regal, slightly stiff set of Sarah's angular shoulders reminded me, I thought, of the natural grace of Ella's; the detached ice of Sarah's blue eyes made me think of her cousin's, green and sparkling in my memory. Yet Sarah was not without a certain compelling air of her own, though her methods were subtly authoritarian and Ella's were not.

'My grandfather,' she said, 'was a very poor man with a very grand name. And my grandmother was a very rich woman with no name at all, to speak of. She was also American.'

'I don't see the connection.'

'Oh it's a simple one, really. My grandmother's father thought a title for his daughter was just the thing to ensure the respectability of his money; and his future son-in-law

42

had an ancient, weather-beaten house to run. So a match was arranged. A bargain was struck. Each side got what they wanted: titled grandchildren for my great-grand-father; a brand new roof for my grandfather. The only person they neglected to consult was my grandmother, Blanche, who arrived in England at the age of eighteen, was married at nineteen, and had conceived a complete and not entirely irrational aversion to her husband by the time she was twenty.'

I nodded.

'That didn't stop her from producing four healthy children for him. An heir and three spares, if you like. She understood that that was her end of the bargain.' Sarah paused. 'But she was a woman who needed people and life about them. The decaying house, a castle in fact, was in Cornwall. And her father wouldn't finance a place in London that befitted the status of the new couple, so in Cornwall she languished, painted once by Sargent, but otherwise left undisturbed by the fashionable world.'

'And what did she do with her time?'

'Well, she wrote letters; she redesigned the garden; she saw to the upbringing and education of her children. She got in the way, as much as she could, of her husband's philandering.'

'I see.'

'But her mind needed more of an outlet than these activities could provide.' Sarah smiled. 'Blanche was not a domesticated woman. That was the thing. And she was highly gifted, which made things worse.'

'So what happened to her in the end? What did she find to do?'

'She didn't find anything at all. That was her tragedy. And there's only so much solitude a woman of that kind can bear.'

'What happened to her?'

Blanche's granddaughter was quiet for a moment, looking silently out over the cheerful, boat-filled lake.

'She killed herself eventually,' she said at last. 'Jumped out of a window on to the terrace. Caused a huge scandal at the time.'

'How awful.'

'Isn't it? I think it affected her children profoundly.'

There was a pause.

'And there,' she said briskly, looking directly at me once more, 'you have the story of how I come to have an American grandmother. I hope I didn't tell you more than you care to know.'

'Not at all. I found it fascinating. And tragic.'

'Yes,' she said thoughtfully. 'It certainly has both of those qualities.' She turned to me, confidential suddenly. 'I have an idea, you know, of writing Blanche's biography one day. She was a woman who gave to everything she did the kind of glamour one usually finds only in fiction.'

'I'm sure it would make a very interesting book.'

'Do you really think so?'

'I do,' I said, rising. 'But I've kept you from your reading far too long.'

'Goodbye.' She held out her hand.

'You couldn't pass on a message to your cousin could you?'

'Of course, though I'm not sure when I'll next see her. We don't see very much of each other.'

'And why is that?'

'Frankly, we don't get on. But if I see her before you do, what should I say?'

'Tell her you saw James Farrell.' I realized that until now I had not offered my name to Sarah and she had not asked for it. 'Tell her that you saw James Farrell and that he wondered how life on her island was suiting her.'

'Is that all, Mr Farrell?'

'That's all. She'll understand.'

'I hope so.'

'Well, goodbye again.'

'Goodbye.'

And with that I left her and walked once more over the bridge and down the carriage track. I felt Sarah's cold blue eyes on me as I went and I turned on the far side of the bridge to wave. But she was seated, her nose in her book once more. If she saw me, she gave no indication of having done so.

5

As it happened, none of the Harcourts gave any sign of acknowledging my existence in the days that followed my meeting with Sarah, days I spent practising my violin and thinking of Ella. I found to my delight that I was able to transform the bitter-sweet frustration hopeless love produces into the energy serious work requires, and even my parents were impressed by the ardour of my diligence. Throughout that hot August I was never far from the airless room at the top of the house where my violin was kept; and as I practised I played to an imaginary audience of one, hoping as I did so that the sheer dexterity of this or that scale would impress her, or that this or that sonata would make her smile. I played a good deal of Brahms at that time, and I remember finding in the drama of the music a fitting accompaniment to my own secret dreams of rescue and valour.

Ella, the unwitting object of all my thoughts, remained nowhere to be found or seen. She was never at home to my telephone calls; she never gave any sign of having received a message from me. The forbidding Georgian portals of the house in Chester Square never yielded up her slim frame when I happened to be passing, as I frequently was. But the effortless way in which she had entered my mind, the strange, unlooked-for meeting with her cousin, the occasional photographs of her and Charles Stanhope that appeared in the magazines I read while having my hair cut, all fanned the flames of my interest in her. I continued to play and dream and be disappointed.

But even the interest of an unusually impressionable boy begins to wane. With no encouragement from the unknowing object of my devotion, without so much as a note or a look from her – either of which might have conquered me for ever – the intensity of my enthusiasm could not be maintained indefinitely. It might, I suppose, have faded and finally died, consigned to history as a last memory of fiery adolescence, had Fate, if such a force exists, not decreed otherwise.

The instrument Fate selected to bring Ella and me together again was chosen with exquisite taste. It was Camilla Boardman; and she telephoned just as I was deciding that there was nothing to be done, and that if Ella wished to waste herself on Charlie Stanhope she was welcome to do so.

'*Daaarling!*' cooed the voice I had not heard since it had given me Ella's telephone number many weeks before.

'Camilla. How are you?'

'How are *you*? That's *far* more to the point.'

'I'm well, thank you.'

'So why have you been hiding away? Positively *ignoring* all your friends.'

I knew Camilla well enough to be suspicious of her tone of mock injury. Cautiously I replied that I had not been hiding away, but practising hard in preparation for the Guildhall.

'Oh, I forget you're off to be a famous musician. You'll still remember me when you're famous, won't you, darling? Even with all those glamorous women throwing themselves at you.'

I sensed that a compliment was appropriate. Hesitatingly, I attempted one. 'They couldn't possibly be more glamorous than you, Camilla ... darling.'

'Oh Jamie, you're *so* sweet. *So* lovely. You *always* are.'

The frequency of Camilla's emphases prepared me for her inevitable climax.

'In fact, that's *just* why I've called you. Ed Saunders has left me *completely* in the lurch, as he always does.'

Ed Saunders was Camilla's current man, I gathered, and I pretended to recognize his name.

'Oh, Ed,' I said.

'Yes, the *toad*.' A petulant Camilla was even more alarming than usual. 'And Ella Harcourt's engagement party starts in an hour, would you believe?'

'Ella Harcourt, did you say?' I caught my breath, hoping against hope.

'Yes, her parents are giving a lunch for her and Charlie. *Everyone's* going to be there. Pamela (that's Ella's stepmother) is a *fabulous* hostess. And Eddie's just rung me up and told me he's got laryngitis and can't possibly come. *Laryngitis.* Honestly!' said Camilla, as though it numbered amongst the rarest of tropical diseases. 'In August! And *so*,' her voice changed tone, 'I wondered whether you might *possibly* be free. I couldn't *bear* the thought of going alone. And,' realizing that this sounded selfish, 'I haven't seen you for *ages* and I remembered how well you and Ella got on at my party.'

I wondered privately how many people she had called before trying me. Aloud I said, 'I'm not sure, Camilla. Of course I'd love to see you, but it's very short notice.'

Camilla respected people with multiple engagements. 'I *know*, darling,' she said. 'And if his laryngitis doesn't kill Eddie you may be sure I will. But I would *so* like to see you. And if it's any consolation, I'm sure it'll be a very brilliant affair. Wonderful food . . .'

Camilla was tenacious in pursuit of her social goals.

'And there are bound to be *lots* of Oxford people. And . . .' She considered what further inducements she could offer.

'Ella's cousin will be there, of course. She's very pretty. An odd fish, by all accounts' – for Camilla was a strictly truthful person – 'but very pretty.'

'I know,' I said, thinking of Sarah's cold beauty.

'So you'll take me, then?'

An hour later I found myself on the steps of the house in Chester Square. Camilla, beside me, squeezed my hand with relief and smiled a practised and perfectly-formed smile of red lips and white teeth, expensively arranged.

'Darling, you're a *saviour*,' she whispered in my ear as I rang the bell.

We were late, for it was part of Camilla's creed always to be missed, and we entered the drawing room just as the other guests were beginning to shuffle hungrily and glance at their watches.

There were perhaps thirty of us in all: a dowdy but respectable pair in tweeds whom I took, correctly, to be the Stanhopes; several people my own age, amongst whom I recognized the girl with the villa in Biarritz; and the

Harcourts themselves, tall and stately, precisely as I had imagined them, talking to Sarah by one of the long windows that gave on to the square. Neither Ella nor Charlie were anywhere to be seen.

Camilla moved straight towards her host and hostess, her arms flung out in a gesture of greeting. Trailing in her wake, I noticed that conversation had died.

'Lady Harcourt,' she said, embracing a tall, angular woman with red hair scraped off her face and piled in complicated wreaths on her head. 'How *lovely* to see you.'

The voice that replied told her, in the drawling tones of a Bostonian, that she was divine to have come. Alexander Harcourt had the same colouring as his daughter, although on him the blond hair was thinning and the cheeks were ruddy rather than rosy. His eyes were blue, like Sarah's, but shone like Ella's; and he moved with the confidence of a handsome man who has always been thought one. His hands were large, his shoulders broad, his manner frank. I liked him.

'Here they are now,' he said, nodding amiably at and past me, towards the drawing-room doors. His wife, Pamela, very erect in a green dress which did not suit her, went forward to greet her stepdaughter.

'How lovely you look,' I heard her say as she kissed her cheek.

If Ella did look lovely, I could not see it. In an old-fashioned dress with a high lace neck she looked like an Edwardian doll and moved with the stiffness of one. She did not appear to see me.

Camilla, as ever, was the first in the impromptu line that formed to greet the engaged pair. Stanhope, standing behind Ella in a dark suit, his hair severely parted, glowed with pleasure as his fiancée submitted to the embraces of his friend. I waited with the other guests as he and Ella, relinquished with reluctance by Camilla, came down the line, receiving the congratulations of their parents' friends and their own.

Ella saw me while three people still separated us. She was kissing Sarah formally on both cheeks when her eyes, straying down the line, met mine. Instantly she looked away, and I glowed at this secret triumph.

'I didn't know you'd be here,' she said as she reached me, and made a point of offering her hand rather than her cheek.

'Camilla invited me, and I haven't had a chance to congratulate you.'

She looked at me for a moment, more embarrassed than hostile, and passed on.

Stanhope, when he reached me, greeted me as an old friend.

'So this is the splendid girl I wasn't to talk about?' I asked, smiling.

'This is the girl,' he replied, looking down the line at Ella. 'And she is splendid, isn't she?'

'Congratulations.'

He moved on.

The afternoon proceeded. Lunch was served on a long, silver-laden table in the dining room, a lofty, red-papered space with a large chandelier and a view of the garden. Outside it was raining.

I sat between Camilla and Sarah, and opposite the girl with the villa in Biarritz. The food, as Camilla had predicted, was excellent; the wine, too, was good. Vases of roses filled the room with their scent. Occasionally I heard snatches of Ella's conversation, three places down on my left, tantalizingly close.

But it was only as the meal progressed and I heard more that I realized that every phrase I caught was precisely as it should have been; that my love was speaking with precisely the same thoughtless, practised ease of which she had been so critical a few weeks before. Her thanks for people's presents were pretty, her secrecy about her dress conventional. Nowhere could I detect any trace of the woman with the gaunt face who had spoken to me of drowning in the darkness of the Boardman stairwell. This transformation infuriated me. It seemed that Ella had decided to swim with the current rather than against it, and she was swimming with a rehearsed grace that reminded me of Stanhope's and impressed me as little as his had done.

Yet I did not despair of her wholly. Something in her voice reminded me of the voice I had listened to in the park and in the alcove. I heard again the confusion of her words then, the sincerity with which she had railed against the forces which were . . . How had she put it? 'Pulling her under'. And Ella pulled under had resolved to put a brave face on it.

So I thought, and in so thinking I was half right; I came closer to the truth in that conclusion than in any of my flights of medieval fantasy. I was wrong only in thinking that I knew what had pulled her down.

Tantalizing though Ella's presence was, however, I did not forget my duties as Camilla Boardman's partner; nor was I allowed to. The infectious laughter of the woman who had brought me, the intimate way in which she confided other people's indiscretions, the complete and gratifying attention she paid to my responses, all combined to put me in an agreeable mood. Ella was not the only one, I thought, who could conceal her feelings behind a flow of effortless patter. I would show her I was as adept as anyone.

And so I talked: to Camilla; to Sarah; to the girl with the villa in Biarritz; all the while wondering how to get Ella to myself for a moment and resolving not to leave the house without making an attempt to do so.

Sarah Harcourt, rigid in blue linen on my left, spoke to me of her distaste for roses. Her criticism, inaudible to her hostess, was more for Pamela than for Pamela's flowers, I suspected; and I thought that I understood where the disapproval came from. Pamela, for Sarah, was an invader. To begin with, her accent was American and thus hardly to her credit; but what was more to be deplored was her self-conscious attention to the anglicizing of every other personal detail. Her hair, piled above her head, was impressively Edwardian; her jewellery was heavy and old-fashioned; she addressed the footman with just the correct amount of polite disdain.

All this, I could see, irritated Sarah almost as much as her cousin's charming conversation irritated me. And although she said nothing, I felt within her the hostility to foreigners, particularly usurping foreigners, which is latent in certain English souls. She sat by my side, hardly touching the food that was put before her, splendidly regal. I noticed that no one spoke to her but that her presence was very much felt, and I thought again that she was someone to be treated with deference but no intimacy: an outsider by choice and circumstance.

Even Camilla, though nothing and no one could upset her iron self-assurance, seemed disinclined to engage Sarah in conversation, sensing her to be a difficult conquest. And I, looking at the set lines of Sarah's mouth and wondering how I could ever have found in her an exact likeness of Ella, felt sorry for her in a way I would never have dared to express.

Only once did the girl with the villa in Biarritz attempt conversation with Sarah, and her choice of opening was unfortunate.

'Do you know,' she said from across the roses, 'I never knew Ella had a sister. Are you very close?'

There was the slightest suggestion of a pause; but it was frosty enough to halt the conversation around it for a moment before Sarah smiled and said that she and Ella were only cousins.

'But you could almost be twins,' the girl blundered on, smiling still.

'We could *not* be twins,' came the acid reply, just loud enough for Ella to overhear; and by the forced cheerfulness of her conversation it seemed to me that the object of the slight had heard and was consciously ignoring it.

'Oh, but you *could* be,' the hapless girl persisted. 'You're almost identical.'

'But our styles are quite different,' came the sweetly damning reply.

Sarah leaned back in her chair, languid and serene, and smiled at her cousin. It was left to Camilla to cover the ensuing silence by redirecting our attention to the splendours of the Chelsea Flower Show.

We returned to the drawing room after lunch, an ocean of uncomfortable sofas of ornate wood and sombre pattern. Almost at once the party began to split up, and I saw that Sarah was one of the first to say her goodbyes. Instead of kissing Pamela she shook her hand. Alexander she kissed, and Ella, too, although the brushing of the cousins' cheeks which passed for a kiss did not suggest much unspoken affection. Stanhope, rising, leaned forward to kiss Sarah and was rewarded by the quick outstretching of her fine white hand.

When she had gone, Camilla found a place next to me on a sofa and said, softly enough for only one or two people who would share her opinion to hear, 'Well, I said she was an odd fish. You can see I was right. ' She considered the question gravely for a moment. 'I think she's superior,' she said at last, with an air of finality. 'And frankly I don't see any reason why she should be, do you?'

But her question was merely rhetorical; I was not expected to answer it and when I did not she let the matter drop and spoke of other things. I listened to her vaguely, concentrating most of my attention on the question of how I could possibly get Ella to myself for a moment. A moment was all it would take, I thought. But one by one the guests got up to leave and I felt my time of opportunity dwindling. Ella showed no inclination to talk to me and I had no desire to cross the expanse of carpet and sit with her and Charles Stanhope. I wanted her alone or not at all.

Again it was Camilla who came to my rescue with

her suggestion of seeing the engagement presents. 'Ella, darling,' she called from our sofa, 'aren't you *dying* to see what everyone's brought you?'

'Of course she is,' said Pamela, smiling.

Sensing my chance and seeing Ella about to protest, I joined the chorus with a well-timed 'So are we.'

'Well, why don't we open them now, sweetheart?' said Stanhope on cue.

Ella looked doubtful. 'We could, I suppose,' she said.

'Then let's,' said Pamela decisively, rising. To the few guests who remained, she said, 'You won't mind coming upstairs, will you? They're in the Blue Room.'

And with a laugh, taking the arm of her future son-in-law, she led the way to the stairs. Alexander followed with Camilla and the girl with the villa in Biarritz. A plump relation, the only other member of the party still present, had gone to sleep in an armchair.

Ella and I were left alone.

'So,' I said quickly, my irritation at lunch giving an edge to my voice, 'this is it?'

'What?'

'Is this the island?'

There was a pause. The relation in the armchair gave a gentle snore.

'Is this what you meant by events overtaking you?' I was courageous after weeks of pent-up frustration and excitement.

With a sharp nod Ella motioned me out of the room and on to the landing. 'I don't know what you mean,' she said, putting her foot on the first stair.

'No, of course you don't. I forget that in our particular

school of fish one should never admit to having said anything real.'

There was a note of sarcasm in my voice, which I saw made her uncomfortable.

'Particularly if one hasn't said it to someone one's known since childhood.'

'Don't talk to me about schools of fish.'

'Why not?'

'It's a tired metaphor.'

'All right then, I'll ask you plainly. What on earth are you doing?'

'I am marrying the man I love, James.'

But even as she said it, her tone rang false. We both observed this.

'And anyway,' she whispered almost fiercely, angry herself now, 'I don't see what business it is of yours whether I'm happy or not.'

'It's only my business in as far as you've made it my business,' I said quietly.

'Well, I'm sorry I mentioned anything.'

'I don't think you are.'

'I beg your pardon?'

'I said I don't think you are. When you first met me, that day in the park, you were looking for a solution. I think you wanted me to help you find one.'

It was wise of me at this point not to have come out with any of my wilder theories on the question of Ella's motives; as it was, the gist of what I had said was correct and she did not contradict it.

'And then when your engagement was finally announced,' I continued, warming to my theme, 'and things were truly out of hand, you decided there was no escape and so you gave in. To use your own phrase, you decided it was easier to swim with the current than against it.'

'Hush,' she said, 'they'll hear you.'

I lowered my voice but went on, 'Even now, though, you despise yourself for being so weak, don't you?'

'How dare you—'

'Tell me you don't despise yourself. Tell me you relish wearing that silly dress and being made to look like a child that can't think for itself. Tell me that,' I concluded triumphantly, 'and I'll go into the Blue Room and gawp politely at your engagement presents and not bother you again.'

She looked at me, speechless, and I saw to my mingled horror and relief that there were tears in her eyes.

'Tell me,' I insisted, 'and I'll go. Tell me,' for now I was in full stride, 'that you can't imagine ever loving anyone more than you love Charles Stanhope now and I will go. I won't even say goodbye, if you like. I'll just leave.'

'I will tell you nothing of the sort,' she said, with an attempt at dignity. 'But you had better go all the same.'

'Not until you tell me why,' I replied, seizing on a new angle of attack, 'if only to satisfy my curiosity. Tell me why you're marrying him.'

Confident I knew the answer, I expected her finally to crumble into the safety of confession. I was disappointed. Instead, she drew herself up to her full height and looked me squarely in the eyes.

'Ella, darling!' came a shrill voice from upstairs.

'Go on,' I persisted, 'tell me.'

Ignoring all I had said up to this point, she made a visible effort to recover herself and when she spoke it was in a tone of quiet command. 'You have no right to expect me to answer you. You are a guest in my parents' house. You have certain obligations. Fulfill them and oblige me by doing what I say.'

'What is that?'

'I want you to go and thank my stepmother for a delicious lunch,' she said evenly. 'Then I want you to take Camilla home, see her safely in at her front door, and go home yourself. Forget my metaphors; forget everything I said in the park; forget our conversation at the Boardmans'. Put it all down to the confusion of a young girl about to get engaged. Put it down to anything you like, but stop asking me about it.'

'Ella!'

The call was louder this time; a man's voice. I heard the creaking of wood as someone with a tread I recognized came down to find her. 'Ella, sweetheart, where have you got to?' The voice was Stanhope's, cheerful as ever.

'I hope you have understood me.'

Our eyes met.

'Please, James,' she said, her attitude changing, 'not now.'

Seeing the light of hope in my eyes she went on hurriedly, 'Not ever. I've made my bed, I've come this far. Now I intend to lie on it.'

'It's not too late. You've got your whole life to get through. Spending it washed up on an island with Charles Stanhope can't be a tempting prospect.'

'Don't talk to me about islands.'

'Why not? It's your word.'

'I've told you. The metaphor is tired.'

'But it's still apt, I think.'

'Think what you will,' she hissed, and there was exasperation in her voice.

'Your whole life is ahead of you, Ella, don't you see?' I went on more gently.

'That's what you kept on saying that night,' she said, as Stanhope appeared on the stairs.

'You two been nattering down here all this time?' he said jovially.

'It's still true,' I muttered.

'What is?' asked Stanhope.

'Only that trains wait for no man,' said Ella brightly, putting her arm through her fiancé's, 'and that James, no matter how much we beg him, won't miss his.'

'Too bad,' said Stanhope as I followed them both upstairs to say my goodbyes.

6

Thus far I had been defeated, crushed by the determination of those steely green eyes. And you may be sure I took my defeat to heart in the days that followed the party at Chester Square. But you may also be sure I remained unshaken in my romantic beliefs and that I returned to my thoughts of Ella and her predicament with renewed vigour.

I had, I thought, done myself credit on the rainy day of her engagement party; I felt that the bond between us had strengthened in some indefinable yet concrete way, despite all evidence to the contrary. Youth is optimistic; that is its consolation. And I waited patiently to allow events, if only they would, to follow their natural course.

In so doing I was not arrogant enough to suppose that Ella could not resist the temptation of seeing me again. Rather, I suspected that she could not for long resist a temptation of a different kind: she would want an opportunity to justify herself more effectively than she had done at her engagement lunch. So I settled down to wait and resolved to bide my time.

The Stanhope–Harcourt wedding was set for the following March, seven months away; and as the days since the Harcourts' lunch party stretched into a week, I comforted myself with the thought that time, at least, was on my side. Ella Harcourt, I suspected, was a proud woman, and I held firmly to this suspicion for it served to explain her continuing silence. I told myself that it would be foolish to badger the house in Chester Square. No more chance encounters with any members of the Harcourt family ensued, though I looked out for them as eagerly as ever. For a week I waited, unencouraged.

On the eighth day I received her letter. I have it with me now, with all the others she wrote me; and looking at its jagged writing, its heavy paper, its brown ink, I think with a sharp sorrow of the girl who wrote it and wish, as so many have wished before me, that the past were more fluid, that it might be possible to return, by a route other than memory, to the day so long ago when Ella's letter found its way on to the mat in my parents' hall.

It is dated Saturday; the scrawled address reads 23 Chester Square, SW.

Dear James,

You will be glad to discover that our conversation last week had, if no other effect, at least that of making me see the light about that awful dress. You were right, I looked ghastly. I needed someone insulting and presumptuous enough to tell me so and I thank you for your rudeness – I thought it had been socialized out of you. Perhaps it has and I got the last drop of it; I hope not. How American, I hear you say. Well, I guess I am an American and proud of it. But I have an English name and you will remember how we agreed that a name is the least private thing about a person. That, perhaps, will form the beginning of my answer to your question of last week.

'Why?' you asked me. 'Why are you marrying Charles?'

Why indeed? But before you get on your high horse I think you should put yourself in my position, if only for a moment. If your (I don't know how many times great) great-grandmother had also seduced Charles II, you might understand what I'm saying. Your name, like mine, might stop describing and begin defining you, along strict lines you don't altogether like. I, heaven knows, am defined by my name. Do you honestly expect that the Hon. Ella, daughter of Lord and Lady Harcourt, niece of the Earl and Countess of Seton, with her very own mention in *Debrett's*, <u>could possibly</u> marry anyone other than Charles Stanhope, eldest son of Sir Lachlan and Lady Stanhope, of Barton Manor, Wilts, and Windham Road, Fulham, ed. Eton and Oxford?

I suppose the time has come to be frank with you. I have got myself, as I said that day in the park, into a mess. And it is a mess of my own making. This I freely admit. That's why I've been forging ahead with everything over the past few weeks, because I made my bed and I should lie on it.

Quite why I insisted on making it, on setting this whole bizarre machinery in motion, I cannot explain to you completely. I have asked myself why a thousand times and if I never get a straight answer, why should you? But there is an answer nevertheless, or rather several little answers, which together might explain what I've done.

If you'd really like to know why I'm marrying Charles, and think you might have any bright ideas – once you know all the little answers to that very big question – of how I might get myself out of this ludicrous predicament, then meet me under the departure board at Paddington at two o'clock tomorrow afternoon. You should bring an overnight case. If I don't see you, I'll know that you have quite wisely decided to steer clear. I would probably do the same in your position.

Sincerely,
Ella Harcourt

No endearment, nothing more personal than her name. But, of course, I went. Who wouldn't have gone in my position? And I went with joy in my heart and music on my lips.

Ella was standing under the departure board at Paddington, small and lost in the crowd. She could not have looked more different from the woman who had spoken so demurely of engagement gifts and wedding plans a week before.

'Hello, James,' she said when she saw me.
'Hello, Ella.'
We looked at each other.
'Thank you for coming.'
'There's no need to thank me.'
It was she who bought the tickets and, as she did so,

said to me, half apologetically, 'I'm afraid it's rather a long journey. But I can promise you excellent fare when we reach our destination. There's a sweet inn in the village I'm sure you'll like. Until then, you'll have to submit to the standard train sandwiches.'

And taking my hand, she led me down the platform towards the Cornish Express.

I remember her in that train. I remember the green wool of her sweater against the cream of her skin; the sweep of her newly washed hair; the scent of her soap. Here was Ella unadorned: not the decadent figure in the park, nor the decorative guest at Camilla Boardman's party, nor still the Edwardian little girl at her stepmother's lunch.

Ella Harcourt was a woman of many facets. She possessed a quality of aesthetic malleability I have known in no one but her. Sitting in the drabness of a second-class railway carriage, she seemed as lovely to me as she had been on a park bench and in the half-light of a book-lined alcove. As I stared, trying to explain to myself why this was so, I discovered the truth that beauty is elusive and defies description. Prettiness lends itself to words but beauty is something finer, a thing apart. Ella was beautiful.

She was also inclined to be communicative. And with only a little encouragement from me she gave me an outline of her life.

'If you really want to know,' she began, smiling, 'I was born in London on a misty day in November almost twenty-four years ago. Exhibited by my proud parents as an example of all that is wondrous in childhood, I was in fact an ugly, filthy-tempered baby with no hair but healthy lungs. I was inclined to scream.'

I laughed and she gave me a wry smile.

Lighting a cigarette, she continued, 'When I was nine my mother, a perfectly respectable nice young English girl, took the liberty of dying in an accident. Most regrettable. For her, of course, and also for my father who happened to be very much in love with her, but chiefly for the family at large. Unable to do anything, they watched as poor Alexander, in his grief, transferred himself, bag and baggage, to America in the hopes of starting afresh and finding happiness once more. Very poor taste, everyone thought, giving in to your emotions like that. And what was worse, he insisted on taking his little girl with him, who, under the influence of some barbarian colonials, absorbed, as everyone had feared, some unfortunate habits which have tainted her to this day. It was felt – though such things are never said, of course – that she could only bring disgrace on the family name.

'When poor Alexander committed the supreme treachery, nine years later, of returning to London with a new American wife,' Ella continued, her face distorting into an expression of chill disapproval, 'the family despaired. And what was more, his daughter had gone over to the other side. Her vowels were rounded no longer; her manners (never excellent) had deteriorated sharply. Clearly something had to be done. But she was eighteen and very headstrong, altogether unwilling to listen to good advice. An ungrateful child. Yet the fact remained that she was a Harcourt, and showed every sign of remaining one indefinitely. So it was vital that she was taught to behave like one without delay.'

She took a meditative drag.

66

'How to mould her correctly remained a problem. Her education completed and cultured conversation acquired, she was taken under various wings, introduced to endless people, given a sufficiently smart set of lifelong friends. By the time she was twenty-three she knew people like Camilla Boardman, supreme arbiter of all that is best in young England today, and was engaged to a very nice young man. Even her accent, though it remained far from perfect, had improved. She could at last be married off without shame.'

'And Charles Stanhope was the nice young man?'

'Yes.'

'I see.'

There was a pause.

'What do you think of my story?' asked Ella. 'Do you like it? Is it as you imagined?'

'Yes,' I said, happily, thinking how correct I had been in my theories all along.

'The unfortunate thing,' she went on, 'is that what I have just told you is not the whole story. By no means is it the whole story.'

'What do you mean?' I asked, surprised by the change in her.

'Well . . . you remember my letter?'

I nodded.

'How I said that there were lots of little reasons, which, taken all together, might possibly explain how things have come to turn out as they have?'

I nodded again.

'The explanation I have just given you is one of those little reasons. Perhaps the smallest.'

'What are the others?'

'There aren't many others, in fact. I was exaggerating. There's just one really.' She took a deep breath. 'And it is, on the whole, a little murkier than what I've just told you.' She paused and raised her eyes to mine. 'The two reasons are related, of course, but substantially different. The one you don't know is a little more ... cold-blooded.'

She looked at me steadily and I felt the challenge in her eyes.

Silently I met it. 'Go on,' I said.

'Are you sure you want me to?' She lit the cigarette and inhaled deeply, blowing the smoke out of her nostrils in a defiant swirl.

I felt the tingling vertigo of one standing on a knife-edge.

'Go on.'

'Very well, then. But you'll have to wait until we get there.' She smiled at me and I saw her shoulders relax. 'There's something I want to show you, something that will explain things far more eloquently than I could.'

It is from that moment, on that journey (a journey I have since repeated more times than I can count), that I date the beginning of it all.

In London I had been fascinated, it is true, but mine had been a fascination based on romantic notions of plight and salvation. Ella had filled my thoughts, but more as a princess in a fairy-tale might have done than as a being of blood and flesh. Her aura was ethereal and I, a mortal, had succumbed to it. But I had been held at arm's length and largely ignored. What intimacy there had been had been haphazard and insubstantial, completely at the mercy of coincidence and whim. But now I had passed a test I only dimly understood but which I knew enough to value. I had promised myself and had been given in return a right to claim something. What I might claim I hardly knew, but no longer was I peripheral.

This mysterious woman with the changing eyes and smiling lips had plucked me from my life, on a whim, and had taken me on a six-hour journey to be told something I might not even understand. From everyone she knew, of all the people in her life, she had selected me to be her confidant. It was to me that she had chosen to explain the tangle of motive and error that had led to her engagement; it was to me that she looked for help in extricating herself from the depths in which she floundered. From the school of fish that flashed its scales before her eyes, she had selected me to swim with her, to brave currents, tides and oceans by her side.

So slid Ella's metaphors in my mind: colliding; joining; mingling with my own romantic dreams of passion and valour. Yes I was a dreamer; to that charge I plead guilty. And as I dreamed I stared at her smooth white neck and felt that there was nothing I would not do to be worthy of her trust.

We passed the remainder of that journey in silence, watching the blur of passing towns from our carriage window; listening to the rattle of the train; allowing its gentle rhythm to lull us to near sleep. We spoke little. Ella smoked a great deal. I watched her fingers as she lit and disposed of her cigarettes.

7

The train followed the coast for the last half-hour of its journey to Penzance. Ella and I sat in complete silence in a carriage which gradually emptied as it passed through Devon.

She had stopped smoking. I watched her profile as she gazed at the view, occasionally following the direction of her unblinking eyes, feeling her intent with expectation and wondering what it might be for.

She had told me nothing of our destination and I, enjoying the suspense, had not asked. Then I saw it and knew as I did so that I saw what she had been waiting for. Rising tall and many-turreted above the sea, the windows of the Castle of Seton winked at us in the sunset. Behind its bell tower the sun, a scarlet ball, dipped towards the Atlantic, sending rays of gold fanning outwards in a mauve sky, turning the castle's grey granite to a rosy pink, catching the gilt on its weathercocks as they spun in the wind.

'There it is,' said Ella softly. 'Our island.'

I was to hear the same words, with a different emphasis and meaning, as I made the same journey years later as a married man. Seeing Seton for the first time, however, my thoughts turned not to my future but to its past, to the centuries that had come and gone while it, impassive, had commanded the steep cliffs of its small, jagged island, unmoved by the human dramas played out within its walls.

It is strange for me now to think that this place was ever new to me: that as I passed it for the first time in the shabbiness of a second-class railway carriage it held no associations, nor even much promise of them. Seton is austere and cold, brilliant but aloof. It is cautious of intimacy. Yet its trust, once given, is eternal.

Ella and I sat in silence as the train sped on, watching the fairy-tale image recede into the distance.

'It's like Camelot, don't you think?' she whispered.

'Like Camelot,' I echoed.

The station at Penzance was a bustle of people and bags and lines waiting for taxis.

'Come on,' said Ella, tugging my arm. 'Let's walk. It'll only take an hour or so. And the last boat to the island doesn't leave until ten.'

So we walked through and out of the town. A light drizzle began to fall. Hot and tired from travelling, we welcomed the rain and the air and the smell of the sea. We walked together, smiling, a little awkward now that we had actually arrived. At last we had left the crowds and clustered buildings behind, and Ella led me from the main road and on to a smaller track which led down to the beach.

'Look here,' she said, pointing.

I looked and saw the castle, rising from its cone-shaped island, a natural progression of the granite, ringed by blue sea.

'So this is the view Blanche saw,' I said.

'What do you know about Blanche?' She looked at me sharply.

'Not much. Only that she was your grandmother and that she lived here.'

'Who told you?'

'Sarah.'

'I see.' There was a pause. 'So she's got to you already.'

'I don't know what you mean.'

'No, you couldn't.'

'Tell me then.'

'Not now, James.'

And before I could speak Ella had moved abruptly on, first walking and then running down the steep incline, thick with binding grass, that led to the beach.

'I think we can make it to the boats from here. Run!'

Her command came to me over the wind. So through the rain I ran, my clothes sticking to me from the combination of sweaty train hours and the damp of the drizzle. It began to rain heavily now. I ran on. And always Ella was before me, crying out, a long unbroken shout of something lost between joy and rage; a sound I could not explain or understand but which held me in its thrall, even as the sand spilled into my shoes and the rainwater ran down my neck. Running behind her, always nearing, always eluded: it is how I have spent my life. Even now I can taste the salt in the air and feel the pounding of my blood.

We were taken to the island by a bearded fisherman obviously surprised by our lack of luggage.

'This is the larst boat, sir,' he said, 'if you's thinkin' of comin' back tonight.'

'We weren't,' Ella replied for me.

'Very well, miss.'

And in a rickety boat that smelled of mackerel we made the short crossing to the island's harbour as the last of the sun dipped below the horizon. I was half surprised to find a village beneath the castle walls, for in my mind I had already cast Seton as a self-sufficient entity, removed from our world. But I was glad of a beer and a plate of steaming cod, drowned in batter, in the 'sweet little inn' of which Ella had told me. She reserved two rooms before we sat down to dinner, giving her surname as Warrington.

'My mother's name,' she said quietly as she passed the register. 'Only a fool would sign Harcourt on this island. Wouldn't have a moment's sleep for all the attention.'

I nodded, understood, and signed my own name.

When we were sitting at a table in the cosy bar, listening to the rain beat steadily on the window-panes, she smiled at me. 'So, here we are.'

'Is this what you wanted to show me?' 'It is, partly,' said Ella. 'I wanted to show you the island and the castle. But there's something much more specific I want you to see.'

Our fish arrived. She paused.

'But it must wait until tomorrow. Everything's closed to tourists until tomorrow morning.'

'But,' I began, a little surprised, 'I thought this was your castle? Surely you're not a tourist in your own family's home?'

'No,' she replied, smiling at my innocence. 'Of course I could take you to lunch with Uncle Cyril and Aunt Elizabeth if I liked. I don't imagine they'd be delighted to see me, particularly, though they wouldn't show that. But I can't, of course, for obvious reasons.'

'Amongst which are?'

'Well, for starters, you blind boy, the fact that you aren't Charlie Stanhope. It would never do for them to see me here with anyone but him.'

'At least not until you've extricated yourself?'

'At least not until I have, as you say, extricated myself.'

'I see.'

'But there's another reason too.'

'Which is?'

'I'd much rather show you it in private. The painting, I mean. That's what I've brought you here to see. It might make things clearer. One should never underestimate the importance of visual aids.' She smiled. 'And privacy is important. Not that I mind day-trippers; they won't affect us. It's family presence I want to avoid if I can. I want the anonymity of the tourist. And you've been seeing quite enough of my relations as it is.'

Something about the brittle laugh that followed this made me know of whom she was speaking.

'I've only spoken to Sarah properly once,' I said. 'I mistook her for you, in fact.'

'At my own engagement party?' Ella raised an eyebrow.

'No. Before that.'

The eyebrow came to rest again; Ella looked at me steadily.

'Well, you must have got very chummy,' she said finally. 'She seems to have told you all the family history you need to know.'

'She told me about your grandmother. I'm sorry.'

Ella paused. 'I never knew her,' she said finally, discarding my sympathy.

'I really wanted Sarah to tell me about you.'

'I bet she was happy to advise in that respect. Did she tell you I was a vulgar little upstart? Or was I just crass?'

'She said you two didn't see much of each other.'

There was a silence. I felt Ella's eyes on me and busied myself with my cod. Across the table she lit a cigarette, with a murmured, 'You don't mind, do you?'

I shook my head.

'Thanks.'

More silence.

'I wish you'd look at me,' she remarked.

I looked up. There was a moment of hesitation on her part, as though things hung in the balance; perhaps, even then, they did.

Then she said, in a quiet, low voice, 'Do you know anything about jealousy, James? About what it does to people?'

I shook my head. Feeling as I did so that I was not so naive, I said, 'Yes. I understand jealousy.'

'Ah, but have you ever felt it?'

'Yes,' I said.

'But only briefly, spasmodically. The feeling hasn't lasted long, has it? It hasn't built up into something consuming; it hasn't spread. Has it?'

'No,' I said, truthfully.

'Well, the jealousy you're talking about is only a distant relation of the kind I'm concerned with. You don't mind my boring you with this?'

I shook my head.

'The kind I mean is an illness, a disease. It eats away,

75

spreading into everything a person does, into everything a person thinks.'

She exhaled, blowing her smoke to the ceiling.

'The jealousy you experience, and I hope you won't take offence at this, is of the common or garden variety by comparison. Like the cold it affects everyone at some point, and though it may even affect them badly it seldom leads to anything more serious. It's not a virulent strain of disease; one shakes it off easily. There may not be a cure for it, but its symptoms can be alleviated, suppressed. Do you follow me?'

I nodded. 'Another of your metaphors.'

'The jealousy I am trying to describe is extreme. It's dangerous in a way in which your jealousy is not dangerous. It's out of control, in some ways like a disease. What cures there are for it must be administered in its early stages or all is lost. If allowed to fester, it spreads.'

'Why are you telling me this?'

'So that you will understand what I tell you tomorrow.'

'Tell me whatever it is now,' I said, suddenly decisive, gripping her hand as she rose to leave the table. 'I can't wait another night.'

She looked at me, her eyes narrowing. 'Don't be imperious, James. It doesn't suit you.'

'I don't care.' I was suddenly exasperated. 'You've brought me on a six-hour journey to an island I never knew existed. You've talked to me of oceans and families and . . . and mysterious paintings which might make things "clearer". I don't want paintings. I don't want metaphors. I don't even thrive much on mystery. Just tell me why you've brought me here.'

76

'Let go of me.'

'I won't.'

'You're making a scene.'

'I don't care.'

I looked up at her in steady earnest and met the command in her pursed lips and blazing eyes unflinchingly. Slowly she sat down again.

'I brought you here because I thought you would help me,' she said after a moment, almost grudgingly.

'And so I will,' I replied, relaxing my grip on her hand. 'But you can't keep me in the dark like this.'

'I haven't.'

'You have. I get odd snippets here and there, I admit. You talk to me about the pressure of convention and the tide of public opinion. You talk to me about your family and a world I don't understand. And then you talk about jealousy, about your particular kind of jealousy.'

'It's not mine,' she hissed.

'Then whose is it?'

'It's not mine alone, at least. It's ... Well, if you must know it's mine and Sarah's.'

'*Sarah's?*'

'I know you don't believe me. That's why you must wait until tomorrow. You don't believe because you don't understand. You *can't* understand. I have told you as much as I can—'

'About what? About why you got engaged to Charles Stanhope?'

'About much more than that. But yes, about that too.'

'Then why won't you tell me the rest now?'

'Because you won't believe me. And you might not respect me if you did.'

She pulled her hand away from mine.

'I wish that a metaphor about currents and tides explained the mess I've made of things with Charles,' she began. 'And it does a bit, you know. It does. But only a bit.'

She smiled, calmer now. I listened.

'Of course my family are delighted I'm marrying. Of course they'd be horrified if I married anyone who wasn't as "suitable" as Charlie. That's all true. But there's more to it than that. I've got myself deep into something I can't quite explain but which frightens me much more than marrying Charlie could possibly frighten me. Something in my past – a habit, if you like – is out of control. I've lost the ability to stop. The fact I might have married Charlie has made me see that. It – this thing – is taking me over. I can see that because it has made me do something concrete which I despise myself for having done. Have you any idea what it's like to despise yourself? Not only for what you've already done but for what you see you might do? I've been shown that blackness. But I can't see where it ends. And I'm frightened of it.'

'"It" being jealousy?'

'Oh, no, James. Well, yes ... But it's more complex than that. All my explanations, even my metaphors, can't do justice to it. It's alive in me, not in a physical way, but it's there nonetheless. It's subtle and elusive; it's not obvious. No one would recognize it, save perhaps one other person. I have difficulty in recognizing it myself. But it frightens me, I tell you that frankly.'

78

'Why me?'

'What?'

'When you could have shared this with anyone in the world, why did you choose to share it with me?'

My question broke the flow of her tumble of words.

'I don't know,' she said slowly. 'You came when you were asked for, I suppose. As I sat on that bench, in an empty park, feeling more alone than I had ever felt in my life, you appeared. Oh, I don't mean I thought you were an angel, not in those rugby shorts. And anyway, an angel would have been no use. The help I need is of the most human kind.'

She smiled shyly.

'I almost told you everything then. I would have done if you'd only asked. But you didn't; and then something made me hesitate. I knew that before I could explain it to anybody, I had to be able to explain it to myself. So I didn't tell you.'

She lit another cigarette.

I watched her draw on it, thinking of the one she had smoked in Hyde Park on that warm morning weeks ago. I felt that years had passed since then, that the cardboard figure of Ella that I had made three-dimensional in private hours of daydream was being dismantled before my eyes. From the wreck of the romantic doll I had created I saw a woman emerge who had no notion of dashing saviours. Yet she was frightened and alone, as my creation had been, though for reasons other than the ones I had devised. This new woman was reaching out to me and I took her hand, not knowing where she might lead or pull.

'But then you appeared again at Camilla Boardman's,'

79

she said, 'just when I was trying to pretend that nothing was really wrong. And you made up that silly excuse about a handbag and endeared yourself instantly. Then you listened to me as I talked, and I felt that here was someone who might throw me a rope. But I didn't want it. You need to admit to yourself that you're drowning before you can be rescued and I couldn't do that. It was up to you to tie the rope around my wrists, by force if needs be. I couldn't come to you. And perhaps I wouldn't ever have been able to. But as things turned out, you – you of all people – appeared at my engagement party, and there you did tie the rope around my wrists, in a manner of speaking.'

She put her hand on mine.

'Of course I could see it terrified you to do it. You've been brought up to believe one shouldn't speak to a woman as you spoke to me that day. But you made me see you might be strong enough to help me, and I know that the hand that pulls the rope must be firm and the arms that hold it strong. I thought you might be strong. I wrote to you, not knowing whether you would meet me at the station or not. But you did. And now you're here.'

She leaned towards me.

'Thank you,' she said softly. And she kissed me.

Even from a distance of almost sixty years I can feel the touch of those soft lips, the tingling that ran through me as they leaned down to touch mine. Ella's lips: long-observed, long-imagined, finally given. Our kiss: shivering, electric, long, deliberate, gentle. I can taste the cigarette smoke of it.

'Thank you,' I said in my turn.

'And now you know a little more than you did.'

'I do.'

'And the rest you shall know tomorrow.'

'If you say so.'

'I do.'

'Goodnight, James.'

'Goodnight, Ella.'

She got up slowly and left the bar, deserted now but for a few loyal patrons who had been locked in to continue their drinking uninterrupted. It was long past midnight.

8

The next day was cold. A chilly wind whipped the small streets of the island, sending the tourists scurrying to shelter in tea-shops with Tudor beams and low doors. The islanders themselves paid no attention to the weather, moving with ruddy cheeks through the gusts that ripped the tiles from their roofs and sent sprays of sea into gardens and boats.

Above the village, aloof, stood the castle, casting a disdainful eye on the new army that trooped up its steep hill and paid the uniformed attendants at its gates for admission. The weapons of these invaders were not the bayonets of bygone ages; they were the guidebooks of the modern era. Their leaders did not exhort their followers fearlessly on snow-white chargers; instead they explained that there was a gift shop selling postcards at attractive prices on the left past the Italian fountain.

I listened to snatches of Seton's history from these guides as Ella and I walked behind them. I heard how it had been a monastery since the early twelve hundreds; how in 1536 the monks had been expelled by a vengeful Henry and his cardinal; how the great rooms had lain empty for almost a hundred years. I heard too how the seventeenth century had brought the place fitfully back to life, first as barracks, then as ammunition store and finally as prison. It was Ella who told me how the castle had then been given – by a guilty or grateful king, who is to say? – to Adelaide, Countess of Seton in 1670 for 'services rendered', as her descendant put it with a wry smile.

As I listened to all this I felt the castle watching. If cannon balls and shot had failed to cripple it in the Civil War, it seemed to say, what hope had we? Hewn from ancient granite, its walls four feet thick in places, it had the air of grim permanence that only eight centuries' exposure to cold wind and cold sea can impart.

Walking with Ella under the delicate swirls of its wrought-iron gates, a Victorian addition, I felt that no alterations, however cosy, could change the primeval nature of the place. Seton would not be moulded; it would not bend to the most persuasive of hands. One might install hot water and electricity; heat and furnish as one liked; but the character of the castle was immutable: cast in the very stone of its crenellations, expressed in the thick set of its towers and the defiance of its walls.

Inside we passed heavy rooms of solid furniture cordoned off by silk ropes, the American lilt of Ella's voice making me think of another young American girl, long ago, walking the corridors we walked then. Taking my hand, Ella led me through splendours of library and drawing room, past the dusty brocade and Chinese screens of the King's Bedroom, up stairs and along corridors. At length we emerged in the Great Hall, a high, cold, magnificent room of flagstones and mullioned panes. The hunting trophies of the Victorian gentleman lined its lengths. At its furthest extreme, set between two huge windows, was a portrait.

'There it is,' said Ella softly, nodding towards its heavy gilt frame. 'That's what I've brought you so far to see.'

The Great Hall at Seton is a long, rectangular room on the first floor, once the monastery refectory, and you enter it in the middle of its west side. The two walls to the north and south hold pairs of great windows that reach almost to the floor. One of these pairs gives on to a narrow balcony with a low balustrade, a quite inexplicable Victorian addition, from which a terrace, far beneath, is visible. The other is exposed to the sea, which pounds on the cliffs a hundred feet below it.

It is a large, dramatic room, not entirely without charm. A magnificent Elizabethan table, of ships' timbers salvaged from the Armada, stands in its centre. Otherwise the hall has no furniture, nothing in fact save the stags' heads on the walls and the painting of Blanche.

Ella's grandmother gazed out at the room towards the windows on the opposite wall and the sea that crashed below them. Her portrait hangs, whether as memorial or cruel joke I do not know, between the windows that give on to the balcony. It is from this balcony that she threw herself, and her death (though not its means) are commemorated by a bronze, Latin plaque set in the flagstones below. The castle guides translate it by rote.

I remember seeing Blanche's picture for the first time. I remember looking up at the features of Ella and Sarah, neither one, yet both, distilled in a face of extraordinary charm. I remember the brush strokes of her blonde hair, luxuriant and long, piled high above her face with its small nose and high cheekbones. She is wearing a pale blue dress and one small hand is visible, clasping a closed book. She stares out at the sea, a wistful look in her eyes. Perhaps she is thinking of home.

'Do you see now?' asked Ella quietly.

I felt the beginnings of understanding stir within me, but they were nebulous and incomplete. I looked at the woman by my side, the living, breathing woman whose hand held mine; and I looked at her again, this time immobile, a thing of canvas and oils in a heavy frame. I started to speak then stopped.

'Explain to me,' I said finally.

Ella led me out of the room and into the long gallery that houses the Seton china. I saw that several corridors opened off it, and that the opening of each was protected by a red silk rope. A guard sat sleepily on a high-backed chair at the far end of the corridor. Looking at him sharply to make sure he did not see, Ella stepped over the first of the ropes and motioned for me to follow.

'Quickly,' she hissed.

And quickly, almost running, I followed her down the corridor, through a door and up the spiral staircase behind it. Up and up we climbed, the darkness relieved on each complete revolution by a small arrow slit of window, through which we could see the blue sea, further and further away as we circled upwards. We passed first one then two doors set into the stone. Outside the third we stopped.

'I'm just hoping this is open,' said Ella as she tried its wrought-iron handle. 'Come on, James, push.'

So I pushed, and forced the unlocked door open on

rusty hinges. We were in a small, oddly shaped sitting room tucked between the staircase and the tower wall. It was obviously unused. Dust sheets covered the furniture and I saw, as Ella removed one of them, that there was a large doll's house in one corner.

'Spooky, don't you think?' she whispered delightedly as she removed another sheet to reveal a moth-eaten sofa.

'Very.'

'It was my favourite room as a child. My father used to bring me here sometimes, you know. I colonized this room for myself. There're so many it was never missed.' She smiled wistfully at the doll's house. 'My mother gave me that. You know, you're the only person, besides my father, whom I've ever shown this room to? At least while it's been mine.'

'Thank you.'

'I wonder why they've left it just as I did.'

'I don't suppose they need the space. Why should they bother to clear it?'

'You're probably right. Why bother? There're enough rooms to dust as it is.'

'I'm sure.'

'Something like three hundred, as a matter of fact.'

Settling herself on a window-ledge she motioned me towards the dusty sofa.

'What did you think of that painting?'

'Artistically or ...' I hesitated. 'Or in the context of what you were saying last night?'

'Both.'

'Well, I thought it was beautiful, as a painting.'

'It's by Sargent, you know.'

86

I nodded. 'Sarah told me about it.'

'She told you? What on earth did she tell you for?' Ella's eyes were bright with instant fury.

'No idea. She didn't tell me much, anyway.'

'What did she say?'

'Nothing really. Not much more than that Sargent had painted your grandmother. I presume you didn't bring me to see it for its artistic merit alone.'

'No I didn't.'

'Well then ...'

Ella got up and walked to another of the room's low windows. Sitting on its ledge, her knees pulled up under her chin, she began to speak.

I can see her there, framed by the blue of the sea far below; I can hear her carefully chosen words, feel the tension between us, a tension of confidence dared and understanding attempted.

'I've been trying to answer for myself the question of how it began, of what it grew from,' said Ella. 'Do you understand?'

I nodded.

'And I think the answer is in that picture.'

'In what way?'

'In lots of ways.' She paused, thinking. 'That picture is about family,' she said at last, 'about my family. It's about unhappiness and brilliance and madness and ...'

In a few words she told me the story of Blanche's life and death, which I had already heard from Sarah.

'When I was nine and Sarah ten,' Ella continued, 'my mother and both Sarah's parents died together in a train accident.'

'How awful. I'm sorry.' Even as I spoke, the words seemed inadequate.

'It was awful.'

Ella looked at me; for a long moment neither of us moved.

'And how terrible for Sarah, too,' I said at last. 'Losing both her parents when she was ... how old did you say?'

'Ten.'

I paused, a faint realization crystallizing slowly in my mind.

'This is to do with Sarah, isn't it?'

'Yes, James. My life to date has been to do with Sarah.'

'Go on.'

'I shouldn't jump around like this. First I told you about my grandmother; now I'm telling you about me and Sarah. It might help if I told you about the generation that went between us.'

'All right.'

'Well, Blanche had four children: Cyril, the eldest, who now lives here with his wife; Alexander, my father; Anna, my father's twin; and Cynthia, Sarah's mother. Cyril was ten years old when his mother died. My father and Anna were eight. Cynthia was six. You can imagine what it must have been like for them.'

She looked out to sea.

'They each reacted in their different ways, but it scarred them all. Cyril took refuge in eccentricity. My father stopped talking much about how he really felt. So did Cynthia. Anna, on the other hand, was like Blanche: brilliant, but not stable. She became obsessed by her mother's death.'

88

Ella took a cigarette from a case in her pocket and lit it.

'She devoted her life to being as much like her mother as she could be.' She exhaled. 'She was devoted to Blanche's memory, but not in a healthy way; not in a normal way. She wore her mother's dresses. She did her hair in the same way her mother had done hers. And she hated her father as much as it is possible for one person to hate another.' She paused. 'This house has plenty of dark secrets.'

I sat silently, waiting for her to continue.

'Anna killed herself eventually. She also jumped out of a window. Just like her mother. They buried her at Seton, of course, and the train crash in which my mother and Sarah's parents were killed happened as they were coming back from her funeral.'

'God.'

'So, you see, my father lost his twin and his wife within a week of each other. That was why he took me away to America as soon as we had won the war. I'm afraid I was a bit flippant about it all on the train. I wasn't sure I was going to tell you everything then. Now I see it's all spilling out.'

She looked at me and I smiled.

'Anyway, he hates this place. I think he feels Seton is somehow to blame for what happened to his family. Or perhaps it's just too full of memories. I don't know. What I do know is that he's terrified of me turning out like Anna or his mother. That's why he took me to America. First to California and then, when he met Pamela, to Boston. You couldn't get further from Seton than San Francisco, I assure you. He tried to forget he ever knew this place. And although he had to visit it every so often, he kept his visits to a minimum.'

'I can understand that,' I said.

'Can you? I'm glad. Because it's now that my own story starts.'

She took a long drag on her cigarette.

'You can see the tremendous influence Blanche had over her whole family, particularly in death. Though no one said it – the Harcourts don't talk, you know – everyone thought about insanity and mental illness. They brooded on violent death. So many of them had died so horribly, you see: their mother; two sisters; my mother; Sarah's father. And Sarah and I, the only children in the family, could feel that pressure as we grew up. We knew that people worried about us, that they feared for us. And we knew why, too. We knew that our grandmother and our aunt had both killed themselves. It's not a knowledge that's easy to deal with when you're young.'

She paused, considering something.

'Of course it might have brought us together, I suppose, if we had seen more of each other at that crucial time. And if we hadn't both grown up looking so like our grandmother. As it was, the way we looked was a constant reminder of how we might turn out. Sarah felt it even more than I. She saw that picture downstairs every day of her life.'

'You mean she lived here?'

'Yes. Uncle Cyril and Aunt Elizabeth took her in after her parents died. They didn't have children of their own.'

'And Sarah grew up here . . .'

'Yes.'

'Poor girl.'

'Yes.'

'And I grew up in America, away from all this. But I knew of it, of course. I came to Seton to visit, I saw that painting, I watched myself turn into its image.'

'And?'

'And I watched Sarah, too. She watched me.'

'And you saw the same person.'

'Precisely.'

'I think I'm beginning to see.'

'We felt like two halves of one whole, so to speak, but it didn't make for closeness. We weren't like twins. We each needed, I think, to conquer the other before we could feel like a complete person. Do you understand that? The feeling that, far away, another possible version of you is living, thinking, growing. If we'd never seen much of each other it might have been all right. But when I was eighteen Daddy married Pamela, who couldn't resist the temptations of London for long, especially with a name like Harcourt to open doors for her. So we came back.'

'And you and Sarah were thrown together again. The two halves were reunited.'

'That was how it felt, sometimes. And such different halves we were.'

'You had had such different lives.'

'Of course. She had lived here, on this island, steeped in tradition, in the cult of our family.'

'I see.'

'No you don't. You've no idea how the Harcourts are treated here. It's positively feudal, a little kingdom cut off from the world. A society of obligation and duty and ritual and ... all the things I was free from in America. Away from it I could be myself. Growing up within it, Sarah could only be one person: the future chatelaine, the keeper-in-waiting of the castle. And that's who she became.'

I nodded. Ella lit another cigarette.

'The tragedy, though,' she went on, 'is that Sarah never will have Seton. When Cyril dies, if he has no children, which seems increasingly likely, it will be my father's. And then it will be mine. It was given to a woman, you see. An Act of Parliament was passed to make sure it could be inherited by one too. Oh, there are plenty of provisions, of course. No Catholic can inherit; no divorcée; no convicted criminal. That last clause was added by the Victorians, I think. Typical. But since I am neither Catholic nor divorced nor a felon, in the course of time it will all be mine.'

'Which explains Sarah's—'

'Hatred. Hatred of me.'

'I see.'

'And it's worse because she loves this place, she under-stands it in a way I never could or will. I'll never be anything more than a tourist here. With my accent and my ideas, how could I ever be anything else?'

'So far I follow you.'

I was quiet for a moment, trying to straighten things in my mind.

'But what did you mean yesterday when you talked about a pattern of behaviour you couldn't change? You likened it to an addiction, didn't you?'

She nodded.

'What did you mean?'

92

'I was talking about me and Sarah, James. You've no idea of the extent to which each of our lives is dictated by the other's. I know that Seton will be mine one day. And I know I'm not worthy of it. Have you any idea what that feels like?'

Seeing me about to reply, she went on quickly, opening the window behind her and letting in a gust of sharp, cold air.

'You couldn't and I'm glad you couldn't. My family has lived here for more than three hundred years. Can you imagine how much responsibility it carries with it?'

I shook my head.

'And to know that you're not equal to it, but that someone else is, that you haven't had the training required, but that someone else has. I sometimes think it would be much better for us both if Sarah and I just swapped places. If only I could get rid of my accent and she could acquire it, she could have my name and I hers. Then I could think as I liked, do what I pleased with my life, have the freedom I so badly want and which Sarah's got. And Sarah could fulfil her destiny.'

She ran a distracted hand through her hair.

'But the roles are switched. Fate has tricked us. She can never have what I have. And I'm left striving to acquire what she has. That rigid poise, that certainty of the world and her place in it. It's so alien to my nature but I want it so badly. I want to prove to her that I deserve her blessed Seton, that I will take care of it. I want to acquit myself honourably, for heaven's sake.'

She paused.

'Can't you understand that?'

93

'I do understand it, Ella,' I said. 'I understand it completely.'

'Then tell me why I might have married Charlie,' she said sharply.

'You got engaged,' I said slowly, thinking carefully, choosing my words with caution, 'because Charles Stanhope is precisely the sort of man Sarah might have married. Eton, Oxford, just charming enough without being too clever. He would have been the perfect partner for the Countess of Seton. I presume you get the title with the house?'

She nodded.

'But in the end you won't marry him. Ultimately your sense of self is too strong.'

'I hope so, James.'

I got up from my sofa and crossed the room to kiss her. She held up a hand to stop me.

'No. You should know one more thing first.'

'What's that?' I asked, standing over her.

'Charlie Stanhope was not just the kind of person Sarah *might* have married. She would have married him, had I not . . .' Her voice tailed off.

I drew away. 'Had you not . . .'

'Sarah was in love with him, James. Completely in love with him, in that passionate way people who are usually cold fall in love, if they ever do. I took Charlie away from Sarah. I took Charlie from Sarah only because she wanted him so badly. Coldly, quite calculatedly, I set about taking him from her; and I got him.'

She looked at me.

'Do you see how frightening this thing is? I would have

94

done anything, sacrificed anything – my future, Charlie's future – just to hurt Sarah, just to show her that all her training, all her perfect breeding, counts for nothing.' Ella was crying now. 'I can't believe what I've done.'

It was not a time for words. Not yet. I went over to the cold ledge on which she sat and put my arms around her shaking shoulders.

'Come on,' I said softly. 'It's not too late. At least you understand it, at least you know it was wrong.'

And I thought as I said it that understanding was tantamount to absolution. I omitted the step of confession, which can come before or after understanding but which must come at some point on the path to peace. So too did I ignore the making of amends, which alone makes forgiveness acceptable, even if it remains possible without it.

I would not make the same omissions now. When we sin we pay in a multitude of ways. Sometimes acknowledgement and confession can help us towards absolution, but nothing is possible without reparation.

Ella was fortunate, even if she did not choose to make use of her good fortune. She could have made her reparations and asked forgiveness from Sarah. She could have confessed, and thus she might have found peace. From a distance of sixty years I envy her that freedom.

I have no one with whom to make amends, at least not in this world. And thus there is no one to forgive me. My guilt is ever with me and I must accept that fact. Eric, who alone might have forgiven me, is dead.

As I held Ella on that cold window-ledge, watching the waters of the sea as my neck grew wet from her tears,

I thought that I could save her, that my help, my understanding, was all that she would need. I did not tell her to go to Sarah. I did not wish her to share the intimacy of confession with anyone but me. Already I was jealous of her trust. And so I held her as she cried, and answered 'No' when she asked 'Do you hate me?' and murmured words of love and forgiveness and hope, only the first of which was mine to give.

But they had their effect. Ella stopped crying, believing what I said, and in thus believing she made her grave mistake. She did not know, perhaps did not care to know – and I who suspected did not tell her – that the only person within whose power forgiveness lay was Sarah.

Ella was a proud woman, and pride is the undoing of many. But pride, as it turned out, was not ultimately to be Ella's undoing. It was the lack of trust in the world which comes from betraying yourself that was to be her downfall. Those who give expect much to be given to them; those who take expect much to be taken from them.

By comforting Ella I disguised the dangers of what she had done in the protective gentleness of soothing words. I did not do her a service. Far better that I should have made her – for in that brief moment she would have done anything I suggested – return to London by the next train and confess all to Sarah and to Charles Stanhope. Then there would have been a scene; tears and bitterness would have flowed. And something would have been released. The festering wounds in both cousins would have been opened. They might have been made clean again.

But my soothing of Ella did much to cover over her guilt and so Sarah's injury was allowed to fester undisturbed.

As I stroked her hair and kissed the soft skin of her neck, I thought only of stopping her tears and healing her pain. I was too young to know that tears can purify and too unsure to guide Ella rather than comfort her.

My soothing made confession, and thus forgiveness, at first unnecessary and then impossible. How could I have known that it might have saved us all?

9

I had not been long back from Cornwall, perhaps only a day or two, when the telephone rang and I answered it to Camilla Boardman's breathless cadences and elongated vowels.

'Daaarling. Where have you *been*?' she cooed.

It was an accepted fiction between us that after periods of non-communication it was to me that the blame for this lapse should fall. It was ten days since I had taken her to the Harcourts' lunch and ten days since, smiling and deferential, I had deposited her at her door and we had promised to see each other soon.

'I've been here, Camilla,' I lied. 'Just very busy.'

'Musicking again?' Camilla separated artistic endeavour into three broad categories: musicking; artying; and literaturing.

'Yes. Got to practise. The Guildhall starts soon.'

'I *know*, darling.'

'What can I do for you?'

'It's more what I can do for you. I've just had the most *fantastic* idea.'

'Ye-es.'

I was cautious of Camilla's fantastic ideas.

'I can't *think* why it hasn't occurred to me before.'

'Ye-es.'

'There's someone you simply must meet. You'd enjoy each other such a lot.'

Camilla was wholehearted and sincere – though not always completely disinterested – in her social benevolence.

'Who?' I asked, interested; her enthusiasm was infectious.

'My mother,' she said simply.

And so it was that I attended my first Boardman 'morning'.

The house in Cadogan Square appeared to have sustained little damage as a result of Camilla's birthday party. If cigarettes had been dropped or champagne cocktails spilled, the results of such disasters had been artfully concealed or removed. But the feel of expansive emptiness had gone.

I sensed this the following day as I was admitted by a maid who disappeared with a smile as soon as the door had closed behind me. Furniture and ornament had returned to hall and drawing room, both now a clutter of Victoriana; and through the bibelots, past the open doors to what had been the dancing room, I saw a group of six or seven men and women on uncomfortable chairs pulled in a semicircle around their hostess. Regina Boardman, like her name, was stately and well preserved. She spoke with the attentive yet authoritative tones of the society patron.

'I think salon is such an awful word to use in England,' she was saying as I entered.

Silently I waited for her to notice me, and when she showed no sign of doing so I coughed. She turned slowly, as though careful not to unsettle her hair.

'You must be Mr Farrell,' she said warmly, and offered me her right hand to shake as she indicated a chair with her left. 'My daughter speaks very highly of your talents.'

'Thank you,' I said, as I took my place in the chattering circle.

But sparkling though the conversation of that morning was, its subject matter is not what has remained in my mind; nor can I remember the faces of the people who contributed so eloquently to it. I rack my brain for a memory of Eric and am cheated. It is rather the tableau as a whole which has remained vivid.

I see Regina Boardman, patron saint of struggling artists and other hopeless causes, holding forth to a group of her devoted supplicants. It is a scene which, properly allegorized, might have hung on one of the walls of her heavily Victorian house: *Charity Throned in Splendour.* Yet Regina's style was not Victorian, though her taste in furniture was; and her approach to us, as to all her causes, was thoroughly modern. She was efficient and hard-nosed, with a beady eye for opportunity. When not dealing with the management of public appeals, she had the leisure and the inclination for private patronage.

That morning I was welcomed under the banner of her protection with a gracious smile and a cup of coffee. I accepted both gladly and joined the discussion with enthusiasm, for I recognized my side of the bargain: Regina, unlike her daughter, had a high respect for culture and though not a thinker herself, she liked to seem one. So she took care to listen to people who thought and to support those who put their thoughts into words for her benefit.

There was a more concrete system of reciprocation in operation, too, though I only learned of it as I was leaving. Regina Boardman was one of the wise who understand that generosity that is not reciprocated is stifling and by the time we were in the hall, departing en masse, she had extracted a promise from each of her guests to contribute to a cause quite distinct from their own professional advancement. There was nothing stated about this arrangement; it simply existed. Regina asked and you said yes.

She did not expect you to support her causes with your money but with your expertise and your time. And the cause for which she was marshalling support that morning, as we said our goodbyes, was the restoration of decaying religious buildings. Not for Regina Boardman were the jewels of St Paul's or the Abbey; such national monuments would be no test of her fund-raising prowess. She was interested, instead, in the smaller churches; in the buildings which, as they crumble, are the price a secular age must pay for its indifference to organized religion.

She was organizing a concert at St Peter's, Eaton Square. The success of her appeal depended on it and someone had failed her.

'I had three Beethoven violin sonatas all lined up,' she said to me, her face a picture of pain, 'and the soloist I had in mind has gone off to Berlin to play at a party for that little man with the funny moustache. Herr Hitler. Very good for him, and I'm quite thrilled, of course, but the timing of it's a nuisance nevertheless.'

It happened that the violin sonatas in question were required pieces for my Guildhall course and I had been working on them for some months. In a flash of clarity

I realized that Mrs Boardman probably knew this from her daughter, and that it was not only chance or affection that had brought me to Cadogan Square.

But Regina had mastered an art with which Camilla was still struggling. She had a way of presenting her own desires so that they coincided precisely with the interests of the person from whom she was extracting a favour. Inducement was her forte. As she stood chatting with me on the steps of her house, waving to her other guests as they walked away across the square, she skirted prettily around, and then offered me directly, a sizeable inducement indeed. Michael Fullerton, a reviewer from *The Times*, would be covering the concert at St Peter's.

'He thinks he's coming to hear Heinrich von Hammersmark,' said Regina lightly.

Von Hammersmark, I took it, was the protégé, recently discovered, who had promised to play and now could not.

'Michael's writing a piece on rising talent. I see no reason why you shouldn't be the rising talent instead of Heinrich, who seems to have risen quite nicely without Michael's help.' She smiled benignly upon me. 'Of course we needn't say anything about the change of programme,' she added archly, 'until the last moment. You know what these critics are like.'

I nodded, though I had no idea.

She beamed at me encouragingly. 'If you'd like the chance to play, it's yours.'

I had one reservation. 'Are you sure you wouldn't like to hear me before you put the success of the concert into my hands?'

'Oh darling,' she said, laughing, 'what do *I* know about

music? If you're good enough for the Guildhall, you're good enough for me.'

'In that case,' I said, 'I'm yours.'

'But that's *marvellous*. Thank you so much.'

'And when is it?'

'The concert?'

I nodded.

'Next Friday.'

We shook hands.

As I walked down the steps on to the street she called to me.

'Excuse me, James,' her voice rang out, high and clear.

We were already on first-name terms, for immediate intimacy was the key to Regina's technique.

'I haven't told you who your accompanist is to be.' She smiled at me. 'How silly. His name is Eric de Vaugirard, a really delightful young man. Very French. Very artistic. He was at my "morning", in fact.'

She produced a pen and paper from her voluminous handbag.

'Here is his telephone number. I shall give him yours, too, so that you can contact each other and rehearse over the week.'

'Thank you,' I said, pocketing the paper.

'The thanks are *all* from me,' she replied, kissing me firmly on both cheeks.

And waving me down the remaining stairs, she went back into the house, closing its gleaming door briskly behind her.

IO

It is cold in this room now; the fire is dying and the radiators are useless. This place resists all heating. But I will stay here until I have the events of my life in some kind of order I can understand. For not only must the strands of experience be unravelled; they must be twisted into place again and understood. It is a laborious process, but a rewarding one, though I am continuously distracted by the poor quality of the tools at my disposal. If you spend sixty years trying not to remember you eventually succeed.

It has been a struggle to learn how not to speak of important things; but it is a challenge to which I have risen with success. With so much success, in fact, that now, when I try to remember, my faculties fail me. The frustrating thing about recollection, even once its wheels have been coaxed into motion, is its sketchiness. About some things, some of them inconsequential, my memory is complete. About others, there is hardly anything at all.

Ella was burned into my mind. Remembering her has not been difficult. Sarah lived with me for almost sixty years; I could not forget her. It is Eric who has fallen away. My guilt obscures him. It is to him that I would make amends, if only I could. But he is dead and I hardly remember what he looked like. That is an ugly thought.

I know I must have met him at some time in the week that followed my attendance at that first Boardman 'morning'. He was, after all, to be my accompanist for the concert at St Peter's. And I know also that as I walked down Sloane Street on that blazing August day, whistling, I had his telephone number on a piece of paper in my pocket. I suppose I must have telephoned him and that our rehearsals together must have gone well, for the concert itself was a success; and as the first quasi-professional performance of my career it will always have a special place in my affections.

I have played at many concerts since, in concert halls far grander than the dank church I played in that night and to audiences far more receptive than the one that gathered to hear me then. But viewed from a distance of sixty years, and at the end of a career that has seen a certain amount of success, I find myself thinking of that evening with nostalgia, for the chill of nerves and the thrill of applause grow more commonplace as the years pass.

I see the dark columns of the church, feel its cool, damp air. I hear the expectant hush as I take my place by the piano on an improvised stage in the nave. And now, looking over to him as I signal that I am ready to begin, I see Eric. In this memory, though I do not know him well – perhaps because I do not know him well – I see him unobscured. He is a dignified figure in evening tails and white tie, his unruly hair tamed for the occasion.

Eric was tall and more thickly built than I, with a strong neck. His skin was almost olive – there was a touch of the Spaniard in him – and his eyes were dark. They and his hands distinguished him from the line of gentleman farmers who had tilled the Vaugirard lands for centuries. Large and dark, almost black, his eyes danced. They were joyful.

I remember the applause that night. I remember Ella's face, glowing with pleasure, in the front row beside her father and stepmother. I remember bowing and motioning to Eric to bow also and I remember . . .

But what is the use of all this memory? Remembering that concert will not help my understanding of the events I wish to explain. My career is not a mystery to me. Search though I might, I can find no glimpse of an oracle on that happy night who might have whispered silently that in three months – was it four? – Eric would be dead.

No, I find no sign. And as I look for one my mind fills instead with the memory of that first interview with Michael Fullerton. It is his face – so meaningless to me now – that returns to me, not Eric's; it is his bulging belly I see, his whisky-reeking breath I smell.

Regina Boardman was detailed and frank in her instructions.

'Michael Fullerton,' she told me the day before the concert, 'is an old queen. An absolute dear,' she hastened to assure me (for Regina Boardman had nothing, absolutely nothing against homosexuals), 'but the fact that you're a good-looking young man isn't going to do your chances any harm. Make sure you look dashing and don't mind if he flirts with you. A little judicious smiling – it's all that's required, on top of an inspired performance, of course – and you never know what he might do for you. He's an influential man, knows lots of people. Lots of the right people. He's certainly someone to get on your side. So do try. Make sure you do.'

I did. When Michael told me that I really should be photographed for a feature he was writing, I smiled; when he praised my control of my instrument ('Very masculine, Mr Farrell, but so sensual, quite erotic') I smiled; when he asked me to tea at the Ritz the following day to talk further, I smiled also and accepted. When he had gone, I told Regina verbatim what he had said.

'But, James, that's *marvellous*,' she cried. 'You know that means a real interview, not one of these "quick chats" he has with everyone after the concerts he goes to. He's obviously taken a shine to you, my boy. You won't need *my* help any longer. Once Michael Fullerton thinks you're good, things start happening of their own accord. He told me,' she added confidentially, 'that he wasn't a *bit* upset I didn't tell him about the change in soloist. He told me you had raw talent. Those were his precise words.'

And so Regina Boardman went home delighted and I, delighted myself, was free to keep the clandestine appointment in Eaton Square gardens that Ella and I had made the afternoon before.

I have no recollection of saying goodbye to Eric nor of thanking him, though I must have done both before I left the church. I have no difficulty in remembering my tea with Michael Fullerton, however; or how on expenses I drank tea and ate strawberries, and talked to him of music and passion and the uncertainties of youth. A photographer from *The Times* appeared and took photographs of me, windswept in the breeze, in Green Park. That was that.

It was not until a week later that any results appeared, and it was not I who saw them first but Camilla Boardman, who came in person to show them to me and who arrived on my doorstep, waving a sheet of newspaper, at half past nine one warm morning.

'Hello, *darling*! You *splendid* boy.'

'Morning, Camilla,' I said, wondering what she was doing on my doorstep; then I saw the newspaper in her hand. 'Give me that.' I was awake at once.

'Uh, uh, *uh*. What's the magic word?'

'Don't be coy. Give it to me.' Morning irritability mixed with excitement made me impatient.

'I shan't show you at *all* if you insist on being so rude. I think the *least* you could do is ask me in and offer me a cup of tea. I've come halfway across London to show you this.'

This was not strictly true, but details of geography had never troubled Camilla.

'Oh all right, then,' she said, giving in with a pout, as I remained impassive in the doorway. She handed me the newspaper. And on seeing the look of pleasure on my face she hugged me, with a sincerity that reminded me why I liked her, and told me I was *superb*.

I certainly felt so. Michael Fullerton's feature on me, entitled 'New Star in the Firmament', offered an end to the war with my parents over my future; and the victory was mine.

Our struggle had lasted almost two years and had grown bloody in the two months since I had left Oxford. I had explained, cajoled and finally insulted. They had told me, calmly at first and then frostily, that I was an impulsive boy who did not know his own mind.

I ran into the breakfast room with Camilla behind me and showed them the article, whooping with schoolboy joy. I have it still today; I have kept it all these years.

'This passionate young man,' Michael Fullerton had written, 'seems set to take London and the world by storm. At times controlled, at times abandoned, frequently inspired, his playing belies his years.'

My mother, to her credit, cried. My father shook my hand. The war was over.

But it was Ella I most wanted to see, Ella by whom I most wished to be praised. I was like a gun dog with a pheasant. So I telephoned the house in Chester Square and asked her to meet me on the steps of the National Gallery in half an hour.

'You have got it, haven't you? He did write it, didn't he?'

I was silent.

'I'm off to buy *The Times* right this minute. Oh God, this is wonderful. What's he said? What's the photograph like?'

But I was enigmatic to the last. 'Meet me in half an hour,' I said again.

'Of course, my love. In half an hour.'

Hearing Ella's voice made up for all my anxieties over our future. She still was not free. We had returned from Cornwall, locked in discussion for six hours on the train, and parted, as we had decided, with the restrained politeness of virtual strangers. It would not do for us to be seen or for our hands to be forced.

'It's better like this,' she had said. 'I have to ease myself out of this slowly. There are a lot of people I've got to consider before myself. Charlie, Sarah, my parents, my family. No one must see us. No one must suspect about you and me.'

And I had agreed with her.

I number the few weeks of illicit meetings that followed as amongst the happiest of my life. Ella and I snatched our kisses in art galleries and shared our souls on park benches. We touched in the furtive dark of cinemas. We were living in the calm before the storm, and the difficulty of our meetings only added to their pleasure.

For Ella and me, as for all who experience the first rush of illicit love, the enchantment was in the present. It had no future in its first, unaltered state; but it bound us nevertheless with a force that has lasted to this day, despite all that has happened. In those weeks I came truly to life, as I had never done before and would not do again. I was not a fish in a school; or, if I was, then Ella and I had made a school for ourselves alone, and we swam the ocean together.

It was a time of manifold consummations, for love was a varied catalyst; and it came particularly to be the time of my music's real flourishing.

I remember the hours Ella spent on the floor of my cramped attic, listening to me play. I remember how she always sat in the same position, half curled, half upright, on a cushion in the corner where the eaves came almost to the floor: a delicate crumple of limbs, one hand occasionally brushing the fine golden hair from her eyes. I remember how she would be completely still, believing that I played best when hardly conscious of her presence. And although the reverse was true, her quiet exhilaration –

all the more felt for her stillness – first calmed me and then dared me beyond the technical shallows in which I might otherwise have lingered.

Ella would sit, hardly moving, for two or three hours at a time. She would follow me through my scales and exercises; through the seemingly endless repetition of certain phrases; and then she would open the grimy windows and fill the room with the fresh breeze of summer, smiling and laughing and telling me I was wonderful, that I made her happy in ways I could not dream.

We would drink tea together, perhaps, or wine, as the sinking sun filled the room with dusty warmth; and then she would smoke a cigarette, resume her former position in the corner and listen to me, eyes closed, as I played to her: pieces I had grown up with; the Beethoven sonatas I was preparing for the Guildhall; snatches of the violin lines from orchestral works that she loved.

Her tastes were diverse but she had her favourites, and I spent many hours playing them to her, watching the glow of her cheeks as she leaned her head, unseeing, on one bare, folded knee. Bach's fourth sonata for harpsichord and violin was frequently called for, I remember; so too was the waltz from Act I of *Swan Lake*. And it was at Ella's suggestion, and under her encouragement, that I began to learn Mendelssohn's Violin Concerto in E Minor, though I had no way of knowing that it would prove to be the making of my career.

Ella heard me with a delight that taught me the joys of performance. She transformed my natural shyness into a certain delicacy of presence; she taught me to rise to the challenges of my chosen art and helped me to rejoice in the power it gave me to move others.

Relationships grow: their pleasures change and their struggles progress. That first rush of joy, as pure as anything human can be, is never repeated. It develops; it grows; it becomes, I suppose, more real. But in doing so it loses some of its power to intoxicate, for magic must fade in the grim reality of a world beyond the control of lovers.

Throughout those balmy weeks Ella and I were intoxicated, and for many reasons our intoxication did not fade of its own accord. It had no time to do so before we were overtaken by its consequences. We could not lay foundations; our love could not grow as other loves have grown. The joys of a later, more stable age were stifled before they could begin.

Ella blew open my notions about life, my pre-conceptions about how one might live; and I did the same to hers. Together we detonated all history and watched, exhilarated, as worlds of experience and possibility opened in its place and expanded with the frantic energy of romantic fusion. Our nights together – snatched, secretive and few – were eternities. Our days we filled with debate and exploration and music and laughter and ... But why do I try to relive them?

The shadows were lengthening over us even then, just as they were over Europe and the world. For even as we revelled in the power our union gave us, we lost control of its force. Ella and I, in love for the first time, were unprepared for the energy of that first rush. We were children. We behaved with the abandon of children. But our weapons were adult; they were not toys. We smashed our world with the arrogance of gods. Tradition, responsibility, social constriction, all crumbled under the vehemence of our attack. We thought to re-create society in our own image. And in so doing we forgot our place in it and in the heavenly order. Human beings are not gods; they should not play with divine fire. Ella and I committed the sin which the Greeks have taught us is fatal. In our hubris we forgot ourselves. We forgot too that demolition requires rebuilding; that people's hearts are fragile; that to touch them with anything but love returned is evil.

II

My concert at St Peter's was not the last I played under the auspices of one of Regina Boardman's charities, nor was it the only occasion on which Eric accompanied me. That much I know from factual recollection.

If it comes to that, I know, too, that we were both regular in our attendance at Mrs Boardman's 'mornings'. But this I know from what he told me later; I have no memory of him as distinct from the other guests who sat in the library at Cadogan Square and talked with such competitive erudition.

I struggle to think now of anything Eric said. Nothing returns to me. But we must have been on terms of easy familiarity because I was not surprised to receive his invitation to tea.

We had played in two more concerts together since the night of our success at St Peter's and had had another good review in Michael Fullerton's column in *The Times*. I remember reading the slip of blue notepaper from Eric as I sat at home one morning, waiting for Ella; and I remember being vaguely pleased to receive it. Certainly it was no cause for surprise, nor even for particular interest.

That fact, and my memory of the afternoon I spent

with him a few days later, prove, I think, how much of my early friendship with Eric I have forgotten. In recollection, he remains a virtual stranger right up to the day of his great Idea. In actual fact, of course, he was by that stage a friend, and someone who thought of me as a good friend.

I wish I could unearth the details of our first few conversations, of the gradual stages by which we approached intimacy; but the dust of years, conscientiously heaped upon all thoughts of him, has obscured them. They are irretrievable, a fact that frustrates me.

But I do see the tiny flat he lived in now, with its grimy view of Battersea power station. I see its narrow hall and poky kitchen, its cramped sitting room and broom-cupboard bathroom. His bedroom I cannot picture, since I probably never saw it, but the rest comes back with increasing clarity.

Eric had a theory about houses. He argued, and not always flippantly, that like children they should be taught to overcome their limitations. The limitation of his flat was its size. In any given room it was quite possible for two adults, stretching, to touch the tips of each other's fingers with one hand and a pair of opposing walls with the other. Eric rose above this restriction by ignoring it, and his rooms were filled to their seams with oversized furniture.

'Treat a house as though it will grow,' he said, 'and one day it might.'

Thus the small, rather dark flat in which the budget of a starting-out musician forced him to live was furnished with the opulence of a palace, its treasures looted, I gathered, from disreputable auction houses and estate sales.

And although one might not be able to walk with much ease between the Chesterfield and a large potted palm that stood by it, it was impossible to deny that the effect produced by both was anything but impressive. Only Eric's piano stood quite alone, for he believed in showing deference to objects he valued. It was thus that his instrument, unlike his sofa, was not cramped; it stood in an otherwise empty space, aloof from the haphazard indignities to which the other furniture was subjected.

The more I go over that house in my mind, the more I find the character of its occupant returning to me. Eric was not only deferential to things, as so many people are whose intelligence and sensitivity removes them from the world as most understand it. He was not lost in his music, though he lived by it; his mind did not distance him from humanity, though it was superior to most minds. He was someone who engaged with people, whose first thought was more often for the good of his friends than for the satisfaction of his own wants.

He had little of the selfishness that city living can inculcate: what he had, he shared. And his roots were in the country, in the fertile fields of Provence. He had something of the gentleman farmer in him, for all his urbanity, which lent a wholesomeness to his erudition while physical strength gave him presence. Regina Boardman – I am remembering now – called him a 'son of the soil'. Unlike Charles Stanhope, education and social training had not robbed Eric of vitality; and although he was softly spoken, he was vigorous.

I remember his vigour, his enthusiasm, his childlike trust.

I remember, too, the afternoon in early September I spent drinking tea with him. The Anglophile in Eric loved the institution of afternoon tea. Its rituals appealed to his Gallic flair, and the delights of his tea table – which I must have sampled more than once, since I know this to be true – were varied and rich.

On the afternoon I remember I am sitting on a corner of the Chesterfield, my feet positioned gingerly in the tiny space between sofa and tea table. Eric is busying himself with tea strainers and lumps of sugar in an old porcelain bowl. His collection of china was eclectic: invariably of the highest quality, it was nevertheless all second-hand and acquired at random over years. Thus a Spode saucer might go with a Willow Pattern cup – that, in fact, is the combination into which he is pouring my tea as I follow the scene – or a Mason cake plate with a Wedgwood milk jug.

Yes, I'm remembering now: the stuffy sitting room, the delicate china, Eric's large hands moving gracefully between teapot and milk jug. I am in the middle of telling him about Camilla Boardman, whom he has not met, when he asks if I take one lump or two; he can't remember. His English is almost without accent or error; only the occasional lapse in idiom betrays him, and he seems to be humorously aware of his mistakes.

I reply too quietly that I take one lump and he asks me to repeat myself, so that when I continue my anecdote the thread of my account has been broken, and I grow conscious that it is no longer funny. I finish it nevertheless and when I have done so my friend settles himself opposite me on a large wing-backed armchair, suddenly serious. The chair is ramshackle but comfortable; for comfort, as well as opulence, is what Eric looks for in furniture. In his right hand is a slice of buttered toast, in his left a cup of tea. He turns to face me, smiling, but I sense that he has something important to say.

I was right.

'James,' he began slowly, choosing his words carefully, 'how concrete are your plans for the next two or three months?'

'They're cast in stone.'

'Stone can always be broken, can it not?'

'Not this stone.'

He smiled at me. 'Any stone can be broken, if only there is the will.'

'Perhaps, but in this case there is no will. Except,' I paused, thinking aloud, 'possibly on my parents' side, although they seem to have given up their objections to the Guildhall. I've got Michael Fullerton to thank for that.'

'Monsieur Fullerton seems to have become an avid champion of yours in these days. Your discovery seems to be starting.'

I was embarrassed by this and said nothing, for Eric had been only briefly mentioned in the review of our last concert and this was not a point I wished to underline. If my companion minded, however, he showed no sign of doing so.

'Which is *précisément* why I think that you should not cast your plans in stone,' he went on, 'at least not until you have listened with the open ear to my suggestion.'

Resolving not to listen, I told him politely to go on.

'Well,' he began, 'my mother's aunt has died. My great-aunt.'

As words of sympathy formed on my lips he raised a hand to stop them.

'It does not affect me personally. She was old, you see. And besides, I did not know her well.'

As I remember this remark, myself old now, I am struck by the callousness of youth, which thinks itself immortal. It is closer to age than it realizes.

'She was a painter, a woman of some reputation.'

I nodded and asked her name.

'Isabelle Mocsáry,' he told me, and I felt a faint twinge of recognition. 'She was a Frenchwoman who married a Czech. A very cosmopolitan person. Very erudite.'

I nodded again.

'She has left a large apartment in Prague, completely full of furniture and paintings,' he continued. 'Some of her things may be very valuable; many of them will, in any case, need to be sold. I am going there myself in ten days' time to supervise the arrangements.'

'Why you?'

'My mother was Madame Mocsáry's only relative. I am my mother's only son. It is right that I should go.' He paused. 'And I think that you should go with me.' This was said quietly, almost shyly. Seeing my surprise and sensing the beginnings of a refusal, he went on quickly, 'I have a friend at the Prague Conservatory. You will have heard of him.'

I said nothing. Eric looked at me anxiously and smiled.

'Does the name Eduard Mendl mean anything to you?'

My host leaned back, triumphant now; and I saw – as fully as he could have intended – a wizened head of silver hair, a hooked nose, black pointed eyes. Mendl's was a face

I had seen on the covers of gramophone records since my childhood. His was a name I had revered since the day I first touched a violin.

'How do you know him?' I asked, a little awed by such nonchalant mention of greatness.

'He was a friend of my great-aunt,' came the reply. 'When he came to France, he would stay with us between concerts.'

'But that's astounding.'

'You have not let me finish. I think Eduard Mendl is the man to teach you. He takes pupils, now that he has retired from performing. You are getting a little notice in London, thanks to Monsieur Fullerton. Think how useful a term with Eduard Mendl would be. Think how it would sound in Monsieur Fullerton's next column.'

I had already thought how it would sound.

'What makes you think he would want to take me?'

'He would be willing to hear you purely on my recommendation. Although Mendl is a violinist, he has perhaps done more for my piano-playing than any man alive. We have a close relationship; he trusts my judgement.'

'And you think—'

'I think that if I asked him to, he would hear you. The rest would be up to you, of course.'

'Of course.'

Eric saw that he had made the impression he desired. Slowly he smiled.

'Do you really think it could be arranged?' I asked.

It was only after I had spoken that I thought with a pang of how long two months without my love would be, and I remember that as Eric looked at me I almost wished he would say no; that the undreamed-of opportunity he was offering would pass. But then the thought that Ella and I were equal to such a parting made me smile.

And then he spoke.

'I am certain that it could,' he said with confidence. 'But you would have to persuade your professor at the Guildhall to defer your entry by a term.'

At this my face fell again; for I foresaw little hope of success with such an unprecedented request. I brightened a little, but only a little, when Eric told me that he had already spoken to Regina Boardman, who had promised to use her influence.

'England works in a very funny way,' he said. 'Everything is done behind the scene.' He paused. 'Regina knows the head of strings at the Guildhall. He is a dear friend of hers.'

My heart sank. Anyone in a position to be useful to her was a 'dear friend' of Regina Boardman's. The formula was her own; it did not imply intimacy or affection on either side. Eric's next remark, however, revived my hopes.

'He is also the lover of Monsieur Fullerton,' he said smoothly.

'How do you know?'

'That is not for you to mind about, James. But I know. With Monsieur Fullerton and Madame Boardman behind us, it might well be possible to arrange something. And if you came to Prague,' he went on, grinning now, 'would you like to share Madame Mocsáry's apartment with me?'

'It's very kind, but I couldn't impose.'

There was a pause.

'I should be lonely without your company.'

'In that case, I . . . accept with pleasure.'

'And the only rent,' he continued, 'would be a little help with the organization of the sale. Otherwise it would be completely free. Prague is, in any case, a very cheap city. We could live like kings, not like,' he gestured about the room, 'the rats we are in London. I do not like to live in holes, James.'

And in high spirits we shook hands on our plan and I got up to leave, glowing with excitement but telling myself not to allow my hopes to rise too high; that there were many hurdles yet to be leaped. But I thanked Eric for his generosity with sincere warmth.

'Not at all,' he said. 'I like you extremely.'

And I, awkward at such direct affection, was irritated by my own awkwardness. I shook his hand again with renewed vigour; for thus does the Englishman express his regard for his friends. And as I did so I thought of Ella's distaste for physical reserve; it was something we had discussed at length. So I let go of Eric's hand and hugged him, with a certain pride at thus proving my freedom from convention. He returned my hug, pleased but obviously surprised.

'Thank you,' I said again.

'I have told you,' he repeated, looking directly into my eyes, 'it is nothing. To give pleasure to one's friends is to give pleasure to oneself.'

I left him and walked home through the gathering blue dusk, watching pink turn to gold and then to grey as the sun set over the roofs and smog of a great city. And I thought, as I looked at the heavens above me, enormous in their beauty, that all their splendour could not match the splendour of my own happiness, that all their colour was as grey against the riches of my life.

It was a fanciful thought, but Ella had made me fanciful. As the sun set I sat by the river and watched it go, first seeking in its power a metaphor and then resting, quite content, in the pale warmth of its final rays.

12

I n due course the appropriate authorities were appealed to, the appropriate favours were called in and a term's sabbatical granted. Two days later, a telegram arrived from Mendl saying that he would be delighted to take me on for a term.

Camilla Boardman telephoned as soon as she knew. '*Daaarling!* You're *so* fabulous!'

'It's your mother's work, Camilla.'

'Didn't I *say* you two would enjoy each other? Didn't I *say* so?'

'You did.'

'And wasn't I *right?*'

'You were. Thank you.'

Camilla required her own portion of recognition.

My only reservation in all the excitement was the thought of leaving Ella.

I had told her immediately, of course, of Eric's offer; together we had endured the tense few days of Regina Boardman's machinations. Neither of us had believed that they would come to anything, though Ella understood my hopes and hoped with me; and when they did it was Ella whom I wanted to be the first to know. But when I called the house in Chester Square, I was told that the Harcourts were away; and the deep voice at the other end was not at liberty to tell me when they might be back.

For two days I waited, puzzled, while my mother told her friends of my good fortune and undoubted genius. The atmosphere at home had changed now beyond all recognition; for with the instinct of artful losers my parents had come to believe that there had been no struggle between us at all. Of course a little uncertainty on their part was only to have been expected, they told me, but they had never sought to stand in my way. Quite the contrary, in fact, though they still felt it was important not to forget the value of a safe job, whatever I did. With the indifference of youth I listened to their explanations and thought myself very fine for not judging their hypocrisy.

It was only years later that I was able to see beyond the confines of that struggle with my parents; to understand that, though snobbish, they were not hypocritical; to see the love behind our long-drawn-out conflict. Only years later could I appreciate the graciousness of their happiness for me; and then, as so often in life, it was too late to tell them so.

At the time I gave little thought to anything my parents said but concentrated instead on contacting Ella. For three days I was frustrated: again and again I was rebuffed by the deep voice that answered the telephone at Chester Square.

On the third day of fruitless calls a letter arrived from her. Its envelope was heavy, its paper thick, and it was engraved with a blue coronet and an address I did not expect: SETON CASTLE, CORNWALL.

My dearest, Ella had written.

You would be embarrassed to know how much I miss you, or at least to be told so in a letter. (Being at Seton in weather like this, with sparkling views of a sunlit sea, makes me <u>achingly</u> sentimental. I shall be stern with myself and spare you.)

The reason for my presence here is a sad one, I'm afraid. Uncle Cyril has had some sort of seizure; he collapsed four days ago and has been in hospital in Penzance ever since. Things are apparently touch and go and the family has been summoned to squabble by his bedside and awe the villagers. Aunt Elizabeth insists on flaunting unity at times like this 'as an example to the tenants', which of course is a remark guaranteed to make my blood boil. Such is the damage an American education can do, even to members of the best families; and I have been the cause of much collective disquiet.

Aunt Elizabeth and Sarah hum and ha in corners for hours, talking (I'm convinced) of how reprehensible I am and how there is nothing to be done about it. Poor Pamela comes in for most of the reproving looks, however; she doesn't have the protection of blood ties. She's just an interloper whose day will one day come, and Elizabeth knows it. My aunt dreads being sent to the Dower House.

The family disapproval of me and Pamela makes Daddy very angry, naturally; and meals are frosty occasions. I hope Cyril is not sent home to recuperate in an atmosphere like this – it would kill him. But we must stay until he is out of danger, and that will mean at least a week, perhaps two.

This, I think, is good for us. Much as I love our times together (and I <u>do</u> love them) they distract me from the matter in hand. I am still engaged; nothing has changed and I cannot go on behaving as though it has. Charlie is beginning to wonder why I'm always ill when he wants to see me, and my stock of excuses is not endless. I feel Sarah watching me, too, and I wonder how much those cool eyes of hers see. She makes me uncomfortable, as well she might. (You see, I do have a conscience, after all.)

So I shall spend my time here thinking seriously of what is to be done. And I shall think also of you and your tremendous opportunities in Prague. How I shall miss you if you go (damn Regina Boardman – she'll kill herself to arrange things, I know). But with a feeling as strong as ours there is plenty of time.

I love you and love you,
Ella

I did see Ella once before my departure, for studying permits took longer to arrange than Eric and I had anticipated and we remained in London while the bureaucracies of two governments took their time over us. Uncle Cyril came home, recovered, and sent his family away in irritation at the fuss which it made over him. So Ella returned to London and once again the house in Chester Square became a hive of wedding activities.

We met on the day before my departure. Clothes and

books had been carefully packed, friends telephoned and seen. All was ready.

Camilla Boardman had demanded a private interview and, over lunch, had told me that London would be horribly dull without me. Michael Fullerton had telephoned to wish me luck. And Regina Boardman, true to form, had organized a last charity concert, and so seen at least an initial return on her investment in my future.

Ella and I met in the triumphant Victorian splendour of the National Portrait Gallery. It was mid-September, one of the last days of that long, warm summer. Outside in Trafalgar Square and Charing Cross Road the crowds were sweaty and loud; inside, in the sepulchral cool of the gallery and its deserted rooms, there was silence. I can see her as she walked up the stairs towards me, see the expectant haste of her quick, light step, the smile on her lips, the glow of her cheeks. I don't remember all we talked of, though she must have told me about her visit to Seton and the suppression of family bitterness – in the invalid's presence at least, if not elsewhere. I remember telling her of Regina Boardman's supremely focused efforts on my behalf; of the fraught days before Mendl's acceptance of me as a pupil; of the fact that Eric's great-aunt had been Isabelle Mocsáry. I remember going next door with her to the National Gallery to see its small collection of Mocsárys and our disappointment on being told that they were on loan to a museum in Paris.

Above all, I remember the intimacy of those few hours, the ease with which we talked and laughed and, over tea in a Covent Garden café, kissed. It was only as evening drew on that our talk grew serious, with the seriousness of lovers about to be parted.

'I can't say how glad I am for you,' Ella said. 'And how sad I am for me. But this separation is right.'

She paused to light a cigarette and I watched the elegant arch of her fingers as she clasped it and put it to her lips. She lit it and took two meditative puffs, slowly.

'I think that it should be a complete separation, at least for the moment.'

'In what way?'

'I don't think we should communicate at all, Jamie.'

'What?'

She smiled at me. 'We know what we have. It won't go away. But I want us only to write or speak when I've done what I have to do and not before. This ... hide-and-seek isn't good for either of us, and I'm sick of running around like a guilty child.'

I nodded, though I did not wholeheartedly share her distaste.

'It's time to fix things, once and for all,' Ella continued. 'I haven't thought of Charlie as I ought to have done; I haven't thought of Sarah, either. I know she's watching, watching everything I do. She knows something's up. That's why we mustn't write to each other.'

'I don't understand.'

'Don't you see? When I'm with you I'm too happy to be tragic. And it would be the same if we wrote to each other every day while you were in Prague. You need to be my reward, Jamie, not my distraction. I must extricate myself from this tangle so that I can enjoy you ... unfettered, as it were.'

'But, Ella—'

'Please, Jamie.'

'But—'

'Don't you see how a clean break, even for such a short time, will help me? How it will help me to arrange things?' She took my hand. 'I want us to be permanent. Open, above board, acknowledgeable. I don't want us to sneak around like this any more. And I need an absence of distractions if ever I'm going to sort out this mess. I owe that much at least to Charlie, don't you think?'

I nodded sullenly, beginning to understand.

'Now, don't get like that. We have time. You'll only be away for two months. And when you get back we won't have to skulk around like criminals. You can meet Daddy and Pamela properly; I can meet your parents. We can go down to Seton and not have to stay in the village inn and avoid the guards. Don't you see how different it will be then? How lovely?'

I nodded again, less sullenly this time, slightly mollified.

'So go to Prague and don't write. Your letters – anything from you – make me too happy, as I've said, to be tragic. And tragedy is the least I can do for Charlie. I'm going to have to take my time over this. You can't break off an engagement overnight, particularly with the circumstances as they are.'

I nodded again.

'Do you understand?' She looked at me anxiously from across the table.

'I think I do,' I said. 'I don't like it, but I understand.'

'Good.'

'But you've only got until Christmas. Once Christmas comes you won't be able to get rid of me.'

'I won't want to, stupid.' She squeezed my hand. 'I don't want to now. But for both our sakes I must.'

'I know.'

And we kissed each other lingeringly.

13

Prague: a city of arched bridges, sharp steeples, gracious domes. Bathed in a morning light sharper and colder than the light of London, the mist rising from the Vltava was a brilliant, dreamy ribbon in the grey blanket of the city. I see Eric sitting in the train, his eyes bright with the excitement of travel, his voice softly pointing out the landmarks of a city neither of us had ever seen but which he at least had read about.

Prague and I were yet to be introduced. But even as I saw her for the first time I knew, as sometimes one knows instinctively, that I would not find her as I found London. She was not reserved, not distant, not cold. Proud, yes. But Prague's pride was alluring and shrouded in romantic mystery. Not for her the triumphant boulevards of Paris or the sneering skyscrapers of New York. She was a city of cobbled streets and hidden staircases; of courtyards hung with flowers and filled with whispers. A city where palace and tenement lived side by side, together, and crumbled with picturesque dignity.

Eric and I took a taxi through leafy suburbs with strange, art nouveau houses set in overgrown gardens.

'Where did your aunt live?' I asked Eric. 'Somewhere out here?'

'Oh no. She was a woman who had to be in the thick of things. Without the smell of traffic fumes she was unhappy. Her house – her apartment, I should say – is in the centre and just as she left it, *apparemment.* We will live in the real Prague.'

We descended the steep cobbled avenue that cuts down from the Strahov Monastery to the Malá Strana, the baroque 'little quarter' of winding streets crushed together beneath the castle which was to be my first contact with the city proper. Before us was the Vltava; in the distance the twin towers of the Charles Bridge and its line of statues, sinister and black with age and soot.

It startles me how vividly I see this all. I have never gone back to Prague since Eric and I left it, for its associations are painful; but I have never forgotten it. It strikes me that the city I know and the city it is today must be different. Perhaps all Prague's streets are tarred now; perhaps its corners boast the fast-food outlets of other cities; perhaps its monasteries and palaces are hotels. I do not wish to return. I am content with a mental revisiting of the city that awed a young, impressionable man, quick with life.

Our driver deposited us on the corner of a street of grand old houses. Left on the pavement in the chilly air, I waited while Eric fumbled for keys.

'This,' he told me, 'was once the Sherkansky Palace. Now it is flats.'

'Quite grand flats.' He had found the keys and opened the door, leading the way forward under the arch. In the interior gloom the mouldings on the walls and ceiling loomed like ghostly cherubs smiling when the wind changed, trapped forever in delirious wantonness. Light streamed, muted by dirt, through large windows on both walls. Before us there was a staircase, relic of an age more elegant than our own, which led upwards graciously into darkness. As my eyes grew accustomed to the dim light cast by a weak and solitary bulb I saw the true state of the building: the chipped paint and broken tiles; the cracked plaster. Then all was dark.

With a muttered curse Eric groped for a light switch, found one, and another ineffective light, far away, flickered to life. Thus began our ascent. For intervals of a few seconds at a time it was possible to move up the staircase with something approaching adequate illumination; but the weight and number of our bags meant that we inevitably trod the last few steps of each flight in darkness. On the third and final floor Eric produced another key before another set of heavy doors.

With a grind of rusty bolts the door opened and, on cue, the light in the passage went out. We pushed on in darkness and Eric fumbled once more for a light switch and once more found one and flicked it on. This time we were bathed in a tremendous wave of electric light. The chandelier above our heads – as I later had leisure to count – had thirty bulbs; and it illuminated every corner of the Aladdin's cave in which we stood.

I remember that first glow of light, the physical shock of that brightness, and I remember that my life has not been wholly without adventure.

Eric and I were standing in a long, narrow room, the stone of its floor carpeted haphazardly with Turkish rugs, its walls completely bare and painted a deep, rich red. A film of dust covered everything, hushing the colours of the carpets and the drapes, an imperial yellow, which hung tent-like from the ceilings.

I sneezed and the sound broke the tension and made us laugh.

'My God,' I said, 'I've never seen anything like it.'

Eric's eyes danced. 'Let's explore.'

So together we explored the apartment; and, excitedly, like awed schoolboys in a museum, we went through its rooms, occasionally picking up and showing each other some of the more eccentric examples of Madame Mocsáry's taste: a small golden elephant with sparkling red stones for eyes that sat on the piano; a cheap plastic fan of lime green and pink, which lay, for decoration, on an occasional table.

The room we were in served as a kind of entrance-hall-cum-sitting-room – what purpose it had served in the Sherkanskys' days I could not tell – and from it opened two doors, each set back in pillared alcoves. The first opened on to a dank little passage, which led to a poky kitchen and a bathroom with a large porcelain bath and no taps. The second – which we explored only after a hopeful but disappointing examination of the kitchen equipment – was more rewarding.

'*Mon Dieu*,' said Eric as he opened it. 'Come and see this, James.'

So I came and together we entered the Picture Room for the first time. It was a perfectly proportioned square, its walls twelve feet apart and set at right angles to each other, a false ceiling setting their height at twelve feet, too. Every inch of the four walls – saving only the door through which we had entered and two long casement windows overlooking the street – was covered with canvases. Some framed, some not, they clustered together as if for comfort in the chilly room, hiding the wall – which was a deep red like the hall – in a riot of colour: fantastic, half-realistic shapes painted over many years in a progression which – as I later discovered, could be traced.

'So this is it,' Eric said quietly.

'What?'

'My great-aunt used to write to my mother about her Picture Room. She was convinced she would not finish it before she died.' He paused and looked about him. 'It has something of the grand effect, has it not?'

I nodded.

That room was the single most cohesive creation of a brilliant mind. It housed an explosive outpouring of artistic inspiration, from the first ink sketches of a young girl to the assured, experimental works of an older, more mature artist. The images were varied: some were small, some huge; some in oils, some in ink; most were on canvas, some were on board. They coagulate in my mind though I once knew them so well. I cannot make out their individual subjects, for the passing of the years has cast a film over them which blurs their outline and their detail.

It is strange that I should not remember, for I came to love those paintings and the room which housed them; they came to mean a great deal to me. Perhaps that is why I have forgotten.

The spirit of Madame Mocsáry was everywhere in that eccentric apartment: from the faded yellow drapes which hid the cracked ceiling of its hall to the collection of bric-a-brac that covered every available ledge.

For an hour Eric and I wandered about, fascinated. Only then did the practicalities of our situation occur to us. Madame Mocsáry, it seemed, had had no use for a bed.

'She must have had *one* at least,' said Eric. 'We must find it.'

But search though we did, we could unearth nothing that even resembled a mattress, let alone anything more sophisticated or comfortable than that. It was I who discovered the key to the secret of where Madame Mocsáry had slept, and by the time I had done so Eric and I had been searching fruitlessly for almost an hour.

The dust in the apartment had been making me sneeze, so I decided to air the drapes that covered the furniture. It was when I removed the blue velvet square from the sofa that I discovered that it was not a sofa at all but a single bed pushed against the wall with cushions on its three sides. How we laughed to have been outwitted for so long by a ghost.

I remember Eric's laughs. He abandoned himself to them. They were throaty guffaws of white teeth and dishevelled hair and streaming eyes. They will return to my nightmares with the smile which preceded them and the clap of his hand on my back.

It has taken sixty years to banish all thoughts of Eric, to close my dreams to the sight and sound of him. Now I have undone the work of decades; I have remembered. And Eric will return to haunt me. Who is he? What is he? An image. A sound. A touch. A young man who had a happy life but an unhappy death. He is nothing more than that, surely? He is dead. But he lives on in me; my conscience will not lay him to rest for it no longer stomachs deceit.

And so his laugh shrieks at me, accusingly, across the years.

That afternoon, I heard his laugh with pleasure and laughed, too. We laughed and laughingly wrestled each other for the privilege of the bed. Eric, though broader than I, was the loser; and it was decided that after an adequate cleaning and airing, the velvet drapes with which the apartment was full should be piled on top of each other to provide him with a makeshift mattress.

That important issue resolved, we turned our attention to the prospective difficulties of the job at hand, opening cupboards, examining shelves, exploring the nooks and crannies of an old lady's private world. We discovered that the cleaning of the house, unlived-in since Madame Mocsáry's removal to a nursing home almost a year before, would be no easy task. Whatever skills a boarding-school education had equipped me with, the handling of dusters and detergents was not amongst them. Eric was hardly more skilled than I. Our enthusiasm gave us confidence, however. We went out at once and armed ourselves with mops and buckets – for my friend insisted on viewing the process as a military operation – and returned exhilarated by our expedition to face the immediate task of airing the fabric.

Thus it was that a rather bemused Czech audience was able to observe us, over the course of that afternoon and early evening, dancing wildly in the street below our balcony and tugging huge squares of velvet – red, yellow, blue, purple, green – with all our force. We beat them, with tremendous vigour and a great deal of noise, on anything that presented itself: lamp-posts, buildings, walls, railings. Nothing was safe from our furious efforts. But by nightfall we had finished and were ready to hang the velvet to air on the balustrade of the central staircase – giving it, incidentally, something of the splendour it must have assumed on feast days in the past – and to climb to our apartment, naked without its fine fabrics.

There the furniture stared at us, grimy, bare and un-inviting. We left it in search of dinner and wine, drinking and laughing together until we could barely walk, return-ing unsteady at dawn to the glorious decay of the Sherkansky Palace and the desolate grandeur of Sokolska 21.

It was those public fabric-beatings that first brought Blanca into our lives: Blanca, the wrinkled old woman with the carefully dyed blonde hair who had been Madame Mocsáry's cleaner and confidante. She lived in a much shabbier building further down Sokolska Street, on the opposite side, and we learned from her later that she had watched, horrified, as two unknown men had gone about destroying her old mistress's possessions in the street below her very own apartment.

Our impertinence, she told us afterwards, had required immediate action on her part; and although not a large woman, she, Blanca, was both fierce and unafraid, not frightened of young upstarts, and not about to let their impudence go unavenged. So she had gone to meet us, bent on violence, and she had found us as we were carrying the last of the drapes down the palace staircase. An un-expected, neatly aimed kick at Eric's shins had been enough to incapacitate him, while a loud barrage of enraged Czech had awed me into silence.

We calmed her eventually, but only with great difficulty, repeating our explanations first in English and then in broken German, Eric nursing his ankle all the while, I doing my best to placate our unexpected aggressor with soothing phrases from a half-remembered Czech phrase book.

When at length the situation was clarified, Blanca's apologies were scarcely less alarming than her previous fury had been. On no account were we to clean the apartment by ourselves; she must make amends for her insult. In any case, men were notoriously unreliable. What did we think we were doing without a woman's guidance? There was no knowing what damage we might cause if left to our own devices.

Faced with such an implacable opponent, there was little for Eric or me to do but to submit, so submit we did; and from henceforth Blanca assumed control of the project in hand and worked with expert energy, talking nineteen to the dozen all the while and delegating enthusiastically as she did so. Under her guidance, the days that followed our arrival at Sokolska 21 saw a whirlwind of activity on a par with anything the building could have experienced in the course of two centuries. Arriving promptly at nine o'clock, Blanca worked her troops from the moment she crossed the threshold until late into the night, setting us to scrub, clean and sort with tireless authority.

It was understood that any furniture the Vaugirard family did not want for itself was to be sold with the paintings; and the six days of our house-cleaning were devoted to salvaging the odd treasures from the amorphous heap of junk that Madame Mocsáry had accumulated in the course of nearly eighty years. We found things in curious places. One of the floorboards – suspiciously creakier than the rest – lifted to reveal a bundle of neatly tied letters; the lid of the piano concealed, below the strings of the instrument, a tiny black box with an old amber brooch in it; and taped to the top of a kitchen drawer was a gentleman's pocket watch made of a metal that looked to me like gold.

All these items – and many more – I showed to Eric on discovery, and it was he who decided their fate.

Of the letters he said slowly, 'Love letters. Let us burn them.'

And so, itching with a curiosity I could not satisfy, I placed them in the corner of the balcony we called the bonfire site. There were about fifty in all, written on the same paper and now cracking with age, in a spidery handwriting and a language I did not recognize. Eric cast an eye over them.

'Not my great-uncle's writing,' he said sternly; then he softened. 'But let us preserve an old lady's secret.'

And holding them in his left hand he lit his lighter under them and we watched as they burned brightly and turned to ash.

Isabelle Mocsáry and her unusual style intrigued me, and if I could not read her letters I could at least follow Blanca's unceasing reminiscences with great interest.

'Madame was a very fine lady,' her former cleaner told us in reverential tones as she scrubbed. 'A very fine lady. I was her servant but she treated me like her friend.'

And as Blanca dusted she would tell us a brief history of each object she touched. Eric and I listened, fascinated, as she reeled off the names of the people who had drunk from Madame Mocsáry's teacups; the works of the intellectuals who had frequented her card table; the genius of the musicians, Eduard Mendl foremost amongst them, who had sat at her piano.

'It seems a pity. Her pictures should not be sold and separated. She would not have liked that. They should be put in a museum for people to see.'

I agreed with her. I had spent many hours in the Picture Room amongst the vibrant colours and flowing lines of Madame Mocsáry's personal collection. I came to know her paintings intimately, to appreciate in them a steady progression from the passions of youth to the tranquillity of age; and I saw by their dates that she had painted one a year, quite incidentally to the rest of her output, for almost sixty years.

'There was always a painting. Always she would be painting,' Blanca told us one day. 'She began this room the year she married. She used to say that when she had covered the Picture Room her life's work would be complete. She didn't care what happened to the paintings people bought from her. She cared only about the ones she kept for this room.'

Hearing this, I thought with amusement of the crowds queuing in Paris to see the Mocsáry retrospective there; and I chuckled as I did so, wondering what they would think if only they could hear Blanca's words now, as I did. Eric smiled too and our eyes met, sharing the joke, before a stern word from our self-appointed supervisor sent us back to our work. I returned to my scrubbing, pleased to think that the Picture Room had been finished before its creator's death, that Madame Mocsáry's grand plan, adhered to for so long, had finally borne fruit.

'She lived very alone when she grew older,' continued Blanca, following the train of her own thoughts. 'And her family did not visit her.' A pair of gimlet eyes met us both in a moment of beady interrogation. 'A person needs other people in life, not in death. Once they are dead they have the angels for company.' Blanca paused. 'The good ones, at least,' she added after a moment's consideration.

Eric looked down at the painting in his hands.

'I think, maybe,' the old lady continued, with uncharacteristic gentleness, 'that the best ones have the angels with them on earth too. I think, maybe, that Madame had the angels with her on earth.'

And with that she went on with her work and we returned to ours. No one spoke, and it was only when Blanca sniffed that I saw she was crying.

14

When you're twenty-two and footloose in a foreign city you give no thought to the future. Certainly I did not. I devoted myself instead to adventure and enjoyment and music; and from this last at least I gained something whole, something good.

Our days passed happily, mine divided between the Conservatory and Madame Mocsáry's apartment, where Eric spent his time sorting his great-aunt's papers, arranging the sale of her things, playing her newly tuned piano. Not long into our stay we both bought bicycles and on these it was possible to dodge through the crowds of traffic on Sokolska Street. I remember the hours we spent lounging in the cafés beside the Charles Bridge, talking of everything and nothing.

The machinery of permits and exemptions and death duties necessary to begin the sale of Madame Mocsáry's effects was slow to grind into motion. Eric and I delighted in its inefficiency, for it left us longer undisturbed in the now gleaming splendour of her apartment. Our days were carefree. As I search my memory of them I find no sign that the coils had yet begun to twist. My life was light, then, and I rejoiced in its lightness; I had not learned to look for creeping shadows.

Eduard Mendl extolled the virtues of simplicity and clear thinking in the baroque elegance of his rooms at the Conservatory. He was a small, precise man with a sharp tongue. He told me he was not there to teach me technique – that was my own concern – but to teach me to understand beauty and to express it in a way that was uniquely mine.

'I shall teach you to think,' he told me in his clipped tones. 'To see things in your own way, to hear them in your own way. And I shall teach you also the beauty of expression. But the ease with which you express yourself' (by which he meant the facility of my playing) 'must be your own affair. You must work at it alone.'

I was a conscientious student, as worlds of musical possibility opened before me, illuminated by the genius of that fine old man whose silver hair and creased face, lit occasionally by a smile of praise, are as clear to me now as they were then, when I saw him every day.

I have never forgotten Mendl; he was never buried in my mind; there is no dust to clear from his image. His lessons, though I did not know this as he gave them, later saved me from myself. And I have always been grateful for that.

I played from early morning until late afternoon every day and devoted the remaining hours of daylight to endless walks in the cobbled maze of streets beneath the Hrad or to lazy boating on the Vltava with Eric. We spent our evenings in cafés or in the splendours of the Rudolfinum or the State Opera. Sometimes we stayed at home, experimenting with cooking and praising the results of each other's efforts, however dubious. It was a time of near tangible freedom. We lived as we pleased, revelling in the lives we created for ourselves and each other.

One's twenties are a time of reinvention, of regrouping and rethinking after the battles and fiery uncertainties of adolescence. Eric and I learned that reinvention is easier and more pleasurable when the expectations of those you know are removed. Social ties can stifle growth, or at least alter it, and we relished their absence. We lived serenely in the present, content, with little care for the future or the past.

Slowly we settled into life in Prague and made Sokolska 21 our home, filling its kitchen cupboards, fitting bulbs into unused sockets. Needing somewhere to work, we turned the sitting room into an impromptu rehearsal space, moving the piano from its corner and setting it instead between the two long windows that gave on to the street. Restored once more to its former glory, hung again with the yellow drapes of Madame Mocsáry's day, that room became the focus of our Prague lives, and we spent many happy hours under its haphazard canopy, working hard – together and alone – but talking also. And as the days passed and familiarity (far from breeding contempt) bred intimacy instead, we found in each other and in the bond between us something that sustained us both; which gave us both a sense of excitement and adventure which neither of us, I think, had found in friendship before.

Artistically, Eric and I challenged each other; personally, we supported and upheld; and in retrospect the easy companionship of those nights seems strange, for by nature I am a solitary worker and find the company of others a distraction from my music. Remembering Eric, and my friendship with him, I remember most that curious admixture of frivolity and commitment that characterized all he did.

Once a week we played together in the benignly august presence of Mendl himself; and in his quiet, measured way he took our youthful efforts and made something of them, or pointed the way for us to do so. Praising rarely but warmly, he was no easy master. Certainly he put me through my technical paces at the Conservatory, whatever he said about the facility of my playing being my own affair. But in Eric's presence he unbent a little, rewarding our efforts with a dreamy, glazed look of absorption that was thrilling from one such as he.

Sometimes, when I was practising alone, Eric would assume the role of audience that Ella had made her own in London. On the mattress of velvet squares, his head in his hands, he would sit while I played to him and thought with pleasure of how Ella's hair fell into her eyes when she listened to me; of how her lips curled into half-smiles at the passages she loved most.

Of course I missed her. But Ella did not write, as she had warned me she would not, and I was sure enough of her not to mind, though I thought of her constantly: seeing her supple form in every passing beauty; hoarding my anecdotes for her amusement; remembering my adventures so that one day she might share them. Once or twice I almost wrote or telephoned, but Eric argued against my doing so with a forcefulness I did not understand but which was strong enough to persuade me. So I waited, as Ella herself had told me to wait; and by and large I was content to do so, for there is a certain thrill in the anticipation of intimacy. Prague, I felt, was a fitting setting for a star-cross'd lover.

As time passed we settled down, separated ourselves from the tourist crowd and lived with the discernment of permanent Praguers. We became regular and recognized patrons at a few establishments, patronizing for preference the Café Florian, a bar run by two Czechs who spoke English with American accents.

Florian's patrons were a motley crowd, a cosmopolitan collection of hopeful geniuses who sat in huddles on the sofas and talked in low whispers of coming masterpieces. Art was discussed constantly; politics never. Occasionally one of the groups would explode in passionate argument and the opinions of the other drinkers would be volubly sought by the participants.

Jean, a French-speaking waiter of Yugoslav extraction who had grown up in Warsaw – how he managed this curious combination, he never divulged – was the supreme arbiter of such discussions, and when not waiting at tables he spent his time writing poetry that appeared occasionally in magazines. He seemed to be the only published writer in the place, and as such his opinions carried weight.

It was one of Jean's rules never to talk to customers unless their arguments threatened the peace and required arbitration. He wisely cultivated his aloofness, and thus his mystique, amongst those who provided his tips.

After a time, since we rarely participated in their argu-ments and seldom joined any of the groups on the larger sofas, the other regulars began to ignore us. We didn't mind. In fact we rather enjoyed being left alone, free to talk to each other and to form our own judgements on the issues debated with such passion around us.

I enjoyed talking to Eric, and over many nights ensconced in two armchairs of purple velvet in one of the quieter corners of the café, I learned a great deal about his opinions, for there was much to learn. Of mine he must have learned less, for there was less to know; but Eric possessed the gentle art of making his friends interesting, even to themselves, and he drew me out of my shell as few had done before.

He talked to me of Oxford, of my parents, of my music. He listened with an air of affectionate understanding as I explained my confused but sincere attempts to break free from the path my family had laid out for me to follow; to define and achieve my own place in the world, independent of their influence and prejudice.

'You are a very true person, James,' he told me one evening in the smoky half-light of Florian's. 'I admire you for that. And for the way you want to strike out for yourself. It is not a universal quality.'

I thought as he said this of how Ella and I would strike out for ourselves, of what the future held for us both. And I smiled at the friend who had provoked these happy thoughts.

'Are you not glad you came here? To Prague?'

I nodded. 'Very glad.'

'I think we will remember this as the finest time of our lives, James.'

'I'm sure we will.'

Seeing that Eric's glass was empty, I ordered two more gins from Jean, who brought them with the smiling alacrity with which he honoured his most deserving clients. This pleased me.

After some minutes of silent contemplation, I asked Eric what his own family was like, for it struck me suddenly that he had not spoken much of them. All I knew, in fact, was that he was the elder of two children, and that he came from a line of gentleman farmers who had tilled the lands around Vaugirard and its small château for centuries.

'What are my family like?' He repeated the question, more to himself than to me. 'What are they like?' He paused. 'I will tell you, James, what they are like. And one day, maybe, you will meet them yourself and form judgements of your own.'

Eric's English, excellent since I had first known him, had improved still further. He had developed a style of his own, a curious, considered way of speaking which lent his conversation an appealing gravity and inspired the trust of his audience.

'My sister,' he began at last, choosing his words with care, 'is two years younger than I. She is called Sylvie, and she is very pretty but not so clever—'

'—as you are,' I finished for him, teasingly.

'No. Not so clever as she might be.'

'And why is that?'

'She does not question things, James, which is something any intelligent person must do. Which you do, for example. She accepts. All the time she accepts what she is told.'

'Such as?'

'I don't know. Everything. She lives her life according to a plan someone else has designed for her. She is happily

150

married. She lives near my parents at Vaugirard' – his family still lived in the village and farmed the fields around it, though the château had long since passed out of their hands – 'and knits socks for the foreign legionnaires. A very safe, very narrow little life.'

The disdain in his tone was unusual and real. It surprised me.

'Sylvie is a devout Catholic,' Eric continued. 'She spends her early mornings in prayer, her days in family duties and her nights in the duties of the wife.' He paused. 'She will have many children,' he added wryly.

'And how do you get on?' I asked, though I suspected I knew the answer already.

'Well enough. But it is for the benefit of my parents. We do not discuss the things we disagree on.'

'Things like?'

'You must know me well enough by now, James, to suspect.'

There was an awkward pause, during which I tried to silence the promptings of a social reserve which told me that to ask further would be to pry. But lifelong habits are difficult to break, and rather than pursuing my friend's overture I smiled and signalled to Jean for another gin.

Unlike Eric I did not actively seek out confidences from others. Ella had whetted my appetite for them but I was still cautious. I had a vague fear still – explained, I imagine, by the repression inherent in any privileged English education – of emotional intimacy that might go too far. I did not enjoy prolonged contact with the deeper, more secret sides of people's natures. I still don't. I might listen but I seldom pursue.

With Ella, love and desire made me fearless and I relished her confidence; but with Eric there were no such powers to drive me and I remained wary. I liked people to be what they appeared to be. I shrank from the private fears and insecurities of others because, perhaps, by admitting theirs I had to move closer to admitting my own. I don't know.

But what I do know is that there are certain doors in one's mind that are better left closed. And when they are opened by another, as the doors of Ella's mind were opened by me, and the doors of mine by her, their opening carries with it a great responsibility. I had no wish for the responsibility Eric's secrets might bring. Despite my affection for him I desired no glimpse of what lay behind the secret doors of his mind. I wanted the easy understanding of friends, nothing more.

Eric, taking his cue from me, seemed to understand: for he turned the conversation, with characteristic deftness, from the intimate to the general, and from then on he offered me no more secrets. Instead he talked of his family history and spoke with amusing erudition of the long line of knights in war and farmers in peace who had served their kings and emperors over centuries.

'We have lived at Vaugirard, with brief absences for understandable reasons around the time of 1789,' he told me, smiling, 'since the conquest of England.'

As he talked I thought of another ancient family and another smile and another voice telling me a similar story. And I thought that life was fine.

15

Three weeks later, Eric and I returned from Florian's to learn to our disappointment that the clogged wheels of bureaucracy – for so long our unlikely protectors – had finally ground into motion and produced all the documents required for the Mocsáry sale to begin. Under the smart letterhead of the estate's lawyers we read that Mr Kierczinsky himself, the head of the firm, would call the following day at eleven if that was convenient.

He arrived promptly an hour before noon, an urbane little man with a small moustache and high cheekbones; and he explained the situation to us very patiently in correct but hesitant English.

'You will see that there is much of . . . great value here,' he said as we sat over tea in the sitting room. 'Your family has taken what is of . . . sentimental merit, has it not?'

Eric said that it had.

He and I had dispatched a small parcel to Vaugirard the week before, filled with letters from Eric's grandmother to Madame Mocsáry and one or two pieces of old jewellery, amber and jade mostly. The gold pocket watch had been sent, too. The rest we had left in place.

'We cannot delay the sale of furniture and paintings . . . any longer,' Mr Kierczinsky continued. 'Your grand-aunt was a great lady and she lived . . . beyond her means. I shall have everything here valued. If your family would like any of the pieces I suggest that they inform me with the least possible of delays.'

Within a week chaos reigned on the top floor of the Sherkansky Palace. A large burly Czech had come to direct operations. Men were running up and down the palace stairs, rolling back carpets, screwing doors off hinges, folding, packing, lifting. The grand piano, dismantled, was the first piece of furniture to go, and it was carried down the stairs like a sedated elephant. The other pieces in the apartment followed it: a large dresser that had stood in the kitchen, its china carefully wrapped and packed into boxes; the heavy bed on which I had slept; a prettily carved bookcase, two occasional tables, an armoire and Madame Mocsáry's dilapidated collection of French novels.

The paintings were moved last, when everything else had been carried down to the waiting removals van, and with agonizing, painstaking slowness they were taken from the walls they had graced. As each was lifted off its hook, a square of wall, garish and red, unbleached by the sun, was exposed where the painting had preserved it. Ranged together these gashes looked to me like wounds, like flesh that has been stripped of its skin, but I did not say so.

Eric and I watched the men in dejected silence, as if they were dismantling the house we had been born in.

'This is no place for us any more,' he said, and he led the way abruptly out of the apartment, past the line of workers on the staircase.

He did not stop walking until we had reached Florian's,

where we spent the rest of the day morosely drinking hot chocolate. The café was unusually quiet and we longed for the crowd of debaters with their long words and lank hair. In the smoky gloom of their habitual haunt their voices rang out to us, ghostly in the silence.

Regardless of our despondency, the day of the sale moved inexorably nearer. There was to be a reception for important buyers on the night before the Mocsáry effects went under the gavel, and the sale itself was to take place a week after the paintings went on show for the first time.

That week was perhaps the only time that the collection was ever seen in its entirety by the public. Each day, for the price of the catalogue, a long line of people – Czech and foreign alike – trooped over the parquet floors of the viewing rooms, pointing, admiring, discussing.

It was on the Wednesday before the sale that I discovered from the gallery's visitors' book that the Harcourts were in Prague and staying at the Grand Hotel Europa.

This establishment was perhaps a minute's walk from where I stood. I dodged through the lines of people staring at the paintings and vaulted down the gallery steps into the crush of the square.

Youth demands such instant gratification of its desires. It has not learned patience.

Certainly I found it difficult to be patient as a polite receptionist informed me that the Harcourts were out and I settled down to an hour's long and fruitless wait. Gradually my excitement gave way to frustration. But I waited. And finally I was rewarded by the sight of Pamela's severe form and sculpted hair entering on Alexander's arm. Husband and wife were talking anxiously together.

'Excuse me, Lord and Lady Harcourt,' I said, planting myself on the carpet in front of them, 'I wonder if you remember me. James Farrell. I'm a friend of your daughter's.'

Their minds had so obviously been elsewhere that it took a moment for them to register the unexpected presence of a former guest and for the machinery of polite greeting to slide into motion. Alexander took my proffered hand.

'Mr Farrell,' he said, shaking it. 'Whatever are you doing here?'

The words were jovial enough but their lightness was forced. Without knowing why this was, I explained briefly the reasons for my presence in Prague.

'How is Ella?' I asked, smiling, keeping my voice steady.

Her father's face was drawn and tired, I saw now. There was a note of dulled resignation in Alexander's voice as he said slowly, 'Ella came here with us, but she disappeared yesterday. Went off by herself. We haven't heard a thing from her since then.'

He looked at me as though still struggling to believe that this could be so.

'We don't know what has happened to her.'

'You must be sick with worry.'

'We are,' said Pamela.

'If you hear anything from her, *anything*, you will let us know, won't you?' This from Alexander.

'Of course,' I said.

'That's very kind of you.'

We shook hands.

'Well, we mustn't take up any more of your time, Mr

Farrell. It was good of you to have come to see us.'

'If there's anything I can do—'

'Of course. Thank you. I'm sure she'll turn up any moment now.'

'Yes.'

Outside, the square was full of people laughing and talking, but I moved through them unseeing. In the grip of something between suspicion and hope I walked quickly home and as I let myself into Madame Mocsáry's apartment I found that I had been correct in my assumption. Eric and Ella were sitting on the music-room floor, drinking tea.

The sight of the two of them together comes back clearly to me now, though I thought I had banished it for ever. I see them sitting side by side on the stone of that floor. I see the shining gold of Ella's hair beside the gleaming black of Eric's, the pallor of her creamy skin beside the olive tones of his. It must have been the first time they had met, though they had known of each other for some time.

I see the look in Ella's eyes as I open the door. I watch her put down her cigarette and rise to her feet in one graceful movement, hear the tap of her shoes on the stone as she moves towards me. She is wearing a tweed skirt that clings to her thin legs and a black sweater. In such dark clothes she looks very pale, but the green of her eyes could not be more alive. She is smiling, hugging me, holding me; and then we are kissing, and her taste fills me as I run my hand over the fine bones of her spine and pull her closer.

It is only as I bury my nose in the fine skin of her

lemon-scented neck that I see Eric watching us from the floor with something in his eyes I dismiss because I don't understand; and it is only then that I remember myself and pull away from Ella, happily, all the frustration of my waiting and my worry gone, and introduce her properly to my friend.

'We have met already,' Eric says with a certain curtness.

'Yes we have.'

Ella pulls me to the floor to sit beside her at an improvised tea table of packing crates and short discarded planks.

'Eric's been telling me all about the wonderful time you two've been having.'

I hardly remember the rest of that conversation. What I do remember is that my eyes met Eric's as Ella said this and that I smiled. I remember also that he did not respond at once, but that as I went on smiling his face softened and he grinned at me, and I felt relief at the passing of an awkward moment.

I remember that tea was poured. I remember also that as I took my first sip I thought of Pamela and Alexander, alone on their hotel staircase.

'I've been talking to your parents, Ella,' I said quietly.

'Have you really?' She made an attempt at nonchalance. It was not convincing. 'How are they?'

'Worried sick.'

There was a pause. I watched, excited despite myself, as she opened her bag, found a cigarette, put it to her lips, lit it. Slowly, deeply, she inhaled.

'I know you must think me awful for running off and leaving them like that,' Ella said.

I did not reply.

'But I can't tell you how badly I needed to see you. And they don't let me out of their sight for a minute.'

I began a question but she raised a hand to stop me.

'There's plenty of time for all that later. A lot has happened since I last saw you, James. A lot.'

She looked at Eric and then at me. There was silence.

'I suppose I'd better go and find Daddy and Pamela and let them know I'm all right,' said Ella, finally. 'Oh God, this is awful.' She got up to go. 'If you'll walk with me I'll tell you about it.'

'All right.'

My lover extended a hand to my friend.

'I so enjoyed meeting you,' she said, smiling. 'I hope we'll see much more of each other now that we've finally met.'

Eric took her hand and murmured something. 'I'll see you later,' he said to me.

I nodded.

And together Ella and I left the apartment and made our way down the great shadowy staircase bathed in short bursts of inadequate light. In the dark on the second landing I felt her hand in mine and smelled her scent and kissed her. And as we kissed I knew the sheer joy of reunion, and I did not have the sense to be frightened by it.

16

I struggle now for the precise words Ella used. I can catch her tone, watch her face and trace the changing patterns on it. But her words come back to me only slowly, for when I first listened to them I was distracted by the flick of her hair, the tap of her light, quick step, the neatness of her waist, the outline of her breasts, the ring of her voice.

I don't remember being mystified by her presence in Prague or by the sudden way in which she had deserted her parents. The arrogance of youthful love provided all the explanation I required.

'I can't face Daddy and Pamela just yet,' Ella said, as we threaded our way through the crowds on Sokolska Street and turned left into Wenceslas Square. 'I need to talk properly to you, Jamie. I need your help. Isn't there anywhere we could go? Somewhere where nobody would know us?'

'You forget this is not London,' I replied. 'There's no need for secrecy.'

And smilingly I guided her into a small coffee shop I knew on the corner. Soon we were sitting at a back table and ordering from a waitress with badly dyed blonde hair and alarming eyebrows.

'Now,' I began when the coffee had been placed before

us, 'what do you need to talk to me about?'

'Well, the fact of the matter is that my family are beginning to consider the possibility that I may be a little crazy.'

Ella paused as I took this in.

'And the worst of it is it's my own wretched fault.' She took another drag on her cigarette. 'I suppose I had better begin at the beginning, hadn't I?'

I nodded.

Silence.

'All right. You know about my grandmother and my aunt and the generally shaky mental history of my family.'

'Yes.'

'My father's obsessed by it. Understandably, perhaps. If your mother and twin sister had killed themselves, you'd worry about your own children, wouldn't you? Particularly if your only daughter happened to be the living image of her grandmother. It would be a constant reminder. Do you follow?'

I nodded again.

'Well, Daddy's always on the lookout for danger signs – signs that I might be unhappy. He doesn't want to take any risks with me, which puts a certain amount of pressure on a person. Can you imagine?'

'I can.'

She bit her lip. 'Oh, God, I've been so *stupid*.'

She stubbed out her cigarette, half-smoked, with exasperated violence.

'In what way?'

'I've played *right* into Sarah's hands.'

'How?'

'Well, while you were away Sarah published a little monograph about our family in the *Athenaeum*. She's working it up into a book apparently, a life and times of our grandmother. I dread that being published. Of course the worst sort of papers loved it. All that aristocratic suicide. I thought I saw my chance of getting rid of Charlie. I thought he wouldn't want a madwoman as the mother of his children. Not even if she *did* stand in line to inherit a castle.' She paused. 'So I staged a confession.'

'You did *what*?'

Ella fumbled in her bag for another cigarette and lit it.

'I cried and I told him how unstable my family was, how there was something wrong with our genes. I even said I had a duty never to have children, for fear of passing it on.' She stopped. 'I thought it would scare him off.'

'When in fact it did quite the opposite.'

'Not exactly,' she said quietly. 'At first Charlie wouldn't budge. He was going to stick by me loyally and all that. He kept on saying it was only my family, it wasn't me, I had to rise above it.'

I thought of Charles Stanhope's earnest, uncomprehending eyes and a sudden fear gripped my throat.

'What did you tell him?' I asked quietly.

Ella took a deep drag on her cigarette. For a long moment there was silence. Finally she spoke.

'What did you expect me to tell him?'

'Don't tell me you—'

'All right, I won't. But I did.'

Her voice was small and thin, like a child's.

'You told him you were—'

'Yes. All right. I told him I was worried about *myself*.'

There, I've said it. I told him it wouldn't be fair to marry him.'

'Oh God.'

'And do you know what *he* did?'

I saw with complete clarity how things stood.

'He told your father, didn't he?' I said grimly.

She nodded.

'Oh Ella, you stupid ...'

I could not find the words. Love and anger welled inside me; then pity too as I saw she was crying.

'I thought Sarah was giving me a way out,' she said through her tears. 'For the first time in her life, in her own twisted way, I thought she was being magnanimous. By stirring everyone up and making everything so public, I thought she was offering me a way to escape and so I took it. I had no idea things would turn out like this.'

'Oh no.'

'It seems strange to say it now, I know, but you have no idea how perfect it all seemed at the time. I thought it would be the least painful way of breaking with Charlie. He'd noticed I'd changed towards him, you see; he's not stupid. He needed an explanation. And I could hardly have told him the *truth*.' She paused. 'I didn't think he'd tell anyone.'

'I don't believe you could have been so—'

'Don't judge me, James.' Her voice rang suddenly sharp. 'Don't judge me.'

Mutely we stared at each other. I took her hand.

'If you knew what these past two months have been like you would be kinder,' she said more quietly at last, drying her eyes. 'I've been paying for my freedom, I can

163

tell you. If you knew what it's been like seeing my father so worried, with so little reason, knowing it's my own fault ... If only you *knew*. Seeing him suffer like this has been punishment enough.'

She looked down at the floor, away from me.

'But what could I have done?' Her eyes met mine. 'Short of telling everybody everything, right down to why I got engaged to Charlie in the first place, there was nothing to do but pretend. I was trapped, Jamie; I couldn't go back then. So I pretended.'

I put my hand on her arm.

'And, God, it was awful. I can't tell you how awful. The situation got completely out of hand. I couldn't control it any more. And that was when it got frightening. I tried to be myself again and found that I wasn't allowed to be normal any more. The whole system had already swung into gear, you see.'

She drew breath deeply.

'And then the talking started. You've no idea what that does to you. Knowing that people are always watching: your family; your friends; the newspapers. I've been living in a goldfish bowl these past two months.'

I nodded, still lost for words.

'And the worst thing is that I know it's all my own fault. I don't know *how* I could have let it happen.'

'Neither do I.'

Ella gripped my hand. 'Don't say that to me. You've got to help me'

There was a pause. Her eyes met mine unflinchingly.

'I will,' I said. 'Of course I will.'

'Oh, Jamie. Thank you.'

She leaned across the table and kissed me. Our lips met and I knew in that brief sweet touch that I would do anything for her. I knew and like a fool was pleased by that knowledge.

'If you only knew how *draining* it is having to be happy all the time. I've got to be cheerful to convince them I'm sane. I'm not allowed one morose minute to myself before Daddy suggests I see a new doctor or Pamela wants to take me away for a "change of scene". That's how I come to be in Prague, you know. This is a "change of scene".'

She paused.

'And you've no *idea* how many frauds I've been taken to see; I've sat in consulting rooms from one end of Harley Street to the other.' She made an attempt at a smile. 'You can't imagine what it's like. These people ask you to *remember* things, to tell them about traumas you've never had and insecurities you've never dreamed of. And the frightening thing is that things *do* start occurring to you. All this attention *does* make you think that maybe there's a reason for it after all. You start to doubt yourself and those around you. You begin to remember childhood nightmares.'

She lit another cigarette and drew on it deeply.

'And because I thought I should try to seem open with the doctors – they're the ones you have to convince, after all – I told them all about my childhood, all about everything. Except Sarah, of course. I could hardly tell them about her and me.'

I watched her shaking fingers as she put her coffee cup to her lips.

'So what did you tell them?' I asked.

165

'All sorts of things.'

'Give me an example.'

'All right.' She paused, thinking. 'Well, when I was nine or ten I used to have a nightmare about a witch who lived in the closet in my bedroom and could turn people to stone. In this dream she was always just about to catch me and I was always running away from her, running and running through woods and fields and … you get the picture.'

She smiled.

'I was always looking for my father to rescue me. And I always woke up just as the witch caught me. Daddy never appeared.'

'You told the doctors about that?'

She nodded.

'And what did they say?'

'You must remember psychiatrists aren't paid to tell you you're *sane*.'

'What did they make of that dream?'

'Oh, all the usual stuff: lost mother; fear of stepmother; need for father. They told me I was angry with Daddy for marrying Pamela – which couldn't be further from the truth, incidentally – and started talking about Electra complexes and the dangers of repressed grieving for a parent turning to self-mutilation or violence as a sort of attention-seeking. It was quite ridiculous.'

'Go on.'

'So I told Daddy I didn't want any more doctors, that they were filling my mind with all sorts of evil things. You've no idea, as a matter of fact, quite how stable you have to be to emerge unscathed from a session with a respected psychiatrist. And Daddy went and told *them* that. He got very angry, actually, and stormed into Dr Jefferson's rooms and demanded an explanation, which was of course precisely what the odious little man wanted. I was in *denial* now, you see. If I had a pound for every time someone who doesn't know me from a bar of soap has told me I need to "face my demons", I'd be richer than my father.'

She stopped and there were tears in her eyes again.

'Oh God, Jamie. What have I done? What have I *done*?'

'Hush,' I whispered, getting up and taking her in my arms, holding her tightly. 'It'll be all right.'

'Will it?'

'Yes.'

'I can't tell you how badly I need to hear that. Or how much I've missed you.'

She clung to me. I held her until her tears had stopped.

'And now tell me why you ran away from your parents yesterday,' I began when we were sitting opposite each other again.

'That's the final part of the story. After the big blow-up with Dr Jefferson, Pamela suggested one of her "changes of scene". Basically London was no place for the invalid. Everyone was gossiping. Which reminds me. Look at this.'

She took out of her bag a page from an illustrated magazine and handed it to me. In the centre was a large photograph of her at a party. She was standing on a staircase alone, very pale.

'Heaven only knows where they got this from,' she said. 'Read what it says.'

I took it from her and read the column quickly, scanning its melodrama with disgust.

She looked as though she had everything, but Ella Harcourt, heir to one of the country's most stately stately homes, has a dark family history looming over her. Young, beautiful, intelligent, she is the toast of London ... but how many years remain before the tragic curse of the Harcourts claims a new victim?

'That's why they thought a change of scene would do me good,' said Ella drily. 'They were invited to the sale. I thought if I came with them I could see you.'

I thrilled with gladness as she said this. 'But why did you run away?'

She paused. 'I suppose I thought it wouldn't make much difference. We had an argument, at the Mocsáry viewing actually, and Daddy said something ... about my "condition". And I thought: Well, if they're convinced I'm loopy, and will be whatever I do, I might as well take a night's freedom. Have you any *idea* how wonderful it is to be alone when you've spent two months being watched constantly, day and night?' She looked at me. 'Oh, I know it was wrong. But I'm fed up with the kid-glove treatment. Can you understand that?'

I nodded.

'But now you've got to face them,' I said firmly.

'You don't mean you think I should *tell* them, do you? All about Sarah and Charles and ... what I did?'

'No, I don't,' I said slowly, trying to think. 'But when I left them a few hours ago they were sick with worry.

You've got to go home and let them know you're all right. And you've got some heartfelt apologies to make.'

She bowed her head. 'I know.'

'Then let's go and get them over and done with.'

So we got up, paid, and left the café. As we emerged into the crowds of Wenceslas Square, Ella slipped her hand into mine.

'Thank you, Jamie.'

And she kissed me.

Sin is a strong word to use, an ugly one. But I am no longer afraid of it. I know that Ella sinned by taking Charles Stanhope from Sarah. I think perhaps I sinned too by wanting her confession for myself alone. I was jealous of her confidence.

When I might have advised her to tell the truth, to admit what she had done, I did not. I didn't show her the dangers of deceit; I didn't know them myself then. I see now that lies are like the bars of a cage. They solidify with time. Once you have built and left them about you, all is lost.

17

Eric's mother arrived on the day before the sale, a tall, stately woman with fine bones and beautiful hands. I remember the easy elegance of her conversation and dress, the silver of her long hair, her dark, grave eyes. Louise de Vaugirard must have been as old as my own parents or older, but her movements had the easy suppleness of youth. Her face appeared lined only when she smiled. I can see that smile now, and as I see it I remember that it was Eric's smile too; that when mother and son smiled their faces lit up and when they laughed their mirth echoed and rang together. I hear them laughing sometimes, even now, in my dreams. But I heard their laughter later, when I knew the Vaugirards better.

In Prague I saw Louise only twice: on the afternoon of the sale itself; and on the night before it, her first in the city, when she took Eric and me to dinner at Czardas. The haunt of the city's élite, it occupied the first two floors of an old palace block in the Malá Strana and its service was impeccable.

Louise de Vaugirard wore no jewellery but a silver crucifix on a thin silver chain, and as she stood up I knew who she was, even before Eric had kissed her on both cheeks.

'*Maman, je te présente mon ami* James Farrell,' he said.

'But we must not speak in French,' she replied in barely accented English. 'The English do not care for languages not their own. Yes?'

I blushed and said awkwardly that I thought French a beautiful language.

Louise turned to Eric. 'But he is every bit as charming as you said he was.' Turning to me again she gave me her hand. 'I am delighted to meet you at last, Monsieur Farrell. My son has nothing but praise for you. And my husband and I are deeply grateful for all you have done here in Prague. I only wish that Eric's father were here himself to thank you but unfortunately his affairs keep him in France.'

We sat down. Dinner was ordered and arrived, steaming, on gilt-edged dishes. In his mother's company Eric was affectionate, deferential and slightly on edge. He was not as easy with his mother as he was with me; nor, in her company, did he behave with me as he usually did. He watched more and spoke less. His eagerness for us to like each other, expressed in many ways, touched me then. So Louise and I talked – of my childhood, my music, my time in Prague with her son – and Eric did not speak much unless appealed to.

I liked Louise. I enjoyed her easy, uncalculated charm, the precision of her sentences, the irony of her observations. And I talked easily enough, distracted only by the crucifix she wore. It was small and delicately made. But the face of its Christ caught so truly a note of human anguish that I was uncomfortable looking at it, and I was fascinated by my own discomfort. Again and again my eyes returned to it; and my hostess, seeing where I looked, asked me whether I would like to touch it.

I nodded, smiling.

'There is an interesting story attached to this,' she said as she undid the clasp of its silver chain and put the cross in my hand.

'Really?'

'Yes. It was the reward given to an ancestress of my husband's.'

I saw Eric frown slightly and make an effort to hide his irritation.

'What had she done to deserve it?' I asked.

'She was a spy at the Congress of Vienna,' Louise replied, smiling. 'She took the secrets of the foreign negotiators with her feminine wiles and her reward was this cross, amongst other things. She was a great lady. Another Louise, like me.'

'She was a whore, *Maman*,' said Eric quietly, 'as you should know.'

There was an unearthly silence.

Louise gave no outward sign of having heard her son. Calmly, deliberately, she took the crucifix back from me, threaded it through its chain, and hung it once more around her neck. Then quietly, she said, 'I want you never to speak to me again like that, Eric. Am I understood?' And began once more to eat.

The clash of her cutlery was, for a moment, unnaturally loud on the china of her plate; then she controlled it. Turning to me once more, she began to speak again, laughing and smiling as though nothing had happened.

For the rest of the meal Eric did not say a word; and an

hour of strained conversation with Louise, who paid no attention to her son's silence, passed very slowly for me. When our dessert plates and coffee cups had been cleared and the waiter had brought the bill, Eric still showed no signs of movement or of speech. So I thanked Madame de Vaugirard, a little awkwardly, for a lovely dinner and she rose.

'It was a pleasure to meet you at last, James.'

During the course of the evening she had elegantly appropriated the use of my Christian name.

'I look forward to seeing you tomorrow afternoon at the sale.'

'Likewise,' I replied.

Eric got up now from the table and kissed his mother on both cheeks. Then, without another word, he turned and walked out. I shook hands with Louise as though nothing had happened, and followed him.

Outside the restaurant we walked together in silence, my friend setting a furious pace, for ten minutes or more. We were walking along the river, heading for the Charles Bridge and the tram that would take us home; our breath turned to smoke in the icy air of approaching winter. Block after block of cobbled streets and darkened buildings passed. When the floodlights illuminating the castle on the hill above us went out, I registered that it must be midnight. Still Eric did not speak, and as it became obvious that he had no intention of doing so I turned to him and asked him what was wrong.

'Do not bother yourself about it, James,' he said, an ominous note in his voice, which I had never heard before.

We walked on in silence.

'I think you might tell me,' I said at last, doing my best to stem a rising tide of irritation. 'Don't you think I'm entitled to an explanation?'

More silence followed, broken only by the quick regular tap of Eric's step on the hard pavement and the flow of the river.

'Have you any idea how awkward it was for me in there?' I asked finally, exasperated.

My friend turned to me, eyes flashing.

'So it is I who am at fault, is it?' he exploded. 'My mother's hypocrisy earns her nothing but praise. It is I who try to puncture it, I who try to be honest, yet I who get the blame. Even from you.'

I was lost.

'I don't see how the manner in which your ancestors obtained state secrets is a test of how honest you are. And what do you mean by your mother's hypocrisy? You're not making any sense.'

'My mother pretends to be a good Catholic,' he replied tersely. 'She talks endlessly of the sacrament of marriage, about what sex is good and what is wicked. But she praises prostitution, so long as it is done for the glory of France.'

I heard to my alarm that his voice was shaking. Uncomfortable now, my irritation evaporating, I said nothing. Eric sensed my discomfort.

'Do not bother yourself, James,' he said. 'You will not understand.'

His pace increased. The silence was tense and I waited for it to snap as I knew that it must. When he spoke again his words were quick, almost hoarse.

'You will never understand, James. You will never

understand what I mean because you will never leave the safety of your nice, civilized shell. You will never risk yourself or let others risk themselves with you.'

Bewildered by his vehemence, I considered defence and justification; for a moment even, I was angry again.

And I might have spoken, had we not seen our tram rattling down the street towards our stop and run to meet it; but we did. And in silence we went home and to our respective beds without exchanging a further word.

The next day, the day of the sale, patchy rain fell in short bursts on the thronging crowds. Eric and I arrived together at five in the afternoon, an hour before the gavel went up, still not speaking.

We found Louise sitting in the middle of the first row. Her chair, and the two on either side of her which she indicated to us, had large cards on them on which someone, in painstaking copperplate, had written 'Réservé'. She betrayed no signs of unease with her son; it was as if the tension of the evening before had never existed.

'Dear James,' she said to me after she and Eric had exchanged their customary twin kisses, 'before the sale begins and everything gets too – how to say? – frantic,' she smiled at me, 'I wish to make you a little present.'

She took the crucifix from her neck and put it in the palm of my hand, which she closed over it.

'You were admiring this last night. I wish that you would keep it. Christ has watched over the many generations who have worn it.'

I, conscious of Eric's eyes on me, did not know what to

say and began to mumble something about not possibly being able—

'But I insist,' she said. 'You are my son's friend and therefore mine. If Eric does not think it fit that I should wear this, then I should like you to have it.'

And with the air of giving a benediction, she clasped my left hand and Eric's right and squeezed them tightly in hers.

'And now,' she said to the auctioneer, who was awaiting her signal, 'we are ready.'

He in his turn signalled to a flunkey who went ceremoniously to the double doors of the bidding room and threw them open with a flourish. In streamed a long line of people who made their way with much excited chatter to the rows of gilt and velvet chairs. Gradually they filled them; and the auctioneer was just mounting to the podium and beginning his opening address, the crowd was just hushing itself and the doors closing, when in slipped a figure with short, shining blonde hair and excited green eyes. Ella slipped into a seat in the last row. Eric saw me look at her. His mother smiled approvingly as I put the crucifix into my pocket, and the sale began.

The bidding started cautiously. A few of the less prestigious lots went for just under their catalogue estimates: a table; some porcelain; a writing desk that had stood in Madame Mocsáry's hall. Seeing the furniture we had come to know so well go under the gavel, lot by lot, made me nostalgic for lost times in that eclectic apartment, and my resentment gave way to tenderness for the person I had shared them with. I looked past Louise at Eric and smiled at him. His eyes met mine, and after a moment's hesitation he smiled back.

Ella came up to me as the crowds were dispersing and took my hand.

'You were too lovely the other day,' she said. 'I don't know what I'd've done without you.'

'How are things with your parents now?'

'Better. But this must be the last of my little escapades. From now on it's sanity all the way.' She looked up at me and smiled.

'Are they here now?'

I was anxious to meet Alexander and Pamela properly, on the new terms of my intimacy with their daughter.

'No,' she whispered. 'Can you believe it? I told them I'd run away because I was never allowed a moment alone. So they've gone already and left me on my own.'

I can see her shining eyes looking up at mine, can feel her small hand and the tightness of its grip.

'That's brave of them,' I said, grinning.

She kicked me playfully. 'Don't be rude or I shan't say what I've come to ask you.'

'And what is that?'

'Well . . .' She smiled. 'Daddy and Pamela don't want to take me to London for obvious reasons. The fuss still hasn't died down.'

She paused.

'The world must have its pound of flesh, I suppose. What was it Oscar Wilde said? Something about there being only one thing worse than being talked about and that's *not* being talked about.'

'Something like that,' I said, smiling, pleased by her good humour.

'Well, that's how I've decided to view it all.' She reached into her bag for a cigarette. 'But that's not what I wanted to speak to you about.'

'Oh?'

'Don't look at me archly like that, Jamie.'

'But you're a free woman now.' I leaned down and whispered into her ear. 'I want to claim you.'

She put her arm through mine. 'Then why don't you come and stay with me for a few weeks until Christmas? Daddy and Pamela don't want me to be alone. And we've got a place in France I want you to see – I'm going tomorrow.'

'I'd love to,' I said simply.

Then I thought of Eric and our argument. I didn't want to leave him without clearing the air and I suspected that his temper would take a few days to settle.

'But I'm not sure I can leave Eric at such short notice.'

At that moment he joined us.

'Miss Harcourt,' he said stiffly, 'what a delight.'

And he kissed her on both cheeks.

'Just the person I wanted to see,' she said. 'My father and stepmother are going back to London soon and giving me the use of a place we have in France. I want you and James to come and stay, just for a few weeks until Christmas.'

She smiled at me as she said this, and I warmed to her for thus including my friend.

'That would be wonderful,' Eric replied, in a tone so

polite I could not judge the sincerity of what he said. 'But I am afraid that I cannot.'

'But you must,' she went on. 'James has said he won't go if you don't, and I can't be left all on my lonesome in a Godforsaken house in the middle of nowhere.'

Eric looked at me; I looked at Ella; then I looked at him. His dark eyes met mine steadily, almost questioningly. I thought him still angry about the previous night. And anxious to let him see that I had forgotten and forgiven, I put my arm around his shoulders.

'I've got used to having you around,' I said, smiling. 'You've got to come.'

His eyes held mine a moment longer.

'Go on,' Ella said.

'Yes, do.' This from me.

There was a pause while – had we but known it – all our fates hung in the balance.

'Very well,' he said finally, 'I'll come.'

18

Eric and I travelled to France alone, Ella having left Prague some days before us. We said sad goodbyes to people and to places that neither of us would ever forget. At Café Florian we listened sadly to the drunken reminiscences and loud debates which would continue, we knew, whether or not we stayed to hear them.

Alone for the last time at Sokolska 21 we had Blanca to tea and thanked her for all she had done.

In my last few hours in the city I took my leave of Eduard Mendl, who sent me on my way with a piece of 'lucky resin', which I have to this day.

'I have enjoyed teaching you,' he told me gravely as we parted. 'And I do not say that to all my pupils. With dedication you may go far.'

As I put my violin in its case he told me that he had enjoyed my concerts with Eric, also.

'They give me hope for you both,' he said. 'And it pleases an old musician like me to see the rapport which you two have together.'

I thanked him warmly.

'God bless you, James,' he said as we shook hands.

I left his splendid rooms with words of praise ringing in my ears, thinking with pleasure of the excitement of travel, of bags packed and couchettes booked, of Ella waiting for me in France. I remember leaving the Conservatory; remember bounding down its steps in the cold sunlight of that early winter day.

Our last days in Prague were good ones. Neither Eric nor I referred again to the dinner with Louise or to the argument which had followed it; and he, it seemed to me, made as conscious an effort to forget both as I did. Easy relations were re-established between us and our journey to France was light-hearted and happy, full of laughter and jokes and the telling of our first Czech anecdotes.

We arrived at the border in the early morning of a misty, cloud-covered day, and bleary-eyed with sleep we endured an hour of waiting on a freezing railway plat-form – inevitably extended to three by an unexplained delay – and then caught two slow, connecting trains in haphazard succession. Eric had been responsible for choosing our route and he had not chosen well; but his company was too amusing for me to be long irritated by his incompetence with timetables ('Only dull people are good with trains,' he told me) and we arrived at our destination in the late afternoon, grubby but high-spirited.

Ella did not come to meet us at the station; instead she sent the housekeeper's son with a note addressed to me in the jagged brown letters which I had come to know so well.

Darling James, it began,
     As you will have noticed the day is very cold and I have been instructed not to brave the drive or the weather. (Daddy and Pamela have put the village

doctor in attendance, just in case I should do something silly. He's very over-protective.) So I've sent Jacques to collect you and I hope you don't mind. Be sure to give him a tip — it's important to get people on your side in this country.

Can't wait to see you.

E

I read this in the car as we drove from the station and listened absently as Eric and Jacques spoke to each other at intervals in polite French.

As the countryside rattled past and we slowed, approached and passed through a pair of dilapidated stone gateposts I thought excitedly that Ella would soon be in my arms. The drive was long and uneven, the house an ancient block of faded stone dotted by cracked blue shutters. It surprised me that such a house should belong to the Harcourts and that it should be left in such an obvious state of disrepair. Certainly the splendours of 23 Chester Square had led me to expect something grander than this, something less desolate.

I saw Ella as we rounded the final curve. She was waiting for us on the narrow flight of stairs that led to the front door, a fragile figure in pale blue cashmere with ruffled hair and glowing cheeks. I flushed with pleasure as I saw her and looked at Eric to smile too, but he was staring ahead and did not see me. I remember that now. But as the car came to a halt I gave no thought to the firm set of his mouth or to the tension in his shoulders, supposing — if I supposed anything at all — that our long journey had tired him. It had not tired me.

As soon as Jacques had braked I was out of the car and Ella was in my arms and I was holding her and swinging her off the steps and she was laughing and pressing herself against me and pulling my shoulders tight to hers. I remember the bones of her neck, the delicate arch of her nose, the strands of hair flying about her face as we moved together. Even now the sweet thrill of our reunion on that cold day makes my heart race.

It's ironic, you know: that my tears tonight and all this week will not be for my dead wife but for the lost love of her cousin; that Sarah's bloodied body has less power to move me than Ella's sweetly acrid smell of soap and cigarettes, forgotten for so long but now remembered.

As I held her in the icy wind I filled my lungs with it. She was laughing wildly when I let her go and she pushed me playfully away as she offered a rosy cheek to Eric.

'Leave your bags here,' Ella said to us, smiling, as she led the way into a low, dark hall, cheerless despite the vase of flowers on its central table. 'You should see the house before you unpack.'

And so we saw the house, and as she led us through it I thought that her vitality was out of place in its sombre corridors and draughty rooms, that the click of her heels on its flagstones should be heard in a lighter, younger air than that to be found between the unloved walls of that decaying house.

Recollection is curious. I never went back to it after Eric's death, and that was almost sixty years ago; but every detail of Les Varrèges – for that is what the house was called – is etched in my mind still. I can trace the patterns of its thick walls, the sequence of its few large rooms; I can recall the number of doors in its low-ceilinged hall, the musty odour of woodsmoke and dusty rugs that hung heavy in its air. I remember its fireplaces, large enough for a small person to stand upright in; its pock-marked wooden beams made from the timber of sixteenth-century warships and blackened by centuries of soot; the layout of its guest wing, a nineteenth-century addition; the plan of its gardens.

'I'm afraid we haven't opened all the bedrooms,' Ella told us as she led us down a vaulted passage. 'There are only us three in the house. And Doctor Pétin, of course, who's in there.'

She pointed to a door.

'Jacques and Madame Clancy live in the village and we didn't think it worth while opening and airing everything for so few.'

I followed her, delighting in the lilting cadences of her voice.

'You'll meet the good doctor later,' she went on. 'I expect he's gone for one of his rambles.' As she spoke she paused outside a panelled oak door. 'This is your room. I thought I'd put you two in one without any leaks.'

She turned a handle and motioned Eric and me inside a large, airy room, more homely than the others, which gave on to the garden. A strong smell of lavender mingled with the odour of wood and fire met us and Ella, sniffing, pretended to choke.

'Madame Clancy is a great devotee of scented bed-rooms, you know,' she explained as she went to one of the sash windows and opened it. 'But we'll clear the stench soon, don't you worry.'

Outside, fog was creeping over the thick screen of yews at the garden's end. It was a garden past its prime, a once formal grid of gravel walks, hedges and pruned trees in long lines, which had thrown over the yoke of human control and run wild once more. It was ghostly, that garden; romantic and appealing, as all ruins are.

'We don't use the house any more,' Ella said quietly. 'It was my mother's favourite. She and my father bought it just after they married and I don't think Pamela likes it much.' She paused and looked about the room. 'But Daddy would never sell it. He lets it moulder instead and thinks a weekly visit from Madame Clancy is enough to keep it in working order.'

'Do *you* like it?' I asked.

'I do.' Her eyes met mine. 'But I don't like it falling down like this. And it's terribly gloomy at this time of year.'

I nodded.

Ella smiled at me and Eric.

'That's why I'm so pleased you're both here,' she said lightly. 'You can restore yourselves after all your hard work in Prague and we can keep each other company.'

I nodded and looked towards my friend but he was facing away from me, looking out of the window at the long expanse of garden. I could not see his face and as Ella talked easily of towels and bathrooms I noticed the stiffness in his shoulders, which I dismissed as weariness, remembering how little we had slept in the past twenty-four hours. So when Ella asked whether we were tired, I said that I, for one, was exhausted.

'Well, that's hardly surprising after your journey.' Her

small hand squeezed mine. 'Why don't you both have a rest? Shall I see you for a drink at sevenish?'

'That would be perfect,' I replied, thinking with pleasure of all the time that lay ahead of us to be filled as we wished.

Eric, still by the window, said nothing.

'Well, then, till seven.'

And Ella was gone, closing the door gently behind her as she left.

Slowly I unpacked, dreamily examining the room about me as I did so, catching lingering traces of Ella's smell. By the bed were old French novels, nicely bound. An armoire held a large china wash-bowl and a jug with blue flowers painted on it: forget-me-nots, I think. By the fire was a screen embroidered with courtly figures in a stylized rose garden.

The house, I could see now, showed traces of once careful attention only half-forgotten; and I wondered what Ella's mother had been like, the woman who had chosen the furniture for this room, who had placed the novels by the bed for the amusement of her guests. I went to where Eric stood, quite still, and looked at the view with him. What flowers there were, and they were few now, ran amok. I saw row upon row of gravel paths lined with yew hedges stretching to a tall boundary line of trees. In the middle was a fountain, and as I watched it sputtered into life and water poured from the open mouths of its frogs.

'What do you think of it?' I asked.

Eric's only response was a non-committal grunt. There was a pause while I wondered if anything more serious than tiredness had caused the change in his mood, for even I could not pretend that the taciturn figure at the window bore any relation to the laughing companion I had travelled with and I thought that maybe the strange atmosphere of that lonely house had depressed him. Certainly it could not have been further in mood from the eclectic splendours of Sokolska 21 and the deep rich colours of Madame Mocsáry's apartment.

Abruptly he moved away from the glass. 'I think I shall have a walk,' he said, and left me.

'Do you want some company?' I called after him as he shut the door. For a moment he paused, opened the door again and looked back at me through black, unbrushed curls.

'It is not me who you want to keep you company now, James,' he said quietly; and before I could speak again he had closed the door and I could hear the measured tread of his feet on the stone as he went away down the passage.

Alone in the house with Ella I conquered my impulse to go to her, telling myself that there was plenty of time. Instead I had a hot bath and a shave, for a lover's vanity could not be satisfied by my dirty, travel-stained reflection. I wanted to be fresh for the evening.

As I was dressing Eric returned from his walk, more cheerful than he had been when he left for it and full of talk of a deserted quarry beyond the trees at the end of the garden. Pleased at the improvement in his mood I spent a pleasant half-hour talking to him before dinner, which we ate with Ella in a small dining room that led off the kitchen.

I remember that meal: the old-fashioned china on which it was served; the cosy fire which crackled as an accompaniment to our conversation. We were alone, just us three, for Dr Pétin had been called out to deliver a baby in the village and was not expected back until very late.

We ate a selection of cold meats, left that afternoon by Madame Clancy. We talked of Prague, of the Mocsáry sale, of the quarry Eric had seen on his walk.

'It's where they mined the stones for the house,' Ella told us. 'It's very deep; my mother had it flooded for her guests to swim in.' She took a sip of wine. 'You're welcome to a dip, of course, though as December is beginning I wouldn't advise it very strongly.'

It was Eric who said he wanted to see the quarry by moonlight, and when dinner was over and Dr Pétin had still not returned, we decided there was no time like the present.

So the three of us made our way across the gravel paths and through the yew trees, laughing at first – for the atmosphere between us had eased – but gradually falling silent as the spell of the garden took hold over us. Ella's small hand found mine in the darkness and held it tightly. Eric, out in front with the torch, shone it back for us and then forwards. Beyond the screen of yews there was nothing to see but a field with rows of neatly planted apple trees that were sinister in the darkness.

'We're heading up there, past the orchard,' Ella whispered to me and pressed me on over the hard ground.

We passed through another line of trees and as we emerged from their cover Eric flicked off his torch. For a moment all was black. Then the moon appeared from behind a bank of cloud and from far-off schooldays a line of poetry recurred to me, sole survivor of many, and

I thought of Tennyson's *Idylls of the King*, and of the line about 'The barren lake/And the long glories of the winter moon'.

Here was a barren lake; here was a winter moon luminous in pale gold. Before us was the steep cliff of the quarry, dropping away to black water many feet below. From a cloudless heaven the moon cast an eerie light over the scene and turned bushes into hobgoblins and trees into scrawny giants.

We were all silent. In the moonlight I saw Eric's profile: the prominent arch of his Gallic nose, the line of his jaw, the curls of his black gypsy locks. Beside him was Ella, fragile as china, her skin glowing ghost-like, her fingers interlocked. I stood between them, watching her play with her rings.

I remember telling myself as I stood there that here was beauty. But there was something uncomfortable about the beauty of that scene nonetheless, something disturbing about the quarry's isolation and its vast unplumbed depths. I thought of huge beasts moving at its murky bottom, waiting.

When my eyes left, I looked up and saw Eric watching me with something like pain in his eyes. I saw that Ella was watching him, but it was too dark to see the look on her face. My eyes met my friend's and he switched on the torch once more; the spell, cast so delicately, was broken abruptly.

'Come on,' he said, 'I'm cold.'

And he led the way back to the house with quick, defiant steps. Ella and I followed without a murmur.

During that walk a change came over us. Nothing was

said; none of us spoke at all. But when we reached the house things were not as they had been when we left it. There was no comfort in our silence.

As we passed the guest wing on our way to the front door I saw with relief that Dr Pétin's light was on.

Ella walked past his windows without acknowledging them.

'I can't face him now,' she said as we climbed the steps. She looked at me and began to say more but thought better of it. She had not taken my hand or offered me hers on the walk back and as I touched her shoulder now she moved away.

'I have to be vivacious at all times,' she said eventually with a weak attempt at a smile, 'or I don't get a good report sent to Daddy and Pamela. I'll introduce you tomorrow.'

And she let Eric and me into the darkened hall and bolted the great oak door behind us.

'This place gives me the creeps,' she said suddenly, looking about the dim room.

'Me too,' I answered feelingly, wishing that Eric were not with us and that I could be alone with Ella. My friend's presence and the strange mood which had overtaken him on the walk back made me uncomfortable.

'I think it's beautiful.' Eric's voice rang out, unnaturally loud, from the half-darkness. He was standing by the fireplace at the other end of the room, hardly visible in the dying glow of the embers.

'Don't drift off like that,' I said, startled, surprised by my own edginess.

'Are you two frightened of ghosts?'

His tone was derisive. I saw Ella trying to decide

whether the mockery in it was friendly. At length she spoke. 'You're right, this is silly. Goodnight to you both. May you sleep dreamlessly.'

And with a kiss on my cheek she slipped out of the room.

I began to follow her but at the door she turned, looked back, and shook her head. I stood hesitating in the middle of the room. She disappeared.

Irritated suddenly, I turned to Eric.

'Come on, bedtime.'

'Are you sure I'm the person you want to be sharing with?' His tone was coolly level.

'Shut up.'

Silently I led the way to our cosy room, lit now by a coal fire burning in a recently polished grate. The scent of lavender was once again everywhere and I detected the conscientious presence of Madame Clancy. In the warm half-light Eric and I undressed without much conversation and got into our respective beds. The sheets were crisp and cold.

'Sleep well,' I said.

'You too.'

And thus ended that first day.

19

The next was brighter than its predecessor, a cold day of clear winter skies and sparkling light. Frost covered the ground. Eric and I woke early and were the first to take our places at the breakfast table, where a garrulous Frenchwoman (Madame Clancy, we supposed) handed us croissants and made dire predictions about the weather. Her speech was so fast and her accent so new to my ears that when she had gone I looked to Eric for a full translation.

'She says it will get very cold now,' he said. 'And she says also that Ella has gone out for a walk. She will be back shortly.'

As he finished speaking Ella walked in, cheeks apple-red.

'Mornin', boys.'

Her tone was cheerful but she avoided my eyes.

'Good morning.'

I was sullen in her presence, a little sulky after the dismissal of the night before. She ignored this.

'The good doctor Pétin usually comes down at about nine for a cup of coffee and a croissant. I imagine that's him now.'

As she spoke a rather apologetic middle-aged man

walked in, slightly rotund, more than slightly balding, with wispy grey hair grown long at the sides and brushed over his head to hide this.

'Good morning, Mademoiselle Harcourt,' he said in a gentle, ingratiating voice, the tone of one humouring a child. 'I trust you slept well.' His English was perfect.

'Very well, thank you,' she replied, smiling with a brightness I thought studied as she poured the coffee and introduced us.

The doctor nodded his greeting.

'It is important for you to get as much sleep as possible before you return to London.'

Turning to Eric and me, he went on, underlining his points with leisurely jabs of his fat fingers, 'Sleep, rest, warmth; and moderation above all,' he said. 'These are what I believe in, gentlemen; these are my principles.'

And with this he took his place at the table and proceeded to eat four croissants in quick succession.

It was not until the middle of the morning that I was able to get Ella to myself, for she disappeared soon after breakfast and I was left politely observing a game of chess between Dr Pétin and Eric. They played in the salon, a large square room in the middle of the house with long windows that gave on to the gravel paths of the garden.

Sitting on one of its sofas, smiling occasionally to the doctor and my friend to assure them of my continuing interest in their game, thinking continuously of Ella, I saw her emerge from the yew trees and excused myself to the two men. When I reached her she was by the fountain, walking quickly towards the house, tightly muffled in a man's greatcoat, with a pale blue school scarf, that must have been her father's, wound around her neck.

She stopped when she saw me. There was a moment's pause.

'Hello,' she said finally.

'Hello.'

She made as if to move on but I caught her arm.

'Why are you treating me like a stranger?'

The wakeful hours of a frustrated night gave an edge to my voice. 'What's wrong?'

She looked at me steadily for a moment. At last she said, slowly, 'Don't you know?' and looked away from me.

I shook my head. She raised her eyes to mine and studied my face for a moment. The confusion she found there seemed to satisfy her and she felt in her pockets for a cigarette. I watched as she put it to her lips and lit it. She inhaled slowly, deeply, and blew the smoke upwards, tilting her head. I followed it until it was lost in the bright, cold blue above us.

'Talk to me,' I said simply.

Abruptly she turned away. There was a tangible moment of hesitation, which made my heart beat.

'Very well,' she said finally, seeming to resolve on something. 'But follow me. This way.'

She walked quickly down the gravel path and through the line of trees. I followed her, seeing to my relief that the orchard by day was picturesque and unthreatening, its giants apple trees once more.

The frost on the grass glinted in the sunlight and crunched under our feet as we crossed the field. I realized then that I was being taken to the quarry; and as Ella led me through the trees that separated it from the orchard,

I felt a residual shiver from the night before. Like the orchard, the quarry had been robbed of its terror by the daylight; it stretched, a pool of dirty water, nothing more, beneath us.

On its edge was a bench I had not seen the night before. Ella sat down on it and motioned for me to join her.

She lit another cigarette and took two meditative drags on it. There was silence.

Feeling her distance from me and not understanding it, I spoke.

'Why?' I asked, more gentle now than I had been before.

'Why what?' She looked at me sharply.

I blushed but steeled myself.

'Why did you send me to my room last night when I could have been with you?'

I took her hand. She let me keep it, but grudgingly.

'I've wanted you so badly. We've been separated for so long. I didn't write from Prague because you asked me not to. Now I ...'

She took her hand from mine and raised it to stop me.

'You really don't know why, do you?' she said again, ignoring everything but my question, her voice quivering.

I looked at her and saw the tenderness in her face tinged with something I took to be derision. Again I shook my head. Then I looked away and when my eyes returned to hers I saw with a shock that she was on the verge of tears. She saw that I saw and set her thin lips together. When she spoke again her voice was even and firm.

'I don't know how anybody could be so naive,' she said at last.

'What?'

'I think you heard me.' The tenderness had gone from her face now.

'What am I being so naive about?' I asked humbly.

She looked at me steadily. 'Do you really want me to tell you?'

'Of course.'

'And you really don't know?'

'I really do not know.'

'All right.'

She took a deep breath.

'Eric is wildly in love with you,' she said slowly, framing each syllable with deliberate precision.

I can hear her saying it now; can see the way her eyes looked into and held mine; feel the wave of my own surprise and her almost tangible astonishment as I started to laugh. I, who had thought something seriously wrong between us, laughed partly with relief and partly with humour at her error.

'Rubbish,' I said.

And it was only as I said this that I remembered odd moments of my time with Eric in Prague: truths half offered and refused; looks observed but not understood; secret smiles.

'Rubbish,' I said again, more weakly this time.

'It's not rubbish,' she said evenly, still holding my eyes with hers. 'He can't bear the sight of us together; he hates me because you love me. He looks at you when he thinks I don't see.'

'Nonsense.'

'You know it's not, James.'

I sat still, fighting the dawning realization that maybe she was right.

'How can you possibly know?' I asked at last.

She flicked her cigarette, half-smoked, into the quarry.

'Women sense these things,' she said quietly at last. 'It crossed my mind in Prague, but I dismissed it then. I thought he might resent my presence for other reasons. But last night I knew; standing by this bench, I knew.'

As she said this something in her seemed to crack. 'You know it too, Jamie,' she said, her voice wavering again and the suggestion of tears reappearing. 'You know he's in love with you. You may not admit it to yourself but you know.'

There was a pause.

'Since I'm not in love with him, what bearing can Eric's feelings have on us?' I asked hoarsely.

Ella straightened herself. 'How do you *know* you're not in love with him?'

Her eyes met mine coolly now; her tone was more level.

'What?'

'How do you know you're not in love with him?'

'Because I *know*.'

She looked at me steadily.

'No, you don't. The way you've buried your knowledge of his feelings only proves how frightened of them you are.' She breathed deeply. 'You won't admit to yourself that Eric loves you or that you might love him back because you've always been told that one man can't love another.'

'I—'

But she held up a hand to stop me.

'You're frightened, that's all,' she said, and there was derision in her voice again.

Turning to face me squarely, she continued, every word measured and even.

'Before we can go on as before I want to know that it's me you really want.'

'It is you I want.' I took her hand but she pulled it away.

'You can't know that.'

'Oh, yes, I can.'

'No, you can't. You can't make an informed decision unless you—'

But I cut her off. 'I'm not ... like that, Ella.'

'How do you know you're not unless you face the possibility that you might be?'

'I—'

'I don't want to be your safe option, James.'

I looked at her helplessly, incredulous.

'Are you trying to say you want me to sample the alternatives?'

'In a manner of speaking.'

I tried to look into her eyes but she turned from me towards the quarry and wouldn't shift her gaze to meet mine.

'You're crazy,' I said. 'You're completely crazy.'

From the twitch of her shoulders I saw that I had touched a chord. 'Don't *ever* say that to me again.'

'But—'

'But nothing. Don't ever say it again.'

I nodded, humbled by her anger. Mutely I looked at her, searching for an explanation for her words; none was given me. Instead she rose to her feet.

'I cannot love emotional cowards,' she said with slow deliberation.

Fighting a spreading sensation of numbness, I asked her what she meant.

'Precisely what I say.'

There was a pause; my pulse beat a steady tattoo in my head.

'Are you trying to test me?' I ventured at last, lost.

There was silence.

'I suppose so,' she said finally. She turned away. 'I want you to prove to me that it's me you want, that I am not a safe option, that you know yourself and your desires.'

'And how can I do that? How can I prove anything to you if you won't believe what I say?'

There was silence.

'A simple kiss would probably suffice,' she said softly, still not looking at me. 'Once you've kissed him I imagine you'll know how you feel. You'll have forced yourself to face something. Then you'll know whether or not it's me you really want.'

And with that she walked quickly away, and I heard the crunch of her shoes on the gravel as she disappeared into the trees. I sat numbly, staring after her retreating form.

The boy on that bench long ago is a stranger to me now. He does not hear as I call. He sits numbly as wave after conflicting wave crashes over him; he cares nothing for my warnings. I tell him not to be distracted by the letter of what Ella has said, but to look for the meaning hidden in her words. He does not hear me; he cannot. He feels sick and lost and dizzy with the effort of thinking. He is falling, falling into swirling waters he does not understand; and as he falls he reaches out and clutches on to a small shard of unthinking, unexamined resolution. It is to this he clings, for in it he sees his salvation; he clings to it in the mistaken belief that it will help him to float. He does not know treachery yet, nor what it does.

From a distance of sixty years I call to him, for I understand now what Ella said in a way he could never have hoped to do. I see her again in that café in Prague. I hear her as she tells me that I've no idea how sane you have to be to survive a session with a really respected psychiatrist; that doctors with their endless questions could make anyone doubt themselves and those around them. But he will not hear me. He sits impassive as I tell him that when we sin we must accept the possibility of those we love sinning, too; that when she took a man she did not love from her cousin, Ella dealt herself a blow just as damaging as anything she did to Sarah.

I tell him that his love betrayed herself and that, from the moment she had done so, she had to live with the terrible fear that others she loved would betray her in their turn. It was that fear which made Ella push me away; that fear which made her need me to prove – by whatever means – my devotion to her.

I know now that betraying her own trust made Ella lose her trust in the world; and my heart aches for the fragile girl who wanted only the safety of the knowledge that I loved her completely.

I curse the cruelty of a Fate which did not grant me the perception to see that there are some things which even love does not sanction.

I had neither wisdom nor experience; I was a child

playing an adult's game. In my youth and weakness I succumbed to the logic of her insecurity. I came to believe as I sat on that lonely bench that I had been set a challenge, that to prove my worth to Ella I had to pass the test she had set me. And I knew as I sat there that I could not bear the derision of her cool, green eyes. I did not know that what I took for derision was in fact fear; that my love was also a child playing an adult's game; that other proofs might have done in place of the one I finally offered her.

As my world spun before me and all ideals of friendship and faith crumbled under the weight of her challenge, I did not know that the test Ella set me was in fact the reaction of a proud mind to the fear of grave loss, however unfounded that fear might be. I did not know that what she needed so desperately was a proof of my devotion to her and not of my courage with others.

It is true, you know: those who give much expect much to be given to them; those who take much expect much to be taken from them. Ella took the person Sarah valued most from her and after that she could never be sure of anyone completely. As Charles had been taken from Sarah, so might I be taken from Ella: that was her fear, and fear is the undoing of many.

The only way Ella could be sure of me was to drive me away and have me back on her terms. Because she was young and Eric – sweet, trusting Eric – was on hand, he and his love for me were the means she chose. And I, tormented by love for her, driven by the coolness of those haunting eyes – a coolness in which I saw no fear, no weakness – set my mind to the task ahead. I resolved to accept Ella's challenge, to prove myself to her on her terms.

I found Eric alone in the salon, reading; and with a first shiver of treachery I put my hand on his and said that we should leave. I remember his surprise, remember his wide brown eyes and his mouth opened to protest. I remember too how his protest died on his lips, how his look changed from one of mystification to comprehension, how he bounded from his chair and went to pack, spurred on by sudden joy and undreamed-of hope.

I saw Ella for a moment before I left and I kissed her goodbye with a fury that was new to me. It scared her and I was glad that it scared her. I wished her to doubt the outcome of her test so that when I passed it her confidence in me would be all the greater.

Sitting in this icy room now, I can hardly speak.

20

My first memory of the days we spent together is of the train journey Eric and I took after leaving Ella's house. We were going to Vaugirard to stay with his family – though what possessed me to go there, I do not know – and I remember our journey because it contrasted so completely with the one we had so recently taken together from Prague.

I mean, of course, that I contrasted so completely with the excited boy who only the day before had gone to see his lover, full of hope and joy and thoughts of future happiness. I was different on the second journey because I understood Eric's smiles now and returned them; because I knew with absolute clarity that Ella was right and also, though this sickens me to say, that I would pass her test.

I try to remember precisely what I felt beyond this, whether I gave any attention to the possible consequences of my actions, whether I would have cared if I had done so. Behind every thought of mine were my love's eyes, distant and derisive, the eyes I had seen by the quarry that morning. I wanted to make myself worthy of their approval, to make them shine for me again.

The ease with which my ties of friendship with Eric dissolved under Ella's influence shames me now. Then, I'm almost certain it didn't. And as I talk I remember why it didn't. I remember the tricks I used to bypass all considerations that might have weakened my resolution, the cunning by which my possessed mind protected itself and its intentions from all complicating scruple.

I remember now how I taught myself to separate the Eric I knew from the Eric I had been challenged to explore. And I was so successful in this separation that the two sides of his nature – the passionate and the platonic – grew in my mind until they had formed two complete personas, linked of course but ultimately distinct.

Eric the lover I did not know and did not care to know; him I transformed, with deft precision, from a person who might have feelings into a trophy whose sole purpose was to be won. Questions of loyalty and even of gender dissolved in the harsh face of my determination to conquer.

Eric the friend could not, of course, be so dealt with. He was the Eric I knew, the Eric I would have turned to for advice in any situation but this, the Eric I had laughed with, drunk with, fought with and worked with for three heady months in Prague. He could not be made into a trophy and had instead to be separated so completely from the prize I wished to win that no concern for our friendship or history would stand in the way of my desire for victory. I separated Eric the lover from Eric the friend with cold deliberation. With the treachery of a Judas I saw the first fruits of my work even as our train pulled into the small station at Vaugirard. I found myself able to smile without affection, to put meaning into looks that held none.

We arrived in the late afternoon and were met at the station by Eric's sister Sylvie, a large woman, prematurely middle-aged, in whose face the Vaugirard nose and jaw sat incongruously with a weak mouth and tranquil eyes. She kissed her brother and offered me her cheek, pointing as she did so to an old red Citroën parked nearby. As we pulled out of the car park she asked me, in correct but hesitant English, whether I had enjoyed my time in Prague.

'Very much,' I replied.

'I would have liked to go too,' she said. 'It would have been wonderful.' She paused. 'But I have my duties here.'

And as she spoke she looked with a certain smugness at her brother, who ignored her.

After this we drove on in silence, past the modern flats of a growing town and into the cobbled streets of its medieval past. On a hill that commanded the entire district was a château, fortress-like in construction and bearing, which was proudly pointed out to me as the family's own.

'Of course we do not own it any longer,' said Sylvie as we waited at traffic lights, 'but the family stays on here nevertheless. There will always be a Vaugirard in Vaugirard.'

And I thought of another castle, far finer than this one, and of another voice talking of ownership and duty. Eric said nothing.

Louise de Vaugirard welcomed me with open arms and a hearty dinner. The family lived in one of the old houses in the centre of the town, a high narrow building which from the street looked cramped but which was in fact cavernous, with low-ceilinged rooms leading into and out of one another in haphazard profusion. It was longer than it was wide and had been extended at various times into the garden behind it, so that only a small square patch of lawn now remained.

'We play croquet there in the summer,' said Louise, pointing it out to me. 'What a pity you have come in the winter, for I fear the weather will be very harsh.'

I had no desire for lazy summer afternoons with Eric's family and looked at the cloud outside with gratitude. In the comfort of his own home, under the strain of his family's kindness, I felt that my ingenious separation of him into friend and trophy would be difficult to prolong; and as I replied that the weather could be no worse than it would be in England, I wondered why I had come at all and thought with relief that I had only promised to stay five days. For five days the anaesthetic might endure; beyond that I could not be sure and I had no wish for its effects to wear off in the bosom of Eric's family itself.

After Sylvie had left us, Eric's father arrived and shook hands with his son and then with me with heavy dignity. He was a great squat man with huge hands and a powerful, vice-like grip. It was possible to see, as Eric stood beside him, that although my friend resembled his father his features had been softened by his mother's genes, for a prominent nose and strong jaw gave the elder man an air of terrifying caricature, which the younger had escaped. Eric *père* was a friendly giant who sat quietly through dinner while his wife's conversation warmed the room; occasionally he bestowed a hospitable smile on me, but more he did not do or say.

When we had moved upstairs for coffee, however, he pulled me to one side.

'I would like to thank you for what you have done for

my family,' he said in a deep, gruff voice. 'Eric speaks very well of you, as do all who met you in Prague.'

He spoke English slowly with a heavy accent.

'It was a great pleasure to be able to help,' I said. 'An honour.'

'And the paintings were interesting also, no?'

'Fascinating.'

'Yes. It is a pity we could not have kept some of them. But what use do I have for pictures?'

He smiled at me and shook his head while I, trying sincerely not to like him, smiled back.

I don't know why even the polite trivia of that time seems worthy of retelling. I retell it, I suppose, to delay the recounting of what I did. Though it shames me to do so, I linger on the Vaugirards, on the ease with which they accepted me into their home and their lives. I, who intended their son nothing but harm – or who at least was prepared to sacrifice him on the altar of my love for another – was welcomed into their lives; and I accepted their hospitality as Judas might have accepted Christ's at the Last Supper: duplicitously, deviously, deceitfully. I was accepted because I was their son's friend. On that recommendation alone I was welcomed as a member of the family.

The actual taking of my prize was easy, and I say that without vanity. On the evening of my second day with the Vaugirards I decided to act, for I feared their kindness and was uncertain how much longer I could endure it. I knew enough to know that treachery had its limits and I was fearful of testing them. So I sat through a second dinner, which like the first was long and very good, drinking little and watching, waiting for my opportunity.

It came as the last plates were cleared and Eric excused himself and got up to go to bed. I, sensing that it had come, excused myself too and left the room with him, smiling my goodnights to his family.

We ascended the narrow flight of steep stairs that led to our bedrooms in a silence that for me was grimly purposeful. On the landing outside my room, high up in the gods of the house, Eric said goodnight to me and turned to open his own door.

'Goodnight,' I replied.

There was an awkward pause as I steeled myself to take the plunge. Thinking of Ella's eyes, of the smooth hollow beneath her collarbone, I twisted my lips into a smile.

'I'm not very tired,' I said, keeping it fixed.

My friend turned to me, surprised.

Unseeing, I looked through him.

'Come and keep me company for a while,' I went on, walking quickly into my bedroom. As he followed I took a sip from the glass of water by my bed, for my mouth was dry. When I looked up I saw Eric framed in the darkness of the doorway, hesitant, uncertain.

'It is so wonderful to have you here,' he said, at last.

'It's good to be here.'

'And my family likes you so much.'

'I like them.'

'You are an old charmer, James.'

Bolder now, he moved towards me and sat on the foot of my bed. Awkwardly I stood next to him.

'We are very easy around you,' he said, and I knew that

this was true: there had been no further signs of the tension between Eric and his mother which I had seen in Prague, for the family had drawn together to show its best side to its guest.

Slowly, trying not to shake, I sat down on the bed next to him. Our knees touched, as if by accident, but Eric didn't move his away and I forced myself to keep mine where it was. There was silence between us, though inside my head I could not think for sound; above the quick, hard beat of my blood I heard Ella's voice, cool and even, telling me that she could not love emotional cowards.

'You are a mystery to me, James,' Eric was saying.

I looked down, not trusting myself to speak.

'I never know what you mean or what you want. You seem so different since we left Ella's. What happened there? Between you both.'

With a supreme effort of will I forced myself to raise my head. I looked steadily into Eric's eyes, found my voice and said, hoarsely, that I didn't want to speak of Ella. With a deep breath I put my hand on his.

'Now I really do not understand you.'

'I think you do.'

My voice was measured; I was determined to keep it steady. I took his other hand in mine.

The uncertainty on Eric's face resolved slowly into a smile.

'This I cannot believe,' he said, looking at me shyly.

'Why not?'

'Because I ... *Mon Dieu*, how does one say this?' He hesitated and then decided to trust me. 'Because I love you and thought you wanted me only for a friend. I thought she had taken you for ever.'

He spoke quickly, his words falling over themselves in his eagerness to get them out.

I let them glide past me, leaving no mark on my mind. Silently, adrenaline making me light-headed, blood pounding in my brain, I leaned forward to kiss him.

I remember that kiss. Oh God, I remember it. I see Eric's broad, unbelieving face with its frame of dark curls moving towards mine even now. I smell his foreign, unknown scent of sweat and shaving foam; I feel his hands on my shoulders and the violence of his quick embrace. His kiss itself was rough and harsh, as unlike a woman's kiss as anything could be, and suddenly I felt him on top of me, pulling at my buttons, and I was pushing him away and saying 'No' with all the force in me. Ella's voice rang in my brain, saying over and over that a simple kiss would suffice, that once I had kissed him I would know and as I pushed Eric away from me and sat upright, breathing heavily, shaking from what I had done, I knew that I did know, that I had come as far as I could safely go, that I had passed my lover's test, and deserved the sparkling praise of her shining eyes.

It was only then that I saw Eric smiling delightedly at me, his face glowing with a passion I had never seen in it, his body taut with excitement. It was only then that I had the first inklings of what I have since come to know with such certainty: that human beings cannot be divided, separated into distinct halves for the moral convenience of others.

Breathing heavily, eyes dancing, Eric took my hands

and leaned towards me; and as he did so I knew that I had lost my friend for ever. I said nothing, sickened by that thought, but as his lips moved towards mine again I pushed him away and stood up, reeling with what I had done.

There was silence.

'I . . . I'm not ready,' I said at last.

Slowly, respectfully, he released my hands. I could see the effort it cost him to restrain himself, to leash once again the unleashed desire of so many months, and I admired him for it. Sitting upright on the bed once more, he leaned over to where I stood and took my right hand in his again, raising a questioning eyebrow as he did so. I didn't have the heart to refuse it him.

'I love you, James,' Eric said quietly.

I said nothing.

'I have loved you since the day I first saw you, since the minute you walked into Regina Boardman's drawing room.'

My brain was spinning. Eric tried to pull me closer but I pushed him away and went to the window. I could not bear his touch any longer. Far below us the street lights twinkled and cars drove back and forth over the cobbles.

Strange as it may seem, I had given no thought to how I would deal with my prize once it was won. I hadn't thought beyond the passing of Ella's test, beyond the proving of my own emotional courage to her. And I discovered that I could no longer bear even to look at my friend. I knew then, I think, that whatever I did now I would break him.

He left me that night puzzled by my silence but thinking that he understood it.

'Tonight has been enough for me,' he said as I stood by the window, unable to meet his eyes. 'I will leave you now. The rest will come later, in our own time.'

He came up behind me and laid a hand on my shoulder. Feeling me stiffen he removed it.

'Goodnight,' he said.

And at the door he turned and some last vestige of dignity made me turn and face him.

'I am happier now than I have ever been in my life,' he said softly as he left me.

I am trying to remember what I felt as I undressed and got into bed. I know that I turned out the light and tried to think of Ella but that I could no longer see her eyes or feel her lips on my lips. I felt only the harsh energy of Eric's kiss, the fury of his passion. And it was then that I had my first bitter taste of treachery. I knew I could not stay another night in that trusting house, that the next day I must leave, that any lie would be worth my freedom. And sweating, cold with what I had done, I lay awake and tried not to think.

I didn't sleep until the sun was turning the black sky to a misty grey, but when sleep came it was so deep I didn't hear Eric opening my door the next morning. I slept on as he crossed my room and was woken only by him stroking the hair out of my eyes. Then I knew that the night before had not been a dream, that its nightmare logic was part of the real world.

In my desperation, further deceit came smoothly and easily. After a hasty breakfast, during which I forced myself to meet Eric's shining eyes without embarrassment, I went into the village, found the post office, and put through a call to Camilla Boardman. She answered on the third ring, her speech as shrill and her emphases as frequent as ever.

'*Daaarling!*' she squealed. 'I thought you were *never* coming back! Where are you? What are you doing for lunch?'

I explained that I was in France staying with friends and that lunch would thus be impossible, a fact I sorely regretted.

'But how *tiresome*. London's been just *too* deadly without you and I want to know when you're coming back to liven things up for me.'

'Soon, Camilla. Soon. In fact, I'll be home all the sooner if you'll do me a favour.'

Rapidly I invented a story about staying with dull people from whose hospitality I needed a polite excuse to escape. Camilla drank it in greedily, for social intrigue was her forte.

'I want you to help me,' I finished, 'by cabling at once that I must come back to England immediately.'

'But, darling, how *exciting*! What reason shall I give?'

'I don't know. I'm sure that you of all people don't need inspiration from me.'

'Of *course* not, darling. You can trust me.'

'I know. That's why I called.'

And with many kisses blown and endearments exchanged, the conversation ended.

Calmer now, but eager for my abrupt departure from the Vaugirards to be thought unavoidable, I asked Eric if he would like to go for a walk. I wished Louise to receive Camilla's cable, for then I would be beyond suspicion.

He took me over the grounds and buildings of the

castle, a picturesque ruin, and told me the history of the town which it commanded. Thankful for so neutral a topic, I nodded and smiled and in my uneasiness heard nothing and counted the minutes to give Camilla time to send a telegram, and the postmaster's son to deliver it, before we returned. I was at my most relaxed when there was silence between us, for with each word I spoke I felt myself more false. But even the silences were untrue: for Eric they were times of quiet communion; for me they were a brief respite from the pressure to be tender.

Louise, when we arrived, was in a state of great distress. She met us at the front door and led me into the sitting room, taking my hands in hers and asking me to sit down.

'I have some bad news for you, my dear James,' she said gravely.

I looked suitably anxious.

'Leopold is dying,' she said gently. 'He may not have long to live.'

And with infinite tenderness she looked into my eyes and stroked my hand.

'A telegram has just come from your mother. She thinks you should go back to England at once.'

Leopold, it dawned on me, was Camilla's King Charles spaniel. Struggling to overcome the absurdity of the situation, I looked away from Louise.

'Now, now,' said Eric's mother, putting a hand on my shoulder. 'You must be brave.'

'I had better get my things at once,' I said hoarsely.

'Perhaps you had. Eric will drive you to the station.'

And so, light-headed with relief, I went upstairs to pack.

21

I f only great events didn't hinge on trivial ones. If only I hadn't left my violin in Vaugirard. If only ... I don't know. With time, perhaps Eric's passion might have cooled. Ella's trust might have grown. We might, all of us, have had space to breathe. I don't know.

But I did leave my violin in Vaugirard. And because I left it, Eric was told, when he went to the post office that afternoon to telephone my parents to ask whether or not to send it on, that my family knew no one by the name of Leopold and that I had not said anything about coming home before Christmas.

With no idea of how soon events were to overtake me, I made the short train-journey between Eric's house and Ella's, slumped in the corner of a deserted carriage, letting the awful memory of the past two days drain from me, thinking with relief that I had escaped. As the hard fields sped past, I began to think with pleasure that in a matter of hours my beloved's hair would be in my eyes and her fragile body in my arms. As Ella filled my mind the events of recent days took on an air of increasing unreality, and Eric became unreal with them. This calmed me, for it obscured my motives and made it easier for me to forget what I had done to him. I tried hard to put away all thoughts of my friend.

I telephoned Ella from the station when I arrived and her delight touched me and made me feel that all would be well, that all was almost well already. She collected me in Jacques' dusty Renault and for the first time since I had left her in London there was something of the old magic between us, uncomplicated by the company of others. The old house no longer seemed so gloomy with her by my side as we rounded the last curve in its drive; its desolation was a refuge, a protection from all thoughts of the outside world.

I did not give Ella any but the barest details of what had taken place between me and Eric. I had passed her test, that was all I cared her to know; and she, perhaps already guilty for setting it, did not probe me.

After my brief account of the past two days we talked together as if nothing had happened, as if Eric and Sarah and Charles Stanhope did not exist. We touched that afternoon with a passion that was new, even to us; and I basked in the caresses of her warm white body with something approaching perfect joy. Thinking of her now, I miss her supple limbs, her soft breasts, the arch of her nose, her silvery laugh. Even now I miss her, though I am an old man and I sit alone in a darkening room. Despite all that has happened, I want her still.

I cannot speak of the sweet dinner we shared that night, or of the way our delighted laughter and warm words lit up that cold, old house. We ate alone together in the small dining room that led off the hall. Dr Pétin was away again in the village and we were left in delicious peace.

I remember the cosy crackle of our fire, its light on Ella's face, the smell of woodsmoke and cigarettes and sweat and perfume which hung about us. We had not dressed but sat side by side at the small table in dressing gowns, hair dishevelled, touching sometimes as we ate, watching the movement of each other's forks, listening to the muted clash of silver on china, drinking sweet wine.

Remembering that night, I see my love's tousled hair, the line of her cheekbones in the candlelight. I hear our lazy, candid words, her light laugh, my deeper chuckle sounding with hers. I watch her eyebrows furrow as the doorbell rings and hear her say that it must be Dr Pétin back unexpectedly from the village, that it's just like him to come home at a time like this. I hear her giggle and say how compromising our near nakedness is and I see her tie her dressing gown tighter round her slim waist and run a hand quickly through her hair, to little effect. I watch her as she moves past me through the dining-room door and into the hall and I listen for the deferential greeting of the doctor.

There is silence for a moment. Then the scraping of a heavy bolt and the turning of a key in an unoiled lock. Then a short sharp cry and the sound of a man's step on the flagstones and I hear Eric's voice, wild and high, asking for me and Ella's reply that I am not here, that he must go at once. I hear his hurried, forceful steps in the hall and his raised voice calling my name, and I stand up, sick, and go to the dining-room door and open it and see him standing there, in the same clothes I left him in that morning, his hair wild, my violin case in one strong hand.

And then I remember where I left my violin and know

with awful clarity what has happened, how he has found me. And I go to him but he looks at me in horror and throws the faded leather case on the floor with all his might and there is a twanging of strings and I watch him bound through the doorway and down the steps of the house into the cold black night.

What could I have done but follow him?

With a word of caution to Ella, standing silent in the hall, I went down the steps after him in my dressing gown, the wind of that chill night whipping my ears, its frost freezing my feet. I called my friend's name, but there was no reply but the steady beat of his shoes on gravel as he ran away from me. In the dark I followed him, guided by my ears and by the lines of yew hedge which scratched my hands but kept my path straight.

At first I called, but when I knew that my voice only made him run faster I was quiet and listened instead, following the crash of his footsteps and trying to make out his flying form in the dark. As the moon appeared from a bank of clouds, I saw him in the line of trees at the end of the garden and ran towards it; and as I emerged I saw him across the orchard, calling to me to leave him alone, a sharp, wild note in his voice like the cry of a hunted animal.

On I ran, on and on, until I had left the orchard behind and was standing by the edge of the quarry, panting, calling softly to Eric, telling him that I could explain. He appeared quite suddenly as the moon shone once more through a crack in the clouds and I saw that he was standing by the bench. As I called his name he sat down on its rusted seat, his head in his hands, his shoulders shaking. Muffled, breathless sobs came to me through the damp air and I, appalled, moved towards him and put my hand on his shoulder.

'Do not touch me.'

His voice was small and unsteady, almost reedy; I had never heard it like that before.

'Eric . . .' I began, and fell silent. No words would come.

Slowly he turned and looked at me. As my eyes grew accustomed to the dark I saw that his face was wet.

'Why are you here?' he asked; and there was something pathetic in his helpless look and streaming eyes. 'Why are you here, with her?'

I looked at him and said nothing. What was there to say?

'I love you, James.' The man by my side now took my hands in his and held them as I tried to pull away. 'I have loved you since the first moment I saw you.'

'Eric, no—'

'And I know that you love me.' He was talking quickly now. 'I know that you do. I did not think you did at first. I tried to be content with your friendship, with what we had in Prague.'

I got my hands away from his and waited awkwardly, willing him to end. He sensed my unease.

'But . . . last night,' he went on eventually. 'Last night I knew that you loved me, too. No, do not say anything. I knew.'

Mutely I shook my head, my brain reeling.

'What is the use in pretending, James? A love like ours is a fine thing. There is nothing shameful about it.'

'But, Eric—'

'Do not say "But Eric" to me like that. You know that you love me. Say that you do.'

As he took my hands once more and pressed them to his lips, I knew that I had to speak, that I had to make him see.

'Eric,' I began, shaking my hands free from his grasp again, 'I—'

'What, James?'

'I . . .'

I searched vainly for a form of words that might conceal my betrayal of his trust. After a moment's thought I found it.

'You are my friend,' I said, 'one of the people I like most in the world.' I paused, seeing the hope in his eyes. 'I confused my affection for you with something else.'

'No.'

'I did, Eric, and I'm sorry. I do love you, but not in that way. I can never love you in that way.'

'But last night?' He looked up at me in helpless misery.

'Last night was madness. I had no idea what I was doing.'

'I do not believe that.'

'It's the truth, I swear it.'

'But you kissed me.'

'It was a mistake,' I said quietly, numb with self-loathing.

'A mistake?'

'Yes. A mistake. I cannot love you like that.'

'Why not?'

'I'm not made that way.'

There was a brief, awful silence.

'Do you love her?' he said at last.

'Who? Ella?'

'Who else?'

'Yes, I love her.'

Eric looked at me helpless, uncomprehending. 'And you do not love me?'

I sat down on the bench and put my arm around him.

'I like you as much as I have ever liked anyone,' I said.

'But you do not love me.'

'No, I don't.'

He started crying at this point, first slowly and quietly, then fast and loud; and I did not move as he leaned against my shoulder and cried large hot tears which wet my neck and the collar of my dressing gown. Slowly I put my hand on his shaking back and as I did so I realized I was freezing.

'Come on,' I said gently.

As I opened my mouth to say more I saw the sharp beam of a torch in the darkness and heard Ella's voice calling for me. Eric heard it too and clung to me with all his might, burying his face in my neck, his tears still hot and wet on my chest.

'Come on,' I said again; and as I spoke I blinked in the harsh beam of the torch, which caught and then held us. Ella stood beyond it. Dazzled though I was by the brightness of the light, I saw that there was fear in her eyes.

'What are you doing?' Her voice was sharp and brittle.

'It's not what you think.' I began to push Eric away. But as I did so I knew suddenly that I had done proving myself to Ella. She could take me on trust now; I had sacrificed enough to earn her confidence. So I continued to hold my friend as his huge frame shook. Quietly, firmly, I asked Ella to leave us for a moment.

'What are you trying to say?' she replied, her voice quivering now.

'Nothing but what I have said. I'll come back to the house in a moment. Please. Eric and I need to talk in private.'

There was a tense silence, broken only by Eric's whimpering.

'Before I go, tell him it's me you love.'

The sound of Ella's voice roused Eric from his misery and he raised his head and looked at her.

'Tell him,' she said again, her face hard and set.

'Go away.'

The man by my side had stopped crying. Slowly he stood up, and his great bulk loomed, terrible in the moonlight.

'You have done your harm,' he said thickly. 'You have done your damage. You can go now. It is me who James loves. Nothing you can say will change that.'

I watched as they faced each other.

'Please, you two——' I began.

'Tell him, James.'

'Please, Ella. I'll be in in a minute.'

'Tell him now, before I go.'

'Please.'

'Tell him why you kissed him.'

There was silence. Eric looked at me.

'What is it she wishes you to tell me, James?' he said at last.

'Nothing. Nothing, Eric. Now please . . .'

The beam of the torch swung into my eyes again. Behind it Ella's face was pinched and drawn.

'Tell him,' she said again. 'There's no use pretending now. We're past that, we three.'

And as she spoke she walked over to me – I had risen from the bench now, too – and deliberately put her arm through mine.

'What is this, James? What does she mean?'

Eric's voice was quieter now, but I could see the veins on his temples throbbing.

'It's nothing,' I said.

'Oh, yes, it is.' Ella's voice was high and defiant.

'Please, Ella.'

I looked at her, trying to show with my eyes that she had nothing to fear. She looked away from me.

'I won't leave until you've told Eric the truth,' she continued, her voice set. 'I want you to tell him that you love me, that you kissed him to prove yourself to me.'

'It is me he loves.' Eric's voice was angry now. 'You have done your best to cause us harm and you have failed.' He moved towards me. 'Come, James. Come with me.'

He looked at Ella with fury in his eyes.

'Eric . . .' I began, searching for words. 'Eric, I . . . I love Ella.' I stopped.

'Tell him, Jamie.'

'I—'

'But what about last night?' Eric's eyes met mine and I forced myself to face them.

'I . . . I didn't mean it.'

'Tell him, Jamie.'

'It was a test,' I said finally, sick at heart.

'A test?' There was a frightened note in his voice now.

'I had to prove myself.'

'What did you have to prove?'

I knew then, too late, that I had proved nothing but my own weakness.

'He proved that he would do anything for me.'

Ella's eyes were shining now. She put her hand in mine.

Her touch and her smiling lips revolted me; I shook my hand free of hers as a rising tide of nausea washed over me. 'I had no idea what I was doing,' I murmured hoarsely to Eric. 'You must believe that.'

'You had every idea.'

And all three of us knew that he was right.

22

I don't remember how I got away from them that night. I do remember running through the orchard and slipping on its icy grass. I remember also Eric's eyes and Ella's smile, surreal in the moonlight. I ran without thought of direction, past stark trees and ill-pruned hedges and a silent fountain, sinister in the darkness. I ran until the lights of the house loomed before me, and I did not stop running until I was in its bright hall, dripping with sweat, my knees bloody from where I had fallen, my hands red and frozen. I was still in my dressing gown.

I could not face either of them again that night, and I stripped a bed in the bedroom which had been mine and Eric's and put sheets and blankets on the floor of a disused little room off the pantry. I worked quickly, worried that one or the other might return, and breathing hard and nearly in tears I locked myself into cramped darkness like a child hiding from punishment.

Alone at last, I still had no peace, for the room filled with sights and sounds: with the rough scratch of Eric's lips on mine and the acrid sweetness of Ella's smell; with wild laughter and streaming eyes and the sight of Eric's face by the quarry, frightened like a wounded animal's.

From far off I heard the front door open and close and

thought with relief that neither of them would find me until the morning. Sick at heart I tried to sleep.

Sleep came as the sun was rising and when it did it was deep and dreamless. I slept so soundly I didn't hear the shouting; and I had hidden myself so well that Ella had to search the house for me when they found him the next morning. I remember waking to the ache of a night spent on a hard stone floor, to the frantic note in her voice as she pounded on the door.

Eric was lying face down in the water, floating in the depths of the quarry like a piece of timber. It took four men from the village with ropes tied round their chests to abseil down and pull his body to the side and drag it up the steep incline to the little group by the bench.

Ella and I stood watching as they tied their ropes to the yew trees and began to lower themselves downwards. We heard the splash of their rubber dinghy as it was lowered into the murky water. We watched two of them get into it and heard their paddling, saw them heave his body into their boat. Then winches and harnesses appeared and Eric began his jerky, solitary journey upwards, back to us. I remember the ghastly stare of the eyes in his waxy face, the way his mouth hung open, the immense weight of his dripping body as it was laid out on the cold earth.

Dr Pétin signed the death certificate, his rosy face pale and sombre, his hair dishevelled. For the probable cause of death he put drowning and I watched the doctor fill out the forms in silence and saw him kneel over my friend's bloated face, examining his body. It was when I saw the tears in his eyes that I realized I was not crying. I was numb, impervious to the bustle that follows a death.

Calmly, almost mechanically, I greeted the village gendarme; saw them put Eric into an ambulance and drive him away for further examination; listened to the condolences of Madame Clancy and Jacques; thanked the men who had hoisted Eric's body from the quarry. As one in a dream I stood by Ella as she explained to the detective that Eric had followed me from Vaugirard to return my violin; that he had arrived towards the end of dinner and that she and I had offered him coffee and a bed; that he had decided to go for a walk before turning in for the night; that he had seemed perfectly happy, quite his usual self.

When asked, I said that I was one of his greatest friends; that Eric had told me nothing of any unhappiness; that the night had been dark; that I could only think that he had fallen; that he was not the kind of man to take his own life.

It was only when the policeman asked if I knew the address of the deceased's next-of-kin that reality penetrated the cloud. I saw the Vaugirards at once: Louise at the market, examining ingredients for the evening; Eric *père* sitting gravely in his study, looking forward to lunch; Sylvie with her son, collecting him from nursery school, asking him what he had done that day.

'I know them,' I said to the gendarme.

'Then perhaps it would be better if you informed them,' he said. He was a small, anxious man with kind eyes. It was, he told me, the first time he had seen a death.

So it was I who telephoned to the post office at Vaugirard; I who waited while they fetched Louise; I who endured her anxious questioning after Leopold and told her that his illness had been exaggerated and that he was now out of danger; I who endured her joy at this news. It was I who told her that something awful had happened; I who told her that Eric was dead, who listened to the first sharp cry of a mother who has lost her son, who answered the rush of her questions and explained how Eric had gone walking at night without a torch and had fallen into a quarry.

And still I did not cry; I could not. Numb and as calm as the dead, I took my place at the dining-room table with Ella and the gendarme and Dr Pétin and waited for Louise and Eric *père* to arrive, thinking nothing, conscious only of a dull ache and of the steady throbbing beat of the blood in my head. I looked at Ella but did not see her. I watched her smoke cigarette after cigarette but did not register that she moved. I could not smell her.

I knew then that I would never tell anyone of the reason for Eric's death and that she would not either. I told myself it was better for Eric's parents to curse Fate and to rail against the tragedy of an accident than to know that their son had ended his own life.

The Vaugirards arrived in the late afternoon and I submitted to their tearful embraces. Madame Clancy disappeared to make up two bedrooms: one for them and one for me, for I could not bear to re-enter the room that had been Eric's and mine. While we waited for her to return, I sat with Eric's parents and told them how Eric had followed me to return my violin; how he had gone off for a walk in high spirits; how he had not taken a torch; how Ella and I had gone to bed, little thinking that he would not return; how he had been found that morning, face down in the water.

Louise, like me, was calm. She sat stately, in a high-backed chair beside mine, her arm on her husband's, the bones of her shoulders clearly visible, her back rigid. Eric *père* cried like Eric *fils* had cried the night before: the loud ugly sobs of a man unused to tears. His crying, alone of all the sounds I heard that day, penetrated my numbness. I heard Eric crying and felt the warm flood of his tears on my neck. Then I heard his laugh. Distant and quiet at first, then heartier, nearer. And then I saw his eyes streaming with mirth and the flash of his white teeth and his wide smile, and I thought that I would cry but I didn't.

I cried later, when I went into the bedroom which Eric and I had shared, to return the blankets and sheets I had taken from it the night before. Numb as I was, I could think clearly enough to know that it would not do for them to be discovered in a dark room off the pantry so I left Louise and Eric *père* talking to Dr Pétin and crept down the vaulted passage that Ella had led Eric and me along such a short time ago.

Everything in the room was precisely as I remembered it. As I opened the door I smelled the familiar smell of lavender and woodsmoke and another smell, which for a moment I could not place, a smell of sweat and aftershave. And then it hit me and I sank to my knees, burying my face in my arms, my nose in the thick wool of my sweater. I could not bear Eric's smell.

While I was crouching on the floor I heard the door open and felt Louise kneel next to me and hug my heaving back with the long slender arms and bony hands she had given Eric. We rocked together in silence and with horror I felt her tears on my shoulder, mingling perhaps with the salt from her son's.

'You must not blame yourself for letting Eric go out alone last night,' she said. 'He was foolhardy. It was what we loved about him. It was what you loved about him.'

As she spoke I thought I would have preferred the clean thrust of a knife.

The coroner delivered a verdict of accidental death and Eric was buried in hallowed ground in the tiny cemetery adjacent to the château at Vaugirard. I was a pallbearer at his funeral, my eyes the only dry pair in that overcrowded chapel of hard pews and Norman arches, my shoulder the steadiest of the six which lifted his heavy coffin and carried it down the narrow aisle.

I lived through that day with the grim determination of a man beginning a life sentence and I watched the movements of my body with detached interest from a recess in my mind, the only refuge I could find. I had hardly slept for seven consecutive nights. My cheeks were sunken. There were dark purple circles under my eyes. Exhaustion calmed me; it distanced me from my role in the last act of Eric's tragedy.

I remember that small chapel high above the town; the rustle of its black-clad congregation as they took their seats on small pews of dark wood. I remember the stately calm of Louise and the wild red eyes of Eric *père*. I remember the coffin and Eric lying in it: remember the calm, pale dignity of his face, the unnatural neatness of his black curls, brushed for the last time.

Standing before him in the line of people paying their

last respects, I found that I had nothing to say, for the suited body before me was not the Eric I had laughed with so uproariously at Café Florian. His soul was gone from his body. All I could do was hope that it had found peace. In a state of eerie calm I looked at him and tried to say goodbye, but no words would come.

It was not until I saw his shoes that the tears came. They tied the body before me to a living reality, which I missed with a wrenching, crippling pain. I remembered the scene at Florian's when Eric had bought them and heard his laughing voice telling me gravely that he did not like new things. He had bought them from an Englishman who had fallen on hard times. They were brogues, old-fashioned and scuffed in, and had been circulated amongst the regulars of Café Florian with an old tweed suit and some ties that had gone to others. Eric had bought the shoes without haggling over their price as the buyers of other articles had done, for he did not exploit those in need. He had paid their owner the sum requested for them and had put them on at once. It was this that made me cry.

Ella came up to me as the mourners were beginning to stream away from the grave, a line of black figures under a grey sky, shivering in the wind. I had been only dimly aware of her during the past week. I had made sure that I was never alone with her, for that I could not have borne. As she slipped her cold hand into mine in that churchyard, the smoothness of her touch sickened me, for it reminded me of what I had done to win it. I could not meet her eyes.

'Jamie ...' she said at last. 'Please don't do this. Don't pretend I don't exist.'

I walked on faster.

'Please. I can't go on.'

'It was Eric who couldn't go on,' I said quietly. 'Not you. Not me. Eric.'

Her hand tightened its grasp on mine. I shook it away.

'He killed himself because of what we did,' I said, 'because—' I stifled the accusation on my lips.

'Say it.'

'Because of what you made me do.'

There was silence.

'Jamie,' she said at last. 'Jamie, please don't do this.'

There was real pleading in her tone. Still I could not meet her eyes.

'You honestly think we can go on blithely as before?'

'No, not as before perhaps, but ... Can't you see how much we need each other? We need each other now more than ever. You're my only hope. I'm yours.'

We were nearing the other mourners now. I heard the shutting of car doors and the tap of high heels on cobbles.

'What did you tell him?' I asked suddenly, quietly. 'What did you say to him after I left you?'

There was silence.

'What did you say?'

'Please, Jamie ...' She was crying now.

'What did you *say* to him?'

'I ...'

Ella looked at me. I met her eyes stonily and for the first time their beauty did not move me.

'Please don't,' she said again.

'Tell me.'

'I ...' She opened her bag for a cigarette.

I pulled her hand. 'I don't want you to smoke. I want you to tell me what you said to Eric after I left you.'

'I told him the truth,' she said quietly. 'He was very angry after you left. He said that you loved him, that I was trying to do you harm. So I told him why you had kissed him. I made him understand you did it for me.'

'And then?'

'And then I left him.'

We walked on in silence, through the churchyard gate and into the street. I heard the tap of Ella's shoes on the stones, the desultory conversation of the other mourners. I have no words for the numbness that ran through me. I tried to speak but no sound would come. As Ella and I walked on together I felt I was floating, as though the world around me was no more real than a dream. For an instant I clung to this hope. Then I told myself that the world was real, that I was not a shadow but a person who lived and breathed like other people. In a moment of clarity the future stretched before me: a life lived in the shallows of my mind, from whence it would be dangerous to stray.

As the street began to steepen, for we were walking from the castle down the hill to the town, I looked at Ella once more and drank my fill of her fine, delicate face. She looked at me, too, and pressed closer towards me. For the last time I smelled her subtle, complex scent.

'I don't ever want to see you again,' I said slowly.

And then I left her and broke into a run, frightened of the sound of her voice, of its power to sway me. I did not stop running until I was lost in the crowds of the town and she was far behind, an isolated figure in a black dress, face whipped by the wind, eyes expressionless.

23

It is difficult for me to talk of the days and months that followed my homecoming. Eric's friendship and Ella's love had gone from my life at a single stroke and I mourned them both, with a pain I could not share. I did not mourn the loss of my innocence, for I hardly knew that I had had it to lose; but I felt that things had changed, that I was not the boy who had gone to Prague three months before. In that I was correct.

I remember my journey to England on a grey day of choppy waves and circling gulls: the lurching of the boat, the salt of the wind on my face, the crowds of people meeting the ferry. I passed through them all, oblivious, and when I reached home I slept, resolving to rely no longer on the opiate of exhaustion.

Sleep shielded me for a day or two as the Christmas cards mounted on the mat and my mother started to talk of trees and tinsel and mince pies, and of how difficult it was to buy presents for my father. Delighted to have me home earlier than expected, she included me resolutely in her plans for the festivities. Finding me sombre and inclined to solitude, she thought me resentful of her attentions and pressed them on me all the harder.

Day after day my opinion was sought on the pressing

issues of the hour. Should we or should we not give a dinner party on Christmas Eve? Should we or should we not ask Aunt Julia to spend the holiday with us as usual? Should we or should we not invite the vicar to lunch on Boxing Day? (My mother, you see, was strict in her social observance of religious principle; the annual entertainment of such minor clergy as were known to her was a sacred rite.)

Through all this flurry of seasonal enthusiasm I moved numbly, as one in a dream, adding my name to the greetings on the Christmas cards; murmuring my approval of the mince pies that appeared, fragrant and warm, at regular intervals. But I felt removed from the jolly bustle around me. My parents, relentlessly cheerful in my presence, said privately to each other that my music was doing me no good and that I was in need of more fresh air. Exercise was always the solution in my family, so I was encouraged, when Aunt Julia came to stay, to adopt her dog and take it on its daily walks: a solitary task that was my only respite from the forced conviviality of home life.

Aunt Julia was a tall, straight woman with intense brown eyes and pugnacious eyebrows. Traces of risqué chic lingered about her still, though she was approaching seventy; and they manifested themselves in her tastes for smoking and swearing, both of which she indulged with military gusto in the manner of her long-dead brigadier husband. Splendidly indifferent to my mother's disapproval, she took a maternal interest in my father (whose mother's best friend she had been) and she rather enjoyed her courtesy title of aunt, for she used it to assume the licence of a family intimate. Advice for my parents flowed freely from Aunt Julia. On me she lavished a sort of barking kindliness, which she supposed, not having children of her own, to be the correct way of conducting oneself towards members of the younger generation.

An iron will and unchanging habits were two of her most obvious qualities. It was these that made me look forward to her visit more than usual in the bleak weeks which followed my return from France. I needed old assurances then. There was nothing so reassuring as a visit from this time-honoured Christmas habituée, in whose presence life assumed a military efficiency, relieved and made charming by the incongruous irreverence of the old lady herself.

Her movements were exact. She arrived without fail three days before Christmas and left, without variation, on the day after Boxing Day. The method of her arrival was consistent too: she came in two taxis from Waterloo ('One for bags, one for owner and dog') and descended, accompanied by the lazy barks of a sleek basset-hound, to present one wrinkled cheek to my mother before paying the taxi drivers and sending them away with loud wishes for a 'bloody good Christmas'. Inside, safely ensconced by the fire, she would light a small cigar, accept a glass of water – for Aunt Julia didn't drink – and question her audience with a ruthless directness that offended my mother and occasioned the first of the icy silences which inevitably punctuated the five days of her visit.

I remember standing in the hall the day she came, waiting to submit to her inspection and to her two, efficient Christmas kisses. I thought Julia's visit might divert me from myself. I looked forward to the unquestioned authority of her conversation and to the way in which she assumed control of my Christmas entertainment.

It was my mother who suggested I take Jep on his daily walks. The privilege was graciously bestowed on me by Julia, who thought no honour higher than that which came with the entrustment of his care. He was a happy, self-important little dog, with the shiny coat and benevolent eyes of the well loved basset-hound; and his impatience for his daily exercise gave me the opportunity and excuse for solitude, for I pretended to be jealous of Jep's affection and would allow no one to accompany us.

I found something reassuring in the uncalculating, uncomplicated affection of Jep. The solitude of those walks was a welcome release for me because the house was filled with a constant stream of guests whose coats I had to take, whose glasses I had to fill, whose conversation, smooth with the practised fluency of countless Christmas drinks parties, I had to listen to and smile at. In only one room could I be sure of privacy, and that was the tiny one at the top of the house in which I'd spent long summer afternoons playing to Ella. But it, of all places, held no peace for me. Her laugh rang there continually. I could not go near its door.

So, with an irony I didn't appreciate then, I sought solitude amongst the pavement crowds of a large city. With Jep the basset-hound by my side, I walked through the shoppers making hasty purchases on Christmas Eve and the days before it. I listened to frenzied discussions about food and gifts and clothes and lovers and holidays; I saw friends laughing loudly at bus stops and couples arguing quietly about nothing, their faces pinched from cold and irritation. I walked through these vignettes of other people's lives and listened with the frightened enthusiasm of one who is no longer interested in his own life. I tried to care about the nameless faces I saw, about the passions and desires that fuelled their smiles and gave an edge to their angers.

Christmas came and went. I ate and drank and tried to laugh as I was meant to, watching my mother's concealed irritation as Julia lit cigars at the dinner table and fed Jep bits of turkey and called my father an old dog. The vicar's wife came alone to lunch on Boxing Day – her husband being 'terribly run down with flu'– and held forth on the subject of the church bazaar while Julia asked whatever anyone saw in antimacassars.

I took Jep out twice a day: hour-long oases of time alone to which I looked forward with an eagerness I could not quite hide.

It was on the return from one such expedition that I found no guests present and Julia in full flow on the subject of the vicar's wife.

'Ghastly dress,' she was saying as I came in. 'I for one see no reason why ugliness should be next to godliness, do you?'

'None whatever,' replied my father.

Julia was sitting bolt upright in her favourite chair by the fire, a cigar in one hand, her iron-grey hair scraped back from her face. Helping myself to a gin and tonic from the drinks table, I sat down in a dark corner by the window.

'Damned cheek, dressing so badly,' Aunt Julia

continued. 'It must be an awful embarrassment to her husband.'

And I thought with pity of the vicar's dowdy wife and of what she must have suffered at Julia's hands over lunch, a pity that did not prevent me from laughing at her misfortunes. Sitting with Jep on my lap I felt with relief that the cold flagstones and peeling shutters of Ella's house in France were very far away; that the events which had taken place under its blackened beams and in the unloved decay of its gardens had taken on the quality of a nightmare. They belonged to a different world from the one to which I had returned, and in which I was safe once again.

I tried not to think of the Vaugirards' Christmas: of the forlorn group they would make beside the Christmas tree in their narrow, rambling house with its croquet lawn behind. I tried not to think of Eric playing the piano in the impromptu music room at Sokolska 21, of the smell of aftershave and sweat which had lingered in his bedroom at Ella's. I tried to focus on Aunt Julia's acerbic wit, but the room swam before my eyes and all I could hear, listen though I might, was Eric's voice telling me that he loved me completely. All I could see was his swollen body laid out on the hard ground by the quarry with Dr Pétin bending over it in tears.

'My God, the boy's crying.'

It was Julia's voice that spoke and it was her thin arms that circled my shoulders; her cracked voice that told me, with a soft sympathy far from her usual tone, that I should get a grip at once.

24

I did recover. One does. And the recovery I made was remarkable. I see that now. I see what Sarah did for me. I appreciate the skill with which she taught her chill lessons of self-delusion and deceit. Child that I was, I did not suspect then, as I told my family that I was tired and that they should take no notice of me, that I had been initiated into a harsher world. I did not realize that those few weeks in Prague and France had taken me for ever from the cheerful confines of previous feeling; that Ella's love and Eric's death had raised me to a colder, more adult plane of experience.

The pain of those first weeks could not prolong itself indefinitely. The fires burned themselves out in the end, as all fires do, though they left smouldering coals that destroyed my hopes of peace.

At last the Guildhall term began and I was thrown into a busy round of classes and private practice that took some of the immediacy from my misery, for routine is a great palliative. In devoted industry I found some relief. Slowly I learned to laugh at people's jokes again, to listen to their troubles and hear of their loves and their plans with something approaching enthusiasm. I learned to get through the days and gradually they became bearable.

My practice room at the Guildhall, a tatty little space that held no memories, became the centre of my life. I see again its cheaply varnished upright piano, the lime linoleum of its small square floor, the steel music stand that stood beside its dirty windows of frosted glass. I remember the mustiness of its smell, the cigarette burns on its small table, the faded prints of original scores and Viennese waltzers which were all that enlivened its four brown walls. Nothing could have been further from the splendours of Madame Mocsáry's apartment, but I rejoiced in the anonymity of its ugliness. In Room 32 I was safe, you see; and I spent many hours playing in it, undisturbed and alone.

My violin was my chief comfort in those dark days. Sometimes, when I played, Eric faded from my mind as the music filled it; sometimes, for an hour or two, seldom longer, I was free from the memory of what I had done to him. But I could never be so for long. Eric lived in my dreams and sleep ceased to be a refuge. Instead it became a frightening cacophony of sight and sound and smell, of tears and yells and long, steep falls into darkness. I began to lie awake in bed, willing the morning to come; telling myself that nothing is ever so awful by daylight; that even Eric's laugh would not outlast the coming of morning and the chasing of the shadows.

With no one to confide in, I was alone. And I learned the hard truth that isolation has little to do with the number of people who fill your days; that solitude follows you everywhere.

I did not see Ella, though I read of her in the society pages of the press. With disgust I read the florid stories of the Harcourt curse; read also how it had claimed a new victim, a young and promising French pianist, one of the family's guests at their 'picturesque villa in north-western France'.

On such nonsense does the popular imagination feed.

On such nonsense did my imagination feed, too, in a way; for such drivel was the only contact I allowed myself with Ella over the three years of my study at the Guildhall, a time I filled with the intense work that is, for some, one of the by-products of loneliness. She wrote to me, of course: long, frightened letters that grew more frightened as the weeks turned to months and I left each one unanswered, some unopened even.

I missed her; of course I missed her, with a kind of wrenching sorrow. More than once I nearly wrote. But my conscience would not allow me to see Ella; and the greater my desire for her, the more necessary it was to deny myself the comfort of her presence in my life.

Gradually her letters stopped. My life, devoted more and more to music, continued without any concrete reminders of our love. The days merged into one another and I passed through them all, trying not to think, working hard to resist a secret voice which told me that my silence was cruel, that the fragile woman whose photograph I saw in the papers did not deserve to be severed so completely from my life, in which she had shared so briefly but so fully.

Thinking of it now, I see that my treatment of Ella was cruel, that without adding to my own guilt – or to hers – I might have written, at least. And though perhaps it would have been wrong for me to tell her that her image

242

haunted my dreams still, that no day went past without me thinking of her ringing laugh or of the softness of her touch, I might have said that I grieved for her, that I mourned for her, too.

But it is easy to wish that one had acted differently once the time for action is past. Hindsight is notorious for its clarity. The fact is that I did not write. And my silence grew also from the fact that secretly I blamed Ella for Eric's death more than I blamed my own naivety, which was the true culprit.

I was alone in those years. Without the support only Ella could have given, the knowledge of what I had done made me secretive. Over my time at the Guildhall I learned to disguise how I felt, to shield my unhappiness from the concerned enquiries of my friends and my family. As I learned to do this better, I became more adept at deceiving myself. True, I did not become as proficient as I would years later, when Sarah's example had shown me the means to self-deception with such unspoken clarity. But I made a valiant effort, and with that I had to be content.

Try as I might, I could not escape one frightening truth: that human nature needs a punishment to fit its crimes. I came to writhe under the very absence of hardship in my life; to see in every kind word and happy coincidence a reproach that could not be silenced. With no recriminating words to hurt me, deprived of the catharsis of confession, there was nowhere for my guilt to turn but in on itself. So I devised other self-inflicted privations – food I liked; certain pieces of music; access to my violin – all the while knowing that they were not enough, that they never could be enough.

I came increasingly to think that any satisfaction I might derive from my life or my art, was tainted by what I had done to Eric; that I owed it to him to turn my back on all that might please me. But nature was too strong for me in the end; and the harder I tried the more I learned that the human spirit cannot be silenced, even by the sternest foe. Ella had forced me to live; more than that, she had made me alive to the possibilities of life, and such knowledge is impossible to forget.

It was with this knowledge that I grappled as I worked. My soul – which is what I will call it until someone proposes a better word – was resisting its imprisonment, I see that now. As my playing was its only avenue of escape, its only way into the lighter air of a world beyond my sorrow, it came out in my work with a focused intensity denied to happier minds. Slowly I came to realize that the extremes of joy and pain to which I had been exposed, first by Ella and then by Eric, had informed my art and had taken my talent to the threshold of genius.

Such knowledge sickened me.

I do not use words like 'genius' lightly; that last phrase, for example, is not my own but Michael Fullerton's and it is from the headline of a review he wrote of the first concert I played after leaving the Guildhall. I have it somewhere in here, part of a neat bundle tied years ago by Sarah's tireless fingers. But there is no point in finding it or the others with it; they all say much the same thing. I need no reminding of my career or of how much I came to dislike adulation when I received it. I came to be scared of the origins of my musical power. Now I am less so. Time has calmed me; and it is right that I should acknowledge the debt I owe my dead friend.

Great art, though not always born of suffering, can be. Mine was.

25

I graduated from the Guildhall in the summer I turned twenty-five. My next concert, as I have said, was reviewed by Michael Fullerton with much enthusiasm in *The Times*. I keep his review in my desk drawer, for sentimental reasons; and I cannot help but look at the photograph that accompanies it, a severe but dramatic shot of me standing on the stage of the Albert Hall, overlooked by tiers of empty boxes. I am simply dressed, for I have been rehearsing; and although I am holding my violin as if about to play, my face is tense and slightly stern.

My hair was still long, of course, for my agent thought that long hair enhanced what he called my 'romantic appeal'. But save the severity of my haircut now – for flowing locks do not survive middle age with dignity – I am little changed from the man who stares at me from the newspaper on my lap. I was resigned at twenty-five to the sorrows of life and I can see the resignation in my eyes.

Perhaps Ella saw it, too, for by that stage I was in the newspapers almost as frequently as she had been, though for different reasons. Perhaps she looked at my image as I looked at hers, and read in my eyes the signs of a suffering which mirrored her own. Perhaps she followed the progress of my career with excitement; bought my recordings and tried to relive the afternoons we had spent together, in my tiny attic, over the course of that golden summer we shared. All this is possible.

What is certain is that I read of her with interest in the intervals between my practice and recording commitments; but interested though I was, I could not be excited (as I hoped that she might be for me), for the news of the Harcourts was not good. Press interest in them had died down since Ella's return from France, but it picked up again and reached new heights after the publication of Sarah's book – a life of her grandmother – which received much public attention and a certain amount of critical acclaim. *The Times Literary Supplement* pronounced it 'eloquent in its portrayal of the unstable brilliance of a remarkable woman', according to the jacket of my copy at least; and after its launch photographers once again waited at the house in Chester Square in the hopes of capturing the fragile beauty of Seton Castle's youngest heir.

For a week or more the journalists were disappointed. Then a lucky reporter in Harley Street caught Ella in tears, emerging from her psychiatrist's, and the newspapers leaped with glee on both photograph and story. So great, in fact, was the public interest which greeted the ensuing articles that even the broadsheets ran small columns on the Harcourts and their history, while gutter press fantasy on the subject of curses and castles knew no bounds. Throughout the summer of 1937, as idealistic young men slipped off to fight in the Spanish Civil War, Ella and her family assumed an importance in national gossip second only to that enjoyed by the royal family; and the characters in their drama were discussed everywhere with an unthinking, good-natured intrusion it made my blood boil to hear.

Even Camilla Boardman, so indiscreet about her friends in private, felt bound in public to talk loudly about what nonsense it all was, thus subtly underlining her intimacy with celebrity to anyone who cared to hear, while maintaining at the same time a strict loyalty towards her friends.

The years had not changed Camilla, whatever they had done to me. As her twenties progressed she remained as perfectly curled, as effortlessly confident as she had ever been. Her emphases did not decrease in frequency or in strength; her enthusiasms did not dim; her lack of punctuation remained legendary. She remained true to her promise and did not marry Ed Saunders. Instead, with a rare show of mettle, she moved to Chelsea. When I graduated from the Guildhall her shop had already been open – in smart premises of elaborate design – for some time. Originally a dress shop, it had gradually become an outlet for Camilla's own creative flair and soon she had four seamstresses under her and her clothes were being worn by a wider clientele than that provided by her mother's friends and her own.

I, less in awe of her as I grew older, saw her often during those dark times: for Camilla demanded an absolute attention that distracted me from the pressures of my own mind. I was grateful for the unfailing diversion from my own thoughts she offered. Never having known a moment's guilt herself – never, indeed, having experienced any mortification stronger than that of being asked to wait unduly long at her dentist's – Camilla was unvaryingly cheerful in a way that was balm to my depressed spirits. And though she must have itched to know the details of my time in France (for she knew, I think, that I had been there with Ella), she forbore from asking for them with a tact that surprised and pleased me; that made me, in fact, reconsider my view of her and decide that I liked her wholeheartedly.

Over the Boardman dinner table I heard occasional snippets of the news about Ella; but as I did not encourage them, the daughter of the house derived no satisfaction from their retelling and they soon dried up.

I did not encourage them because, easy though her company was, I could enjoy Camilla's conversation on certain subjects only. Her telling me, in hushed tones, that Ella Harcourt was utterly miserable, and secretive in her misery, was more than I could bear to hear. Reliable, uncomplicated friendship was what I needed at that time, and by a happy chance it was what Camilla did best. Over the years our superficial friendship blossomed into a closer one, an amicable bond which came to be important to us both and lasted well into the early years of my marriage.

I do not digress when I speak of Camilla. It is vital that I remember the precise sequence of events that led up to and beyond Ella's trial. Detail is important to me now, for so much happened so quickly. I must penetrate the haze of concerts and competitions, of radio interviews and relentless rehearsals which obscure my view of those few weeks before I won the Hibberdson. I must retrace the progression of my friendship with Camilla and remember my partnership with Regina Boardman, in whose charity concerts I regularly played.

Although memories of Eric prevented me from frequenting her 'mornings', I was always grateful for her kindness and for the expertise which she had once shown in her management of the Guildhall authorities. I owed Mendl's teaching, after all, partly to Regina's influence; and I did not forget this, or the fact that she had given me my first chance. So I played, when asked, in a series of her benefit concerts, my growing fame drawing ever larger audiences; and although I declined to play again at St Peter's, Eaton Square, I came to know the interiors of a good many other London churches in this way.

But my architectural opportunities are not what concern me here. I must remember Regina's words after the annual meeting of her favourite charity, the Society for the Preservation of Ancient Buildings. I must see her again, legs neatly crossed, at her desk in the drawing room at Cadogan Square. She has returned from her meeting bright with enthusiasm for a new series of concerts, held this time in private: an idea which, she assures me, can't *fail* to double the efficacy of her fund-raising.

'After *all*, darling,' she says with an arch smile, 'what *is* the use of having friends with large houses if one doesn't *use* them?'

There is a brief silence while I, to whom the point has never occurred before, can do nothing but ask, 'What, indeed?'

And inevitably I fill the expectant pause by volunteering my services for the first of these concerts, an event which I am told, is set for the day after the Hibberdson semi-finals.

'It will be at Cheverel House,' says Regina with pardonable pride; and she goes on to reward the prompt offer of my time with some mild flattery, which I try not to hear. 'Just *think* what fun it will be to play to a *friendly* audience for a change,' she finishes, smiling. 'You do *far* too many competitions, James.'

I am tempted to say that the Hibberdson is my first; but before I can speak Regina is saying that I'll have carried off the prize before I *know* it and that then I really *will* be too grand for the likes of her.

Thinking that nothing and no one could be too grand for the likes of Regina Boardman, I smile politely at the compliment and promise to come back in a week to finalize the programme.

'That would be *splendid*,' Regina says, rising from her seat to kiss me. 'I'm so grateful, James, for the way you share your genius with us.'

And I, uncomfortable with such gratitude from others, make my excuses and leave and I go home and take out my violin, which I play all afternoon and well into the evening, frightened of sitting alone with my thoughts, Regina's praise burning my ears with its well-intentioned kindness.

It was a busy summer for me, that first one after graduation; but because I continued to find my best escape in music, I did not resent the hours of intense practice which recording commitments (and my progress through the rounds of the Hibberdson prize) demanded. I found freedom in the endless hours of hard work my life required of me; and in the concentration of performance I found a release from myself.

I did not see Ella, though I read and thought of her

frequently. I might never have tried to see her, had not Fortune, with characteristic cruelty, devised otherwise, and tempted me into unleashing the pent-up desires of so many lonely months. But Fortune did; and she chose the night of Regina Boardman's concert at Cheverel House to do so, a night that found me at my weakest, trying guiltily to suppress my delight at having secured a place in the finals of the Hibberdson. I still had not resolved my attitude to success, you see; I had not learned how to accept it with anything approaching ease.

As I played on an improvised stage at the end of a long room filled with respectful faces, I tried not to think of Eric's face, of his glassy stare as his body swung slowly up the sides of that quarry in the chill wind.

I did not see my audience as I played to them; I did not distinguish more than the blur of their heads and the enthusiastic clatter of their applause as I bowed my thanks for their attention. I played well, but cautiously; and after my performance I allowed myself to be led meekly, numbly, to a small dark room where a glass of champagne waited for me. There, telling the attendant I needed to be alone, I remember sitting with my head in my hands, unwilling to face the congratulations of those who had spent their evening listening to me.

'Darling, you were *marvellous*.'

The creaking of the door told me I had been found, and I knew that Regina Boardman's embraces could not be far behind her daughter's.

'Come out and enjoy your success,' Camilla said to me, eyes shining. 'Everyone's *mad* about you. Mummy's told them all you're going to win the Hibberdson and

I shouldn't be a *bit* surprised if you did, after the way you've played tonight.'

She waited, smiling, as I put my violin into its case.

'Come on, James, don't be bashful.' She slipped her arm through mine and opened the door on to the landing. 'You've got to get used to all this if you're going to be famous, you know.'

'I'm not going to be famous,' I said, irritated for once by her cheeriness.

'But you are already,' she said simply, leading the way out of the room. 'And there's not much you can do about it now.'

Certainly I could not politely avoid the crowd that waited for me on the stairs. So I smiled grimly as the men shook my hand and introduced me to their wives: deftly made-up women who told me, according to personality, that I was either as dashing or as good as they had been led to believe. The audience that night was an invited one, you see: a selection of Regina's richest and most influential friends, and her guests seemed to take an introduction to the performer as one of the unspoken rights of their expensive admission. So I was duly introduced, for Mrs Boardman never disappointed her public and as I was led slowly down the overcrowded stairs, smiling awkwardly, trying not to hear the words of adulation, I looked forward to my departure and to solitude as a man in a desert dreams of water.

It was only as I neared the last of the couples waiting to meet me that I saw Alexander and Pamela Harcourt standing near the end of the line. Three years had changed them sadly. Though Pamela's coiffure was as complicated as ever, she had an air of weariness that elaborate grooming and expensive clothes could not disguise. I saw white where the knuckles of her bony hand gripped her husband's arm, an arm that showed thin and almost frail through the sleeve of his dinner jacket. Alexander had lost his vigour also, I saw that at once; I saw too that his eyes no longer shone with the confidence of one used to the admiring glances of others. He looked gaunt and old; and his hand, as it stretched to shake mine, shook slightly.

'Good evening, Lord Harcourt,' I said, thinking of the last time we had met, in the lobby of the Grand Hotel Europa, when Ella's troubles were just beginning.

'Hello, Mr Farrell. How good to see you again.'

It was Alexander who spoke, and his voice was older than I remembered it too.

'We did enjoy hearing you play.' Pamela smiled at me: a formal movement of made-up lips.

There was a moment's silence between us. Then I thanked them both for coming and made as if to move down the staircase, but Alexander's fingers caught at the sleeve of my coat.

'Could I ... see you for a moment? In private?' His blue eyes met mine steadily.

I said nothing.

'Please.'

I felt Regina coming down the stairs behind me, ready to move me on.

'I've almost written to you before now,' said Alexander quickly, seeing her also. 'Please. I can't tell you how much I'd appreciate a few moments alone.'

The quiet dignity of Ella's father touched me, for

Alexander's ageing face had a look about it which caught his daughter's exactly.

I nodded. 'Of course,' I said, as I moved away down the last of the stairs.

He was waiting for me by the steps of the house as I left it. I saw Pamela's face in a disappearing taxi as her husband quickened his stride to match mine and walked with me down the road towards the Underground station. There was a moment of awkward silence; then Alexander spoke, and his voice was trembling.

'Something is very wrong with my daughter,' he said slowly.

More silence.

'What do you mean?' I asked at last, though I knew.

'I mean that she hasn't been the same since she went to France with you and that poor boy who died.'

We walked on a few yards, neither of us speaking.

'You mustn't think I blame you,' her father continued. 'I was worried about Ella before she went away. Even then she wasn't behaving like the person I knew. But when she came back she was much worse. She wouldn't talk to Pamela or to me; she wanted to be alone as much as possible. She seemed to have lost her interest in life.'

He paused.

'We thought at first that that Frenchman's death ... What was his name?'

'Eric de Vaugirard,' I said quietly.

'Quite so. We thought that his death had upset her, as well it might.'

Another pause.

'So we gave her time; we didn't press things. But she

got worse and worse. She stopped seeing anyone; she seemed to lose the ability to enjoy herself. And that was hard, because Ella had always taken such a delight in life before that. She seemed so happy around the time of her engagement.'

Alexander looked down. As he did so I thought of the days and nights of that passionate summer when Ella and I had thought ourselves immortal.

'We all tried to help her,' he went on. 'Her cousin Sarah, in particular, was a great source of strength. But now Ella won't see anyone. And all this attention from the press doesn't help, of course. She spends all day alone now, in her room. She won't talk to me any more. She . . .'

But he could not speak.

'Please James.' His eyes turned to meet mine, and I saw that they were wet with tears. 'I'm worried about my little girl. I've no idea what to do. I feel as if I'm losing her. And the only person she talks of, the only person she says she wants to see, is you.'

We were at Notting Hill Gate now and it had started to rain.

'I've almost written so many times . . . And then tonight, seeing you, I felt I had to tell you. She says you don't answer her letters and I've been anxious not to interfere. But now I'm worried. If only you would see her, it might make a difference.'

There was silence again.

'It's worth a try at least, isn't it?' he said; and there was something tragic about the pleading of this middle-aged man.

'What is there that I can do?' I said slowly, more to myself than to Alexander.

Eagerly he grabbed my arm. 'Write to her, James. Telephone her. Come to see her.' He paused. 'My brother is giving a party at Seton next month. Bring her to that.'

I shook my head.

His eyes fell. 'Please, James. Don't abandon her like this.'

There was a long silence as I stood, my head reeling.

'All right,' I said at last. 'I'll write to her. Tell her I'll write to her.'

'I can't thank you enough.'

Alexander held out his hand to me. I shook it and our eyes met.

'Goodbye,' I said, trying to smile.

And turning quickly, without another word, I went down the steps and into the Underground.

26

I cannot tell you how I felt that night. I can only say I didn't sleep. I went instead to the attic, where I knew my light would not be seen, and sat in the corner where Ella had once sat, trying to think, searching for some raft of resolution to cling to in the storm.

I found one eventually. But the search was hard and success required the confession of my own weakness. I had to admit to myself, in a way I had not done before, that I could not spend the rest of my life as I had spent the last three years; that whatever I had done to Eric, however much I deserved to be punished, I could not resist the pull of my old love any longer.

Alexander's pleading had its effect that night. I sat awake, unable to resist the force of memory any longer; and the darkness of the room filled with sights and sounds and shapes I had thought lost to me.

For the first time since returning from France I tasted the wildness of real hope, the sweetness of love returned again. For the first time in three years I rejoiced – with almost adolescent wonder – in the mysteries of the night, in the beauties of a star-filled sky. I did so because the darkness no longer shrieked at me. It was no longer filled with dreams of Eric, but with thoughts of Ella. Shaking, hardly daring to breathe, I saw her beside me. I watched her as she lit her cigarettes, as she brushed the hair from her eyes. I heard once more the silvery chuckle of her laugh, the gentle accents of her voice. I kissed again the velvet space beneath her collarbone.

Alone in the dark I thought that nothing would keep Ella from me, that our love had earned us a second chance and saved us from oblivion. I swallowed my pride. I admitted my weakness. I accepted I could resist her pull no longer; that if she needed me I would go to her.

I see now what a step that was. In retelling the story of my life I have come to know myself in ways I did not dream of then. Sixty years on, from the vantage point of knowledge, I know that the bonds from which I broke free so briefly were mighty indeed; that they could only have been broken by the force of a love like Ella's and mine. Our passion *did* give us power.

My longing for her flowed with a force I could no longer control as I sat in the attic that night, writing by the light of a small bright lamp, scribbling a letter that covered six sheets of large notepaper with the small dense characters of my cramped hand.

I cannot recall the words I used, for they were chosen long ago and at great speed. I know only the gist of what I said and the fervour with which I said it. I wrote to Ella of love; of my love for her and hers for me. I told her of my sorrow for times past and of my hope for times to come. I told her what I should have told her before: that I had never stopped thinking of her; that I had never stopped dreaming of her; that she was right: that we needed each other more than ever now.

I signed my name as day was breaking with a new splendour; and it was only then, exhausted by words, that I went to bed and had my first hours of dreamless sleep in three long years. I woke late, when the sun was high in the sky, and for the first time since Eric's death I took pleasure in the luxury of quiet observation. I rejoiced in the pattern of the sunshine on my wall, in the colour of the book spines on my shelf. My life was changed. I felt sure of that, sure that things would be well once more.

Slowly, easily, I got up and dressed.

Outside in the sunshine I posted Ella's letter. Then I went to the Guildhall, thinking with wonder how different this morning was from those that had gone before it. I took delight again in the freshness of the world. I was alive once more. Years later, as I sit in the dark, watching the moon rise on the lashing waves of a rolling sea, I remember what that was like; I remember the return of hope as a thirsty man might remember his first sight of water. I had not drunk yet, but I could see the oasis ahead. In my desire I thought that nothing could stand in my way now.

Such feeling was expressed in my playing with a force that was as exhilarating as it was irresistible. I had decided long before, in unconscious homage to Ella, to play the Mendelssohn Violin Concerto in E Minor if ever I got as far as the Hibberdson finals. Remembering my inspiration, I worked with untiring passion. In hours of practice I relived the sunny afternoons on which I had played its first movement to her. I remembered how she had sat, silent with pleasure, on her cushion in the corner of my dingy attic.

Days passed in this way; more than I knew, I think. But I worked on in excited contemplation of the future, giving little thought to the limitations of the present. To be sure, there was no immediate reply to my letter, but I could not be disheartened by a delay of a few days after so many months' unconscious waiting. My suffering had taught me patience. And I told myself – quite rightly, as it turned out – that a thousand things might have prevented Ella from writing at once. I felt sure enough of her once more to face an empty letter-box with cheery equanimity.

Other things happened in that time too: meetings and conversations to which I gave little thought then, but which I must remember now if I am to grasp the facts in anything like their precise order. Precision is important. So I try to remember. And as I try, I hear the emphatic tones of Camilla Boardman's voice, higher than usual; and I feel her hand as she leads me across a crowded room full of loud people and brittle laughter and the hard clink of cutlery on china.

We are in a restaurant in a small street off the King's Road. We have met for lunch and my friend is brimming with excitement. We have barely taken our seats at the window table which my name now secures before she is squeezing my arm and telling me she has fantastic news, that her great opportunity has come.

I remember her that day. I remember her animation, her infectious enthusiasm as she asked me if I had ever been to Seton.

'Because it's *the* most incredible house. An absolutely

vast castle on an island off the Cornish coast. Full of *fabulous* furniture and ...'

There was a pause, for Camilla's stock of adjectives was not inexhaustible.

I waited and said nothing, trying to control my excitement as I heard my friend speak of Ella's island, of the house she and I might one day share.

'It's the Harcourt family seat,' Camilla continued. 'And they're giving a *huge* party to raise money for some charity or other. Mummy's involved. I can't think what it's called now. The Society for the Preservation of Ancient Buildings, probably. But that doesn't matter much in any case. What *does* matter is that it's going to be *the* big party this summer. And between us Mummy and I know practically *everyone* who's going and you can rest assured *I'm* going to design all their dresses.'

Camilla paused, out of breath.

'They don't *know* this yet, of course,' she added with unconscious irony. 'But I'm already doing Ella Harcourt. Everyone else is sure to follow her lead, just you wait and see.'

So saying, she smiled brightly and ordered champagne; and I laughed inwardly, thinking that I had heard of this party from Alexander several days before; that I, for once, was better informed than the omniscient Miss Boardman.

Ten days or so passed without my hearing from Ella. By the end of this time I *was* worried that perhaps she had left my letter unopened as I had left so many of hers. But in spite of creeping misgivings I worked as hard as ever, for the final of the Hibberdson was almost upon me, and my days were filled with rehearsals and conductors and the thousand tiny details of competition preparation.

It was on my return from one especially long rehearsal that I saw her letter: peeping from a pile of others on the entrance-hall mat; a blue envelope this time, though the jagged letters of its address were in the brown ink I knew so well.

I remember the excitement of that moment: the way my throat went dry as I picked up Ella's letter and took it to the tiny room at the top of the house. I remember the touch of the heavy paper as I tore open the envelope, the thickness of the sheet that fell from it, the raised print of the address, which told me that she had written it at Seton. She did not use my name, I remember; and her note was not long. But she said:

Darling, my darling,

I can't believe you've written at last. I thought you were lost for good.

You cannot know how much I've missed you, how badly I've wanted to see you. These have been hard years – though you don't need me to tell you that, I imagine. And I'm sorry for not replying to your letter sooner.

I've not been in London, you see – I'm down here helping Uncle Cyril with his plans for a party. The house is in chaos and the younger generation has been drafted in to help. So I've not been at home and Pamela is very bad about forwarding mail. I only read your words this morning – and since then I've not been able to sit still. I can't wait to see you, to touch you again, my love. I have <u>missed you</u>.

But I can't leave here until next week, when the party's over. Of course you could come to the ball – though on second thoughts I can think of nothing worse than seeing you again in front of thousands of people. It's a Regina Boardman sort of party anyway and I want you alone . . .

So will you wait for me a little longer? And while you're about it, will you take care to win the Hibberdson? I've been following you to the finals and I wonder what you will play. You've no idea how much I want to hear you again.

There is so much to say; so much to tell. A letter is not the way.

I long for our reunion.

Ella

Those were her words; and as I say them I can hear her saying them. Alone in the dark, I hear Ella's voice, calling to me from long ago; I see her eyes, looking for mine.

Events followed thick and fast on each other after that.

And it is the night of the Hibberdson final which fills my mind now, a night of judges and lights, of sweat and nerves and anxious friends. A night of glory for me: for I played with a passion I had not known before. A night when Ella's love gave my playing a lightness it had never yet enjoyed, a delicacy it was not to have again.

I remember how it felt to win: the rush of relief as I set down my violin and took my bow. I remember smiling, thanking the judges and telling the interviewers how delighted I was. And I *was* delighted, for nothing can quite dim the pleasure of playing really well, of pushing one's art beyond oneself. Though I felt still that the victory was not mine alone, that the daring with which I had played would have been impossible without the shrieking memory of Eric's laugh and the sight of his sightless eyes, I felt too that Eric would have wanted me to win; and I thought that Ella's love would protect me henceforth from such demons.

Standing on the podium, the bronze laurels in my hand, my eyes flicked over row upon row of cheering faces and a blur of clapping hands; and as I bowed again I saw a slender, tilting neck and a smile that made the breath catch in my throat.

I looked again. Surer now, reeling a little, smiling still, I moved along the stage, shaking hands with the other finalists, accepting their words of congratulation, thinking only of how to leave the concert hall, to escape into the night with the only person I wanted to see.

Backstage, there were newspaper reporters and my agent telling me to go back on for another bow and as I did so the blood beat furiously in my head and my hands were wet with sweat from the fear that Ella might get lost in the crowd, that I might not find her after all.

I did not go on for a third bow but went straight to the finalists' dressing room, where my fellow competitors were putting away their instruments and taking off their ties. In a frenzy, I said my goodbyes and put my violin into its case; and then I raced through cavernous corridors to the players' entrance, hoping to slip out before the crowds arrived. But as I opened the door I heard with quick exasperation the high-pitched shriek, 'There he is!', and I found myself at the centre of a group of excited well-wishers and reporters, questions and autograph books flying.

Telling myself that Ella would find me, that in fact it was best for me to stay in one, obvious place, I breathed deeply and faced the barrage of words and notebooks. My pulse racing, I took out my pen and began to sign my name, telling myself to be calm.

'May I join your devoted supplicants, Mr Farrell?'

I had seen her before she spoke; and the rounded vowels of an English accent made me pale with disappointment.

Sarah Harcourt smiled up at me as I recovered myself. And as I took another programme and automatically signed my name, I recovered sufficiently to ask her what she was doing there.

'Watching you, of course,' she replied, smiling still; and I noticed that she seemed less forbidding than I remembered her. 'I thought I should demonstrate my acquaintance with the winner if I possibly could.'

'What?'

The din of the crowd drowned out her quiet voice.

'Congratulations,' she called, louder this time. And she leaned forward and kissed my cheek.

Someone took our photograph and a reporter asked who the lovely lady was.

'Come on, give us your name!'

Sarah blushed and I thought with longing how beautiful her cousin was.

'It's been such a long time,' she said as I began to push my way through the autograph hunters.

'Yes.'

'And how have you been since I saw you last?'

266

'Oh ... well. Working hard.'

'Winning prizes.'

'Only one.'

'But what a prize.'

She looked up at me and her blue eyes met mine as though we had known each other always.

'It was kind of you to come and seek me out,' I said finally. 'I thought your family had a three-line whip on their presence at Seton.'

'I've been in London today, collecting a dress.'

'I see.'

She smiled at me again. There was a slight pause.

'Well, goodbye,' she said at last. 'Congratulations on tonight. I'm sure it will be the first of many.'

'Thank you.'

'And now that we've bumped into each other so unexpectedly, we mustn't lose touch again.'

'Of course not.' My key was in my door now.

'Goodbye again, Mr Farrell.'

'Goodbye, Miss Harcourt.'

And I leaned down and kissed her cheek. As I did so I smelled her scent, a scent of different cigarettes, of unknown soap, of strange perfume: the smell I smelled yesterday afternoon, made richer then by the thick sweetness of warm blood, as I bent over her bleeding body.

27

The days between the Hibberdson final and the Harcourts' party were busy ones for me. What time I did have I spent with my family, whose praise was reserved but wholehearted, or with Camilla Boardman, whose predictions of future glory knew no bounds. But the person I really wanted, of course, was Ella; and I chafed at the days which still separated us, though I understood why they must do so. I, like her, had no wish to be reunited under the watchful eyes of her family and our friends. Having waited so long, a week was nothing.

In any case my days passed in a haze of euphoria, the like of which I had not thought to feel again.

By writing to Ella I had admitted defeat: I acknowledged that. I accepted, in my own mind at least, that I had been unable to continue indefinitely in self-inflicted imprisonment for the part I had played in Eric's death. This acceptance freed me. Ella's love, or rather the knowledge that she loved me still, liberated me from the past in a way which I was helpless to resist. Try though I might, I could not silence a quiet, insistent voice which told me that life might be a fine thing after all; that perhaps there were better ways of making amends to Eric than the spiritual mutilation which had been my only recourse until then.

For six nights he disappeared from my dreams, his sightless eyes replaced by the sound of Ella's laugh, the image of his soaking body by the warmth of her cheek against mine.

I almost told Camilla everything in my desire to share my happiness, but she was full of her own news and plans and no opportunity arose for me to speak. For too long I had assumed the role of appreciative listener; and the run-up to her night of glory was no time to choose to alter things.

'It's *so* much work, darling,' she told me one evening on the telephone. 'Even now people are coming for last-minute alterations. And you've never *heard* so much conversation about shoes. It's enough to send the puritan in one insane.'

Camilla's facility for martyrdom, social or commercial, had only increased with the passing of the years.

'You've no *idea* how draining it is.'

'None at all, I'm afraid.'

'Lucky old musicker. I'm sure playing old ditties on a fiddle can't be *half* as difficult as advising Lady Markham on handbags.'

'Not half as difficult.'

'Don't be *cheeky*, young man. We can't all have just won the Hibberdson, you know.'

'Hmmm.'

But I was thinking of Ella and of how she would congratulate me.

'Speaking of which,' my friend continued, 'next

269

Wednesday I'm taking you to dinner to celebrate. Eight-thirty sharp. I'll pick you up.'

And with that she rang off.

At that dinner, a few nights before the ball, I remember Camilla describing her clients to me (' *Terribly* indiscreet, I know, but *such* fun – and you're quite trustworthy'). I remember the hushed tones in which she told me that Ella would not be wearing a dress at *all* but a suit of men's evening clothes, specially cut. I remember her saying that Sarah Harcourt ('You remember her, don't you, Jamie?') had come to her for fittings but had finally chosen some *hideously* obvious red concoction from a rival couturier.

'*Such* a pity, darling, since she's *actually* rather pretty and could have looked quite decent,' whispered Camilla with more than a hint of pique. 'But there's no accounting for taste, *is* there?'

From her mother, my friend had learned details of the party's arrangements, and she related these eagerly too as our food arrived. Over steamed asparagus I learned that there was going to be a bonfire (because Atlantic winds can be *freezing*, even in September) and fireworks and hothouse roses and a huge marquee.

'They're not letting the guests into much of the house itself,' said Camilla confidentially. '*Perfectly* understandable, of course, because there are so many priceless things.'

I nodded and asked whether reports that an American film star was bringing her hairdresser over on the *Normandie* for the night were true.

'*Probably*, darling. That's just the kind of stunt Mummy would dream up. You know how she is.'

I did know; and together we laughed.

I remember Camilla's undisguised excitement, the professional pride that lent a weight to her pronouncements which they had lacked in the early days of our friendship.

'You can count on it that everyone dressed by me will look *fabulous*,' she promised as she asked for the bill – for *she* was taking *me*; it was *her* celebratory treat – and kissed me goodbye. 'I'll show you the pictures when I get back. And I'll tell you all then.'

Wishing that I had written to Ella sooner, for then we could have enjoyed the festivities together, thinking wistfully of how lovely she would look, I left the restaurant and saw my friend into a taxi.

'Bye,' she called from the back window. 'See you soon with lots of news.'

'Goodbye,' I called after her, waving.

But it was not Camilla who told me of that party, though she filled in the details for me later, days later, when most of the events were a matter of public knowledge. It was not from her lips that I learned of what had happened; Fate permitted me no such civilities. I read it all on the front page of a fellow commuter's newspaper in the heat of a crowded Underground train four days after our dinner. PEER MURDERED AT SOCIETY FUND-RAISER bellowed the headline.

My mouth dry, fear catching at my throat, I saw Ella's father staring at me from the centre of the page.

In disbelief I left the train at the next station, moving slowly at first through the crush on the platform; then quickly, impatiently, brushing past the queues on the escalator, swearing at the broken barrier, running at last, with the blood beating on my brain, to the newspaper stall at the station's entrance.

I was sitting at home, numb with disbelief, when Camilla called that afternoon, almost in tears.

'Oh God, James,' she said. 'Oh God. Have you heard?'

I had heard; of course I had. It would have been impossible for me not to have done. The story was in every paper; by now it seemed the subject of every overheard conversation.

'Everyone *saw*, you see,' she said. 'Hundreds of people watched her do it.'

And as I listened, I thought, inconsequentially, as one does think at times like that, that Camilla's voice as she spoke was oddly expressionless for one with such a talent for colourful delivery; that she sounded distant, distracted, unlike her usual self. I listened to her story as though its characters were unknown to me, as though they formed no part of my life and never had done.

Only later, alone, did the delayed realization dawn that Ella was a murderer: that the girl I had loved, the girl for whom I had twice sacrificed my self-respect, the girl with the lilting voice and the bitten fingernails, was the person at the centre of the story Camilla told: the child who had killed her father in cold blood in front of more than two hundred witnesses.

'I couldn't believe it, Jamie,' Camilla told me tearfully. 'And I *wouldn't* have believed it.'

She paused.

'But I *saw* her do it. And in front of so many people. There was no way she could possibly have got away with it.'

I was silent.

'And she must have known that.'

'Tell me what you saw,' I said slowly.

It is difficult for me to call to mind the whole wealth of ugly detail which emerged in the weeks which followed Alexander's murder. Over sixty years I have taken care to bury the details of Ella's trial with those of Eric's death: far from the intrusive scrutiny of easy recall. I have not wished to remember and I have had remarkable success in forgetting. More than ever I understand my debt to Sarah; for it was she who taught me to insulate myself against anything that might ruffle the smooth calm of a placid inner life.

Now I must remember. As I have done with Eric, so must I with Ella and her father's death: I must open locked doors, exhume old ghosts. It is hard for a man of my age, because disillusion is the saddest of life's scars. And there is self-pity in my anger now. Life, so recently offered to me again, was snatched from my grasp before I could sample it once more. I cry for that man – he was a boy no longer – who sat, stupefied, as Camilla Boardman told him what Ella had done. I long to comfort him. But I cannot; and if I could, what would I say? There was nothing he could have done; no steps he might have taken. He was lost already, in ways he could neither have imagined nor understood.

Ella as murderer changed everything. It made a lie of all we had had, a lie of which I could tell no one.

I went up to the attic that evening and sat in the moonlight where she had sat, hearing her voice, watching her smoke her endless cigarettes. I remembered our meeting in the park; the announcement of her engagement to Charlie Stanhope at Camilla's birthday party; the way she had taken me to Seton. I saw her flick the hair out of her eyes and curl up on that window-ledge above the sea. I heard her tell me of Blanche, of the history of her family, of Sarah.

'This house has plenty of dark secrets,' she had said.

I remembered her frightened eyes by the quarry with Eric; the clipped intensity of her voice as she told me to tell him the truth. I saw it all, heard it all. And I felt that some kind of spell had been broken; that the person I had loved had ceased to exist, if ever she had existed at all.

Reading of Alexander's murder in the papers, in the hot and crowded ticket hall of an Underground station, I had clung to the blind faith that had made me draw short of condemning Ella in the years since Eric's death. But listening to Camilla describe what she had seen, in a quiet voice I had not heard before, I understood that I had been wrong. And later, alone in the room where I had played to her, where so recently I had written of love and longing in the language of naive adoration, I felt a wave of disgust sweep over me.

Eric's body, heavy with water, returned in the darkness; I saw it swing jerkily up the sides of the quarry, to be laid out before me. I remembered the tears in Dr Pétin's eyes. And I thought with something like hatred that I had twice sacrificed myself – for a girl who had killed her father. To earn her trust I had betrayed all notions of friendship; to see her again I had undermined three hard years of self-punishment.

And as I cried I wept not for Ella, nor even for Eric, but for myself.

28

Even the horrors of the past deserve some recognition, and the obstacles to Ella's success were great. For a start, the access of guests to the house was strictly limited and the Great Hall itself was locked (since all the most valuable objects in the open rooms were stored there for the night). It is only from the Great Hall that access to the balcony is possible and Cyril Harcourt had the only key to this room, a key later found secure and untouched in his desk by the police.

When it happened, there must have been more than two hundred people on the terrace: standing by the bonfire, talking and laughing, apparently preferring the fresh air, cold though it was, to the heat of the reception rooms. So more than two hundred people watched her do it; more than two hundred people, some of whom knew her well.

It is sad for me to trace the events of that night, because I know the house in which they happened so well now. Everything is so real. When Camilla told me the story I could only imagine how everything must have been; I had none of the feeling for the place that sixty years' kinship has given me. Now I know precisely the layout of the terrace, the angle at which one must tilt one's head if one is to see the balcony that overlooks it far above.

I know the smell of the sea in September, the colour of the stone in bonfire light. I can feel the chill of an Atlantic breeze on my neck. Recounting it now I can see it all, feel it all; and I watch for a sign someone might have seen, a detail they *must* have overlooked. But all I can sense is the happy anticipation of the crowd; all I can hear are its sporadic cheers as Alexander and Ella appear.

The Setons' guests arrived between seven and seven-thirty. They were given champagne cocktails in the ball-room and many, as I have said already, strayed out on to the terrace. Between half and three-quarters of an hour later, immediately before dinner was announced, Ella and her father appeared on the balcony above them, from which access is only possible through the windows of the Great Hall.

According to the testimony of most present, they seemed calm, though it was noticeable that the years had taken their toll on Alexander and he seemed older than many remembered him. An expectant hush fell and cries of 'Speech!' were heard. Some people cheered.

Ella in her dinner jacket moved behind her father and put her hands on his shoulders, a gesture that seemed sweetly affectionate. Standing behind the taller man, little of her was visible but the stylish cut of her sharply parted blonde hair.

Lord Markham called, 'Show yourself, Ella. Don't be shy.'

Someone laughed.

Alexander began to shuffle his notes.

As he did so, with unhurried grace, Ella lifted her arms

and brought them down with a crack on his neck. Her father cried out, startled, and dropped his papers. Some fluttered down into the crush below. People scrambled to catch them; one or two went into the bonfire. Some guests on the edges of the crowd, who could not see, began to laugh. But those in its centre watched, increasingly confused, as Alexander turned in surprise towards his daughter and as they watched they saw her bend down and lift his feet from under him in a quick and practised movement, pushing him over the rail. Clutching wildly as he fell, he caught at the balustrade with one hand and for a sickening moment hung there. Everyone stopped laughing. In the silence Ella bent over him, and it looked to some as though she were holding his arm, pulling him back to safety. A woman screamed. Then he fell.

Alexander fell to his death with a long shout that ended sickeningly on the flagstones of the terrace below. Ella disappeared from the balcony.

When they found her she was in her father's bedroom, calling for him, apparently quite unperturbed by what she had done. At first she seemed shocked to see the policemen. When they made it clear that they had come to arrest her, she went 'quite crazy', as one of the officers described it at her trial. Screaming, hysterical, she refused to be handcuffed. Calling for her father, for Pamela, screaming abuse at Sarah – who was in tears in the entrance hall – she was forcibly taken down the staircase and led out through the front door, watched by silent lines of shocked guests.

'You can't *imagine* how awful it was,' Camilla said the next night. 'That look in her eyes. The way she screamed.

And when Sarah tried to get the policemen to treat her gently, she lashed out like you've never seen.'

On the other end of the telephone I heard my friend begin to cry.

'I've known Ella for nine years,' she said through her sobs. 'Ever since she came back from America. I can't tell you how ghastly it was seeing her like that.'

I listened, sick at heart.

'Perhaps the papers were right after all,' Camilla went on. 'You know about the madness in her family, don't you?'

I said nothing.

'Don't you, Jamie?'

There was silence.

'Yes,' I said at last. 'Yes, I know all about it.'

I listened as Camilla, whose mother had heard it from Pamela, told me how Ella had had to be sedated at Penzance station: 'Kicking and screaming like a wild thing.'

In the ensuing search the police found a key in the pocket of Ella's dinner jacket, a key later shown to be a replica of the one to the Great Hall, the original of which was found safe in her uncle's desk. A London locksmith came forward and testified at the trial that Ella had had two copies made a fortnight before the party; and because the other copy was never found it was assumed that she had hidden it or thrown it into the sea.

'You've no idea how awful it was,' said Camilla. 'Listening to Alexander scream. Watching her push him.'

I went to bed that night with those dreadful words

echoing endlessly in my head. *Watching her push him watching her push him.*

The next morning, news of Ella's arrest was all over the papers and she did not leave the front page more than three times in two months. A trial like hers, I suppose, was not likely to go unnoticed. The press, swooping like vultures on the story's principals, scented in the details of Ella's crime all the beloved staples of popular journalism: celebrity; beauty; violence; death. No paper could resist such ingredients. Insanity, in all its tragedy, became a national obsession. For several weeks Ella's fragile image stared out at me wherever I went. I learned to harden my heart to her eyes and her small face with its delicate bones and ivory skin.

Sick with bitterness, I was helpless as old demons returned. Through nights of wide-eyed wakefulness I heard again the shriek of Eric's laugh, come back to haunt me with renewed force, to punish me for presuming ever to escape the consequences of what I had done to him. Impatient for daylight, for the fading of such sounds, I found when it came that in fact it brought no release: only newspapers bearing fresh news of Ella and her trial, beneath courtroom sketches of her gaunt face and pursed lips. Sitting at breakfast, hunched over my coffee, I read of her case with a sort of morbid fascination; with horror and sadness for a family I might once have claimed as my own. And alone once more, in new and doubly lonely isolation, I felt that I was being punished for my hubris, that nothing would save me now.

It was a strange, disjointed, lonely time: lonely because I had nowhere to turn and no one to tell. The irony was that only Ella or Eric might have shared my grief with me and both were lost to me for ever. Reading of my old love in the papers, I grew disgusted with myself. That disgust has lasted all my life. What self-belief I ever had, already so badly battered by Eric's death, died that autumn and winter as Ella's trial progressed. I lost it for ever. And I was only twenty-five.

She denied all charges, to begin with.

In recognition of the horror of the offence, bail was denied and the defendant, I read in the papers, did not leave her cell except to appear in court. Ella saw no one but her barrister. No visitors came: no family; no friends. She wrote to me once: a long, rambling note of desperate defence and counter-accusation, but I hardly read it and I did not reply. I would be tempted by her no more, I decided; and when I didn't answer she did not write again.

On the witness stand she was unshakeable at first, and the increasing hysteria with which she denied the charge, despite the insurmountable evidence of her guilt, did nothing to endear her to judge or to jury. In her statement she said that she had not known of her father's death until told of it by the police.

Ella claimed to have received a note while she was dressing that asked her to meet her father secretly in his room at eight o'clock and to wait for him if he was late. Under cross-examination she said she had thought he wished to go over the notes for his speech, but she was unable to produce the note as evidence in her defence and was left saying weakly that someone must have taken it from her bedroom.

The evidence of the court psychiatrists came next. I discovered, to my half-surprise, that Ella had told a court-appointed doctor all about her obsession with Sarah; had told him, in fact, all that she had told me in that circular tower room at Seton long ago. Confronted by these expert witnesses, Ella's explanation of her earlier breakdown as a feigned and foolish attempt to break an awkward engagement – the explanation she had given me also in Prague – sounded hollow and insincere. I loathed myself for ever having believed it; for having been seduced by the disarming compliment of her crazy confidences.

At last her lawyers prevailed and persuaded her to admit her guilt and ask for clemency on the grounds of temporary insanity. The alternative was the hangman's noose and she did so. I went to the final day of her trial. I heard the verdict delivered and watched her being led from the court, back down to the cells from which she had come, to spend the rest of her life in a lunatic asylum.

In the crowded, overheated courtroom her face was pale, her eyes bloodshot; she was very thin. I realized, almost to my surprise, that she had aged in the years since I had seen her last. She was no longer the girl of my memory, or even of recent photographs, but a woman with a prematurely lined face and a broken walk.

Moving unsteadily between the hulking policemen who escorted her, she didn't look at anyone, didn't seem even to be aware of the long line of Harcourts in the front row of the visitors' gallery. Her friends, if she still had any, had not come; all London, save the gossip columnists, was eager to wash its hands of her, to rid itself of her taint.

As she reached the door to the cells, Ella stopped and

looked at the public gallery. Her eyes were dulled and red but they had something of their old magnetism. I watched them travel slowly over her family, as if locking their images in her brain for the last time. I saw Pamela look away from her. She took in the reporters, the public, Sarah sitting in the centre of her family, her brown hair falling over the lapels of her coat.

Finally her eyes met mine; and I knew that it was me she had looked for. I didn't look away; I couldn't. But I didn't move either. I didn't smile or mouth any words of endearment or pity. I looked at her and she looked at me.

Abruptly she turned and allowed herself to be led away.

29

In the stream of people leaving the court that day I saw Charles Stanhope, his face taut and unmoving. Standing still, lost in the crowd, he seemed to have no idea of what to do or where to go. I felt for him as journalists brushed past to swoop on Pamela.

Pushing past the cameras, past the clusters of reporters shivering under their umbrellas, I walked quickly down the steps. As the rain began in earnest I hurried down the street, eager for my violin, for the escape which only my practice and my playing could offer me now. As I walked I told myself that I was alone in the world; and that the sooner I accepted this fact the better it would be for me. In the cold wind I pulled my scarf tighter round my neck and moved briskly, trying not to cry.

She caught me at the steps to the Underground. I can see her by the rail now: long hair streaming over her shoulders; her face white; her shoulders shaking. She was shivering. Perhaps I returned her greeting. Perhaps I shook her hand or even kissed her. Perhaps ...

But I can't remember. That first meeting is hazy for me still, for it happened in the midst of so much else and Sarah never encouraged me to remember. Even later, years later, we did not speak much of our early days together and I came to take her silence as a sign of the tactful understanding for which I came to value her so much.

It was that reticence that first drew me to Sarah; that quiet sense she had that things were known and understood but not spoken. It was what I had once, mad with love for Ella, taken for awkwardness; but three hard years had taught me the shallowness of that judgement. I sensed, even that first afternoon, that I might safely rely on that reserve.

My wife, as I was to learn, preserved a comforting silence on all painful matters, a silence that at first relieved and then seduced me. Gradually she taught me to preserve that silence in my own mind also; to preserve and maintain it with diligence and care.

It is the oddest things that recur first: the fact, for example, that Sarah's hair smelled clean as she kissed my cheek in the rain; that we ate frogs' legs and steak at the lunch she insisted we have together.

'I don't want to be alone today,' she told me as she put her arms around me; and her look, so like Ella's that I almost cried, was too much for me to resist.

So I let myself be led through the crowd to a small French restaurant where obsequious waiters whispered in corners and Sarah told me of the trauma of the past two months, her large pale eyes seeking and holding mine, her hands mutely asking to be held as they shook and lit her cigarettes. I noticed with surprise that she was no longer the severe figure she had been in the park, nor the chilly young woman I had seen at Ella's engagement lunch. In some way Ella's trial seemed to have liberated her; and

284

I thought, as I watched, that through her tears she seemed warmer.

She was a woman of many wiles, my wife; a sophisticate whose effects were as calculated as they were concealed. I, a man, was no match for her. Certainly I succumbed to her with ease. Sitting at that corner table, as the rain streamed down on either side and the wine warmed us both, listening to her tell me of Pamela's grief and her own, I was lulled by her smooth, round voice, moved by the tears she could not hold back, thrilled, perhaps – as only now I can admit – by the way in which Ella seemed to have been returned to me.

Human attraction is a complex thing; complex and powerful in ways even a lifetime cannot teach. At my age, when I might be expected to have gained wisdom, I can only begin to make sense of its caprices. I begin to see that we are drawn to physical beauty in ways we cannot always know, and by subtle steps we cannot always trace. Recounting the events of my life, I have come to see the truth in the idea that romantic love is bound intimately with its physical expression; and to know that my love for Ella was inseparable from my fascination with her body and her face.

In the weeks that followed, missing her cousin in ways I could not admit, I came to rejoice in the sight of Sarah's slender form; in the touch of her smooth, pale skin and the feel of her lips on mine. I learned to watch as Sarah, rather than Ella, lit cigarettes with unconscious grace and looked at me from large blue eyes. I learned to find charm in her quiet, diffident humour, affection in the tranquil way she assumed control of my life. I found that her

presence offered me security and I was grateful to her
for her willingness to rescue me from myself. Our times
together were simple and calm: all that my life had not
been for so long. I sank into Sarah's serenity with unthinking relief, hoping that in it I might find peace, knowing
that in her strength I would find shelter. It was she who
lit the way to my forgetting; she who tempted me back to
the safety of the shallows.

And I was grateful.

In the attic that first afternoon she talked to me of
Ella. I can see her now leaning against the wall, smoking,
speaking softly in the rounded tones I would come to
know so well.

'You must have known how much she hated me,' was
how she began. Her voice was soft and unassuming.

'Yes,' I replied, wondering how much Sarah knew of
what had happened between Ella and me. 'Yes, I knew.'

'And she told you I hated her, too, no doubt.'

Watching her against the wall, absorbed by the curve
of her breasts and the delicate bones of her wrist as she
held her cigarette, I said nothing. Perhaps I hesitated, for
almost the last time, before betraying so old a confidence
of Ella's.

'It's all right,' said Sarah, sensing my reluctance and
taking my hand. 'You don't need to tell me.'

I looked at her: at the outline of her nose in profile; at
the curve of her nostrils as she blew out the smoke. Her
skin was very pale against the white wall.

'Poor Ella.'

'Yes,' I said.

I tremble with rage at the thought of Sarah's sympathy

that night. Remembering her face and the way her eyes looked sadly into mine has laid all uncertainties to rest; for I know suddenly, and beyond all doubt, that she deserved to die. My killing her was right. In some way it served a deeper, truer justice than the petty bureaucracy of earthly warders and jails would have done. God will judge her; only He is capable of it. And I, sitting here alone and old and unable to go back, can only wait for His judgement, too.

It is strange: how in twenty-four short hours my whole life should have disintegrated; how the foundations of fifty-seven years of married life should have given way in such a little time. Learning the truth has been destructive. In remembering I have undone Sarah's work; I have removed the cornerstones of her edifice. And although I have hardly rebuilt – for there is nothing and no one left to do so with – I have come to understand, at least, the power she had.

My wife's was a personality that never forgot an injury, that seldom forgave a foe, but that rewarded loyalty with a generosity which bound its recipient to her for ever. Those were Sarah's methods. As I listened to her words that night I was unaware – and I swear that this is true – by what gentle, subtle stages I was being brought under her influence.

'I tried so hard to help Ella,' her cousin said with shy frankness. 'I knew she needed help. You've no idea how much I wanted to prevent ... what happened at Seton. I ... I feel in some ways responsible.'

And I think her eyes even filled with tears.

I remember how Sarah cried; how prettily she did it.

I remember wiping her tears gently away that night.

'Thank you,' she said, and stroked my hair.

'I tried so hard to warn people,' she went on, slowly. 'But no one would listen. No one but Uncle Alex. He was the only one, apart from me perhaps, who recognized Ella's condition. He had seen it in his mother and sister before, you see.'

I nodded, sick at heart.

'He tried to help Ella; he was the one who sent her to all those doctors. I suppose that's why she . . .' Sarah's voice tailed off. 'But Ella wouldn't accept his help, or anybody else's for that matter. She was always stubborn. And when I tried she . . . But I can't tell you what she did; it was too awful.'

'Tell me,' I murmured; and some part of me really did want to know the worst.

'I couldn't.'

'Do.'

She looked at me, her blue eyes filling with tears again. 'Well, if you must know . . .'

'Tell me,' I said gently.

'She threatened to kill me also.'

There was a pause as Sarah waited for her words to take their full effect.

'Of course I never thought she'd do anything,' she went on when she saw that they had done so. 'If only I'd known she was serious . . . I might have been able to do something. I might have been able to—'

'It's not your fault,' I said softly, right on cue.

'But I feel responsible.'

'Well, you shouldn't.'

288

For a long while, in horrible sympathy, I held her close to me.

'No, you're right,' she said eventually. 'I shouldn't.'

With delicate grace Sarah dried her eyes.

'It was Ella, after all, who would never admit her problems. Doctor after doctor told her the same thing: that you have to acknowledge your illness before you can deal with it. That was what Ella refused to do. She was so stubborn. Short of having her committed, what could Alexander or Pamela or I or anyone else have done?'

'Nothing,' I murmured.

I tried not to hear Ella's voice in a crowded Prague café years before; I tried to drown the sound of her asking me, with wry humour, if I knew how stable you had to be to survive a session with a really respected psychiatrist.

'You did your best,' I said to Sarah; and as I did so I resolved to let go of the past. I wanted no part of it.

'Yes, I know,' she said slowly. 'I know I shouldn't blame myself. She was so jealous of me, James, so terribly jealous.'

'I know.'

'Did she tell you?'

'Yes.'

'And what did she say?'

'She talked about your grandmother mainly.'

'And about Seton?'

'Yes.'

'She never could bear the fact that I was better suited to it than she was. She used to hate me for being English, you know; English in a way she never could be.'

I said nothing.

'She hated me for understanding the island in a way

289

she never could. She spent her whole life trying to prove that she could care for it better than me. And the sad thing is she hardly knew it.'

'Really?'

'She only went there for birthdays and the occasional Christmas.'

I looked at Sarah and the tears had gone from her eyes.

'It was a terrible responsibility for her,' she went on, changing tone slightly. 'She was terrified of not rising to the task.'

'Poor Ella.'

And I remembered the warmth of her tears on my neck as she had cried in that tower room above the sea years ago.

'Yes, I was sorry for her also.' Sarah paused. 'Perhaps that's why she killed Uncle Alex so publicly. Perhaps she wanted to get caught. That's how I understand it, at least.'

'Why should she do that?'

'Well, she's saved herself from Seton.'

'What do you mean?'

But even as I spoke I heard from distant memory Ella's voice telling me that no Catholic could inherit, no divorcee, no convicted criminal.

'She can never have it now,' my love's cousin said softly.

'What will happen when your uncle dies? Now that Alexander's dead.'

Sarah's face looked up at mine, suitably grave; but there was something faintly uncomfortable about the intensity of its large blue eyes.

'It'll be mine,' she said slowly. She seemed almost to

caress her words as she spoke them. 'The island, the house, the title,' she said. 'All mine.'

'And Ella?'

'Ella will get nothing.'

She looked at me it was with sudden seriousness.

'May I ask you a question?'

'Of course.'

She said nothing for a moment, as though considering her words. And her voice, when it came, was all disarming gentleness.

'Does it frighten you to think that Ella was mad?'

'What makes you say that?'

'It does, doesn't it?' she went on slowly, ignoring my question.

I did not reply. But in the silence I could feel the tears coming; and blushing, embarrassed for some reason, I nodded as I blinked them away.

'Then we won't ever think of her again,' said Sarah quietly, and her tone, though gentle, was final. Gazing into Ella's face, though it had blue eyes now instead of green and a forehead higher than I remembered, I leaned down to kiss a mouth I hardly knew but which I had fallen in love with years ago.

'Never again,' I said.

And six months later we were married.

30

I find it curious to think that the story of my life seems so nearly told, though I have left more than fifty years of it untouched. Fifty-seven years, in fact; for that was the length of my marriage to Sarah. Talking of it now, it seems a long time; certainly it sounds like one.

My gratitude to Sarah persists, for old habits are hard to break. Ours, by any standards, was a contented marriage. Sarah was, in many ways, an excellent and loving wife. I will not find it hard to cry at her funeral. In fact, my tears will come easily. Standing at my place in the chapel next week, on the Harcourt dais above and at right angles to the congregation, under decaying banners and cob-webbed arches, I will cry. Publicly, appropriately, I will weep for my dead wife, for the mother of my child.

Privately I will cry for us all: for Ella and for Eric as well as for Sarah; for myself also. Perhaps particularly for myself, if now – at this late stage – I can admit to such selfishness. I am the last of us; it is I who must continue unjudged and alone.

The truth, which might have been expected to free me, to have given me a new lease of life, has in fact done neither. The telling of all this, the remembering, the undoing of all that Sarah taught me, has left me … tired, more than anything else. I have had a long day. Part of me is unwilling still to see through all Sarah did, to destroy the edifice she built so carefully over so long. Part of me hankers even now for the security of her deception.

But the foundations have been rocked. Old waters rise again. Having come so far I cannot turn back now; I cannot seek once more the safety of the shallows in which she kept me with such gentle authority. I must remember our marriage. I must see it with the harsh clarity of new knowledge. I cannot comfort myself any longer as Sarah once taught me so well to do.

But what is there to remember? The years, though long, seem curiously free of incident. Emotion frightened her and she taught me to be frightened of it also. She worked to eliminate feeling in both our lives, to reduce the power sensation has to unsettle and provoke. And she was masterful in ways I am only now beginning to suspect.

I remember my first journey here as possessor: the way the sun glinted on the weathercocks as we passed it on the train. I remember Sarah's whispered words of victory: 'There it is, our island.' And remembering that moment, I remember also how she loved this place and I know that she was not frightened of all feeling.

On the contrary, my wife was capable of an intense, possessive love. And what she felt for this house she later transferred to our child; for she was always feudal at heart.

Sarah needed her heir. When Adele was born I was in some way secretly relieved that she was so obviously a Farrell. Blanche's features, so truly preserved in both Sarah and Ella, found no expression in her great-granddaughter. I was pleased by that.

Adele is grown up now with children of her own. She will be here in the morning and her family will come with her. The house will be full of life again, life in the midst of death. I will have to tell her how her mother killed herself; how she shot herself, cleanly through the temple, in her private sitting room. I wonder what the children will be told; but I will leave that to their mother.

Perhaps Sarah's death will bring us closer, for Adele – and her husband, I suppose, whom I do not like – is all I have left in the world; and we were distanced by Sarah's obsessive love for us both, My wife's love was selfish. She wished to be everything to Adele and to me, and as a result we were not allowed to be much to each other. Certainly I, encouraged to be an approving yet distant father, became just that; for Sarah had trained me well by then and I did not think to question her.

It is odd how subject I was to my wife. I find it odd, for though by no means a natural leader I am hardly subservient. It is not in my nature. But subservience was not the keynote of my relationship with her. That was Sarah's trick. She had a way of masking her authority, of making one's quiescence to her wishes seem a case of voluntary self-will. She was similar – in that respect, if in no other – to Regina Boardman; and as Regina had done for the early part of my career, so Sarah did for my later emotional life. She assumed responsibility for it, and I was more than happy to grant it her.

Under Sarah's expert guidance I learned to forget, to block the avenues of recollection and recall. It was what I had tried to do in the years which followed Eric's death; but it was only under my wife's unspoken tutelage, and by her silent example, that I learned to bury my past with anything like success. Uncertain of how much she knew, I was wary of discussing her cousin with her; in fact I said almost nothing about Ella over fifty-seven years and Sarah did not broach the topic. She had meant what she said that first afternoon.

I took her lack of intrusion as illustration, were it needed, of her endless tact. I never analysed her calm beyond my admiration for it. I never thought – and this is where her genius lay – that Sarah's sovereign poise concealed any darker truth, or that there might be secrets beneath her serenity.

I spent the war working as an intelligence officer and Cyril died just before the Germans surrendered. When I was demobbed I came to Seton with Sarah, to the house that might have been Ella's and mine. My wife had weaved her spell on me by then, and after the war I was desperate for peace. I was not troubled by memories of my first visit here or of the girl who had brought me on it; for by then I had come to see my love for Sarah as a saner expression of an earlier, misguided feeling for her cousin. Sarah, by artful stages, had assumed all but a tiny portion of Ella's former place in my life. And though I never went to the tower room again, I did not often think of it either.

Married life changed me. Sarah's strength reshaped me in ways I am only beginning to understand. For the first time I have looked honestly at what really drove my music and can see how Sarah disliked and worked against it. My music was something apart from her, an outlet of feeling beyond her control. She would not have that. For Sarah my violin was a rival, its competition for my devotion keener than any a human being might have offered. She worked against it with determination and a cold deliberation that I realized, perhaps, but did not wish to admit; and to which I succumbed in the end.

Sarah and I did not fight. She was no obvious autocrat. The storms that rock most marriages had no place in ours. Instead, by subtle stages, she drew me into the world of this place and saw to it that Seton's rhythms became mine, that I adopted its code of ancient duty and privileged ritual as my own. The world outside – which Camilla once, in a moment of frustration on a visit, called the *real* world – became less real as a result; the pressures of recording schedules and concert commitments seemed distracting, inconsequential details. Gradually I gave them up.

But I gave up performance for another reason also. Under Sarah's influence I lost respect for my playing, you see; and with respect went all desire to perform. You cannot play without feeling and feeling is precisely what Sarah denied me. My belief in my music, for so long so central to my survival, evaporated with my marriage. It was proper that it should have done so. Having played as I once did, having played as I did the night of the Hibberdson, for example, when it seemed that Ella's love and all it meant were about to be returned, mediocrity was no destiny for me.

Alone tonight, with nothing for company but a yellowed bundle of ageing reviews, such arrogance jars sharply. Who am I to make such pronouncements? But I know that my recording of the Mendelssohn E Minor ranks with the best and that such an achievement carries with it a certain responsibility. I could only have moved forwards after that, not backwards; I could not have permitted myself the dubious luxury of poor but continued performance. I have always been a good judge of my own efforts. Such knowledge saved me years ago from spoiling the one unsullied achievement of my life.

It is a blessing that my music was immune to self-deception. I knew when my playing died; I knew and I mourned it but I did not fight it. When technical prowess was all I had to offer, I stopped. I am glad I did. Technical accomplishment can be learned and it must be practised; but real playing – like real living – requires feeling. And that is what I ceased to have.

My violin was not the only sacrifice I made for a place in Sarah's sanctuary. My friends, few but loyal in the years before my marriage, were given up also, and that I minded more. My wife did not share; certainly she would not share me. One by one, my friends – and even my family – gave way to the icy chill of her smile in welcome and accepted my invitations with less enthusiasm, inviting me instead to parties in London, parties that the duties of Seton life increasingly prevented me from attending.

Camilla Boardman, less enthusiastic at the news of my engagement than I had thought she would be, persevered the longest; she tried, I think, to make friends with Sarah in a way I might have told her was impossible. A frequent guest in our early years here, she was Adele's godmother, for my wife acquiesced easily in small things. There was something comforting about Camilla's consistency, about the way in which her curls stayed as tight, her breasts as prominent (though not perhaps quite as pert), her emphases as wonderfully pronounced in middle age, and after, as they had ever been in youth.

At her last dinner here – I see it so clearly now – she talked loudly of her clients, for success had made her more indiscreet than ever, and she tried to make Sarah accept tickets for one of her charity shows.

'Now Mummy's gone, *someone's* got to take on the mantle, I suppose,' she said, pressing the envelope into Sarah's hands. 'It's *so* tiring having to endure the after-party on one's own. You *must* help me.'

But such effusion only made my wife more severe; and under her cold stare even the energy of as lively a butterfly as Camilla found it difficult to endure. Gradually my friend found that the pressures of business kept her in London far more than she would like, though she continued to invite Sarah and me – and later Adele – to anything she did with the social perseverance that was her hallmark.

'I *know* Sarah doesn't like me,' she told me once, in her cups, perhaps, at one of the few parties – I think it was again her birthday – to which I had been able to go. 'And, truth to tell, I don't like *her* much either.' She took my hand with an affectionate squeeze. 'But that's *no* reason to see so much less of you, Jamie darling. Besides, there's my *divine* god-daughter to think of. And who could *possibly* teach her to survive in London but me?'

'Who indeed?'

But even as I spoke I knew – and Camilla did also, I think – that the days of friendship we had known before my marriage were over and irreclaimable. Sarah's price was loyalty: unquestioning and unbroken. And I needed her too much to break our unspoken compact.

I see in what deep seclusion I have spent the last fifty-seven years: isolated not only from my music and my friends, but from myself. It is that self which the truth has allowed me to reclaim. Painful though they have been to learn, the facts of yesterday have given me a freedom I did not know I had lost.

My wife was subtle in her mastery, subtle and instinctive. It is a tribute to her power that I heard of Ella's death unflinchingly, unmoved almost.

I was in the garden; it was winter. There were workmen to supervise. On a day of grey skies and squabbling gulls I stood by the cliffs, smelling the salt on the breeze, giving instructions, in the sting of the wind. I remember it all. I remember Sarah, her hair in a bun, her face drawn – for maybe, at the last, her conscience pricked her; who is to say? – walking down the steep path from the castle: a quiet, sombre figure; dark against the cloud.

'I must speak to my husband,' she said; and the workmen, mindful of their manners, raised their caps and disappeared, leaving us.

'Yes, darling?'

In even tones she said that Ella was dead, that she had hanged herself in her hospital room the night before. 'I had word from the warden this morning.'

It was almost lunchtime then.

'And he sent her personal things.'

There was silence. Perhaps I nodded.

Sarah stood, hesitating.

'And two letters,' she said at last. 'I've looked into mine.'

'I see.'

'It would only upset you to read yours, darling.'

Again I did not speak. My wife walked towards me, towards the cliff. I saw in her hand an envelope with my name on it in jagged brown letters.

'But of course the choice rests with you. Would you like to see it?'

I know now that this was her supreme moment. This was the apex of her daring.

I was silent.

'I don't think you should,' Sarah went on gently. 'She was raving when she died. It's no way to remember her.'

She looked at me and the request on my lips dissolved.

'There's only one thing to do with it.'

In front of me, a yard or two away, she tore the letter, with slow deliberation, into little pieces. We watched them scatter downwards into the sea.

'Let's go in,' she said, linking her arm with mine.

31

There's little more to be said now. All that remains are the loose ends, and those Sarah tied for me yesterday with chilling egotism. When my wife has been buried, and I have watched her coffin slide slowly into the vault in the presence of a weeping family, all will be over. There is something poignant in that. Also in the fact that when I, too, have died, we three will all lie together, united at last. Ella, Sarah and I, side by side in lead-lined coffins, decaying in harmony.

At my age such symmetries are pleasing.

By then there will be no outward signs of our tragedy; no hint – bar the reports of ageing, inaccurate newspapers – of the bonds that really bind us. That is as it should be. Adele must never know what her mother did and she never will. Better by far for her to think, however sadly, that Sarah ended her own life; that she was not, perhaps, as stable as she seemed. For the truth would destroy her and thus our tragedy – mine and Ella's and Sarah's – would spill into generations in which it has no place.

Pretence, for so long the key to Sarah's methods, must now become the key to mine.

I was expert yesterday. Certainly the police will not

suspect and I say that without smugness. The coroner will be helped towards his verdict of suicide by an array of evidence that quite exonerates me: for my wife's finger-prints are on the weapon that killed her; the gun itself was found in her hand, her grip already vice-like in rigor mortis. Earthly justice and its petty officers will have no hold over me. Having failed to find the truth so long ago, they will have no chance now. I shall go alone, unhindered, to the greater justice that is death.

But I anticipate myself again.

A day's events are all I have left to tell, a week's at most. As I go over them now I am struck by the curious irony of it, by the fact that I might never have found her out had Sarah been less considerate about the arrangements for my birthday party.

It was her thoughtfulness that exposed her in the end, and the little signs by which she intended me to know that she was thoughtful.

I have known for weeks that something was up. But I'm particular about parties. I don't like the tenants invited, and I don't like some of my wife's more fawningly agreeable friends. So it was only natural that I should have tried to consult a guest list, so that by hinting at least I could have made my wishes known. Sarah was always receptive in that way; it was a part of her genius to acquiesce easily over trifles.

I chose last Monday afternoon to search her desk because she was out, supervising the extension to the ticket office. And quite by chance I found the drawer she has kept it in all these years: a tiny drawer, hidden in the scrollwork, opened by a secret spring.

It was an odd key: heavy, large, but made of shining steel that seemed too modern for its design; cut for an old lock.

For a minute I turned it over in my hand, wondering why it was there and for which room it was intended. It seemed strange that my wife should have put it in so secret a drawer; strange also that, though ancient in design, the key itself could have been no more than a few decades old. It bore the stamp of a London shop, though all the house keys are cut – as they have been for generations – by a firm in Penzance.

Curious, though not very, I put the key in my jacket pocket, resolving to ask Sarah about it once my party was over and I could confess – in a moment of lightness – to having searched her desk for a guest list. For the best part of a week it remained there, for though the jacket is a favourite one of mine and I wear it frequently, I give little thought to what its pockets hold. They are always cluttered with things.

It was pure coincidence, really, which showed me the truth. But then life owes more to Chance than we often admit; and it has played too great a part in my story to go unacknowledged now. It was Chance that introduced me to Ella; Chance that brought Eric from Vaugirard on that dreadful night with my forgotten violin; Chance that made me choose this jacket as I changed yesterday for an afternoon of interviews and castle tours. Sarah and I are both particular about guides. Before someone is taken on to the permanent staff we ask them to give a tour, which one of us joins.

It was a young Miss Reid yesterday afternoon and

I joined her tour, preoccupied a little by other estate business but pleasant, as I always am, to the group of tourists that joined it too. Pleasant but detached: that is the way to be with them. Through the house we went: down the China Gallery; past the staircase door, now locked, which leads to Ella's tower room; through the King's Bedroom with its nineteenth-century four-poster and Chinese screens; finally to the Great Hall.

My mind elsewhere, for I had heard and overheard the tour a thousand times before, I paid little attention to the monologue being given; and it was only outside the Great Hall, where the group had gathered to examine the door, that I remembered my duties as observer and listened. The guide, correctly and confidently, was explaining the provenance of the lock, thought to be the oldest still in use in the county. It was only as she finished and we moved on again that I felt the key in my pocket. It was clanking against some change.

Remembering it, and remembering also – as Miss Reid was reminding me – that the lock of the Great Hall is the largest in the house, I took the key out and tried it in the door. Unthinking, unaware, completely unconscious of the significance of what I was doing, I took the key and tried it and was pleased when it fitted so easily. Yes, I was pleased; for I used to think it pleasant to have things neatly explained. With a heavy effort I ground the bolts slowly back.

It was only as I did so that something stirred and even then it was only the faintest creaking of memory. Ella's trial, like Eric's death, belonged to the years before my marriage. I had avoided thinking of them both with careful diligence. Not wanting to remember, I had tried to forget, and by and large I had succeeded.

But I have always had an eye for detail. Something stirred in me as I took that key from the lock yesterday: something deep within me shifted and refused to settle. As the tour proceeded I gradually fell back from it, troubled by something, grasping for a memory I could not quite define but which I knew was there. Slowly, obscurely, lines from a far-off court report recurred to me; and as I tried to make them out I heard a prosecution witness state his name and place of work, and explain how most keys are the same but he had remembered this one.

It was then that I knew.

It is difficult to describe the first impact of that knowing: the way things fell so suddenly, so alarmingly, into place. The quickness of it frightened me; the speed with which so much disintegrated: my past; my marriage; my unthinking, unquestioned trust in my wife.

I was not immediately angry. I was numb at first, and disbelieving. I could not understand. For the first few awful minutes that numbness shielded me. It allowed me to smile encouragingly at Miss Reid, to compose myself before returning to the corridor and nodding goodday to the guards at its far end. The rage came later, as I walked through the long corridors of the house that should have been Ella's and mine. Alone in the sanctuary of my book-lined room the tears came.

Sitting here now the events of yesterday afternoon seem an age away: further than Ella's trial or Eric's death. It seems years ago, though it was only yesterday that I sat crying at my desk amongst the scattered, silver-framed records of my and Sarah's joint past.

It was much later that I went to her sitting room, where I knew she would shortly join me for tea.

I was calmer by then. I was soothed by the thought that everything was in place, that I was properly equipped. I did not trust my nerve; even then, knowing the truth as I did, I knew also my wife's power to move me. I knew that I could not hope to endure a night of tearful explanation without losing all resolve. If I was to act, it should be soon. I steeled myself with the memory of Sarah's quiet voice telling me Ella had hanged herself in her cell and that it would only upset me to read her letter.

Waiting in her room, surrounded by her clutter, I looked at Sarah's things: her books and papers and the pictures scattered about. The photograph of Adele's christening, which stood on her desk. One of me, so conscientiously kept, taking my final bow on the night of the Hibberdson final. I could not believe that the woman to whom all these innocent things belonged, with whom I had shared so many years of my life, for whose security I had sacrificed so much, could possibly have done such a thing. Even then I hoped I was wrong; I was willing to be persuaded. With more self-possession she might have fooled me still, for we were not equals yet.

Waiting in her sitting room I heard the crash of the waves far below: relentless, eternal; relieved, at last, by the tap of her heels on the stone of the corridor; by the creaking of the hinges as she opened the door. Seeing me, she smiled, surprised perhaps by my promptness. I am not usually the first at meals.

32

I t was the look on Sarah's face that betrayed her. The way the colour drained from her cheeks and her hands shook. Not greatly, and she stopped them quickly, but enough for me to know. Now that all else is clear I find, beyond the knowledge of what she did, beyond the revulsion of it, a kind of ... incredulity. A fascination rather, for there was daring in her horror. A distorted courage.

She was raving by the end: moving restlessly about the room. There was something mesmerizing in her lucidity even then. She was relieved to have found an audience at last, I think; relieved and resolved to claim the recognition she had never thought to have. It was that resolve which shocked me most; the pride with which she told me – hoping for what? for praise? – of what she had done. I had expected denial, perhaps, or at least a show of remorse. I had hoped for both. But she was unrepentant to the end, and it never occurred to her that I would have the strength to punish her for what she had done.

My wife began on the offensive, but her attack did not last long.

'Is it customary for a husband to rifle through his wife's desk?'

When I did not reply she shrugged slightly, as if to

admit that indignation was a clumsy defence, unworthy of one such as she. Patting her hair, which was straying from its bun, she came to the sofa and sat down – with every semblance of normality, her composure quite regained – at the tea table. Sarah had a gift for smoothing things over; a gift she had used many times in fifty-seven years of married life. Perhaps she thought she could work her magic again yesterday. She began to pour, and all that betrayed her agitation was the unusual clatter of the cups and saucers as she arranged them.

'What is this?' I said quietly: said, not asked, for I knew.

'I beg your pardon, darling?'

My wife did not look up, pretending to busy herself with the tea things. I see her now, her dark hair streaked with grey, her body as slender and as graceful as it had ever been, bending over the teapot, uncertain. It was that uncertainty that betrayed her; that sudden vulnerability that was not calculated and which exposed the pretty, manipulating tears of the past. Her façade, so long maintained, was cracking. I had pierced it; I knew that even then. And her strength, once seemingly so endless, drained through the puncture before me.

Silently she poured the tea.

As it splashed into the cups I thought, inconsequentially, distractedly almost, that she had grown more beautiful with the years; that the fragile, misleading beauty she had shared with her cousin suited the lines and straight-backed deliberation of age. She was wearing a long, old-fashioned dress of teal blue, a shade darker than her eyes. Her arms seemed thin as they lifted the heavy pot.

'Tell me what this is,' I said again, but less insistently this time; for now that power was mine I found I had no idea how to wield it.

Having deferred to her for so long I was uneasy with this upsetting of the balance between us. Some part of me feared that at the last I would lack the resolve to punish her as she deserved. I was relieved that I had made my plans already. Even in my anger I pitied her. Sarah sensed from my voice that I did so and lifted her eyes to meet mine. She looked at me silently with great art. She was expert in her effects even then, and it took all my strength to resist her mute appeal.

But I said nothing; and in the silence she handed me my tea.

'It's the key to the Great Hall,' she said unexpectedly, a few moments later.

She spoke with quiet consideration, for Sarah knew my weaknesses. She knew I was helpless in the face of her vulnerability. So she sat, the bones of her neck showing taut and delicate above the neck of her dress, her hands in her lap, her head tilted a little.

'Tell me how you got it,' I said.

'I have nothing to hide, James.'

She spoke slowly, a picture of bruised innocence. And then her fragility – so artfully maintained – gave way for a moment to a flicker of pride. For a moment, no longer, she looked proud and unafraid. And although she looked away again, and wiped her eyes as though a tear had trickled from them, it was too late. And Sarah knew it. When she spoke again it was in quite a different tone.

'Have we really come to this?'

'Yes,' I said evenly, drawing strength from my repulsion.

From the sofa my wife continued to look at me, but her spell was broken and she knew it. For the first time in our married life I was immune to the power of her pale blue eyes. They had lost their hold over me. And from that moment I was free.

'In that case ask me any questions you like,' she said almost haughtily. 'I see that you have rifled through my desk and found something you should not have found.'

She rose and walked across the room to the windows. Looking out to sea, or perhaps at the rocks below, she turned her back on me with splendid indifference. All efforts at placation were over now. The lines were drawn. Her last effort at concealment was delivered with the air of a grave warning.

'You would do well to think carefully before asking me anything, because I will tell you the truth. And that is not always as palatable as one might wish it. If you take my advice you will return what you have taken from me and think no more about this.'

But I knew as I listened that I had done with Sarah's forgetting.

'Did you kill Alexander?' I asked quietly.

In the silence that followed I thought that Sarah had probably not expected anything so direct as this; that she would break now into confusion. But her answer, when it came, showed only irritation, annoyance at my rebellion.

'I see you have decided to ignore my warning,' was all she said, icily.

'Yes.' As I spoke I felt something close to exhilaration in my defiance.

'Then you must have my answer.'

'Yes.'

'And my answer, also, is "yes".'

For the first time since she had gone to the window my wife turned to face me. In silhouette against the setting sun I could hardly see her face. Her hair seemed ringed in fire.

'I killed him. And to anticipate your next question ... another "yes". It was no coincidence that Ella was found guilty for her father's murder.'

So it was done; it had been said. I knew the truth more certainly than I had known it hours before, standing in the Great Hall, watching the backs of retreating tourists in disbelief, thinking only of being alone. I knew; I had knowledge. But truth to tell, at that moment – at that precise moment – I hardly felt at all. I was drowning already, perhaps; drowning though I did not know it. It was Sarah's quiet calm – for so long my only lifeline – that was dragging me under. I see that now.

Then I could see nothing. Conscious only of a room beginning to blur as quick, hot, childish tears filled my eyes, I could only ask her why; why she had done it.

There was silence. My wife considered the question and chose her words with chilling succinctness.

'Ella had everything,' she said at last, slowly. 'And from me who had no one and nothing – she took the person I valued most.'

She had moved from the window as she spoke and walked now across the room: very upright in her blue dress, her hair falling in wisps from its neatly pinned bun. As she sat beside me on the sofa I smelled her clean, warm smell: of powder and rosewater. She no longer smoked. But it was her eyes, not her smell, that will stay with me; her eyes and her words. Remembering it now, I cannot bear to think of the hardness in them as she spoke.

I realized, as I listened to her speak, that the Sarah I had known – the Sarah I had loved, even – had never been anything more than an artful façade, designed to preserve my allegiance and prolong my subjection; for Ella's cousin never lost her fear of betrayal. In the glow of the setting sun she came alive. There was something terrible in the contrast between her beauty and her words; something chilling in the way she spoke to me of loss and jealousy and grief and revenge, with such barely containable pride.

'You hardly need me to enumerate Ella's blessings,' Sarah said; stiff still, almost childlike in her stiffness. She sounded like a little girl. 'She had a father who doted on her; freedom; friends; this house. The best of all worlds. And still she took him from me, from me who had no one.'

'Took whom from you?'

'Charlie Stanhope,' said Sarah quietly.

And I thought, for the first time in years, of Charlie Stanhope: tall, awkward, loyal.

'Charlie?'

'Yes.'

My wife looked at me. And she stood up again and crossed once more to the window, restless as she spoke. The sun was slipping over the horizon; the room was hazy now.

'Ella took him away. She took him away and she showed

me she could take him and then she discarded him. She didn't even want him.'

From far-off years I saw Ella by another window looking out on to the same sea and I heard her tell me, in tears, what she had done.

'The day she broke her engagement to him I made myself a promise,' Sarah continued. 'A promise to take all that she loved most from her. To show her what loss is *really* like.'

I said nothing; I could not.

'I think I have kept it.'

Still I could not speak.

'It was no easy task, I assure you. Even as you judge me, understand that.'

'I do.'

And I understood also, I think, that this was Sarah's moment, that now she could not help but claim her glory.

She had told no one. Over long years of enforced secrecy she had remained silent. But the urge to tell had always been there: the urge of a proud nature seeking acknow-ledgement. Yesterday afternoon, her guilt exposed, she was fearless and past caring. She spoke with a readiness made compelling by its lack of shame. Standing at the window, the sun behind her, she glowed with victory. I see her now, though it is dark in here and cold, and she is dead and nearly buried, with a clarity that will never fade.

She began boastfully, exulting coolly in the challenge of it.

'You have no idea how difficult it was: depriving Ella of all she had. It required daring, believe me. Courage.'

She paused, looking out to sea.

'But also a great deal of meticulous planning. That was where success lay and I realized it. Attention to detail is everything; and I think you will agree that although a risk was involved – which, frankly, that was unavoidable – I did all that I could to eliminate it.'

'But—'

'Don't interrupt. It was all such a long time ago. I haven't thought of it for years. Of course Uncle Cyril's party was a blessing. And the fact Ella and I looked so alike. Curiously enough, it was you who proved to me how things might work.'

She turned from the window.

'Me?' I asked hoarsely.

'Long ago. In Hyde Park. A summer's afternoon. Don't you remember? You thought I was Ella. And the way you behaved at the Hibberdson prize-giving just confirmed things. It was so obvious from your disappointment when we spoke that you'd made the same mistake. That gave me confidence.'

She smiled.

'And it made me sure that if *you* could be convinced, from a distance, others might be convinced also, particularly if all the details were right. So without asking Ella, which might have given everything away, I had to find out what she was wearing. That was the first step. And that was where that ridiculous friend of yours was so obliging.'

'Who?'

'Camilla Boardman.'

'I went to her for fittings, counting on her notorious indiscretion. Predictably, she told me on my second appointment, in the *greatest* confidence' – Sarah's eyes sparkled as she imitated my friend – 'that Ella would be wearing a man's dinner jacket. Admirable for my purposes, of course, because at once distinctive and easily obtained.'

'I see.'

'Camilla was hardly happy when I stopped going to her and wore a dress by someone else. But that couldn't be avoided. I needed to be noticeable in the crowd so that enough people would see me to cover my disappearance for five or six minutes. That, I thought, was all it would take if I planned properly, and in the event I was only away for seven. Not a long time in the middle of a party, particularly when you have made certain of speaking to a lot of people.'

'Which you did—'

'Of course.'

'Everything else was planned in advance.'

Sarah was talking quickly now, almost tripping over herself in her eagerness.

'I had the right clothes; a blonde wig of real hair, cut and parted like Ella's; two keys to the Great Hall, one of which was in Ella's pocket before the party even began.'

'The other of which is this?'

'Yes. Kept for a keepsake.'

'I see.'

'Foolish, I know, but an irresistible mistake.'

My tears had gone now. I watched my wife with sickening attention as she moved about the room with restless concentration. The tea things lay forgotten on the table, our cups untouched. She talked fluently and I listened, and thought with dread of what she had done and of what

315

I had yet to do. I am not, by nature, a violent man.

Sarah talked on, oblivious to me and my thoughts. She spoke with pride in an unthinking stream, her usual quiet manner completely overthrown.

'It was easy work to remove the original key from Cyril's desk for a night while I had duplicates made in London. And I wore the wig when I went into the shop to get them done because it's little touches like those that make all the difference. One learns that in detective thrillers. Although it was a slim chance, I thought that if I dressed and spoke like Ella, the man might recognize her from her pictures in the papers later on and come forward.'

'Which he did.'

'Yes.'

'And then there was the physical preparation.'

'Of what sort?'

'Well, Alexander was a big man and I'm not particularly strong, so I had to practise the lift to make sure I got it right. That was weeks before. On the night of the party itself there were endless things to do. So many details, and with such time constraints. Timing was everything.'

'What did you do?'

She stopped, disorientated for a moment; and I saw that I had interrupted her flow.

'While we were all dressing,' she began slowly again, as if trying to remember it all, 'I put a note under Ella's door, asking her to meet her father secretly in his room at eight and to wait for him if he wasn't there. I couldn't have her turning up anywhere while I was on the balcony with Uncle Xander, you see.'

My wife smiled at me.

'I got him to come up by saying that the speeches were going to be made from the Great Hall, not in the marquee, which he thought rather a good idea. He waited for me while I changed. I think he was quite amused by my clothes, in fact. I told him Ella and I were dressing identically as a joke.'

'Go on.'

'Well, so far so good, but the point of highest risk was still to come.'

My wife looked at me and I wondered suddenly how I could have lived with her for as long as I had done with so little idea of who she was.

'I couldn't be visible to everyone for too long,' she was saying. 'A moment was all right, but more than that was an unacceptable risk. On the balcony itself I stood behind him as much as I could, and I can't tell you how it unsettled me when old Lord Markham called out for Ella to show herself. I had to act quickly then.'

'So you pushed him.'

'Lifted, *then* pushed him. It was quite a complex manoeuvre. But it caught him so completely by surprise and the balustrade in any case is very low. It wasn't difficult in the end. I almost lost my nerve when he clung on like he did, so I had to loosen his grip as quickly as I could.'

'That was when people thought you were helping him.'

'Yes, though I can't imagine why. It was ludicrously clear what was happening. That was the point. As soon as he had fallen I went in and ran to my room, took off the wig and my clothes, put them in a bag and the bag into a drawer, where no one would think to look for it. I put on my dress and went downstairs. No more than seven minutes, the whole thing. Oh, and on my way I liberated the note I had given Ella, which fortunately was on the dressing table in her room. It was typed, of course, so no real harm would have come of anyone finding it. The police would have thought it was a fake she had written to herself. But I was glad to get it, nonetheless. And the next day, when all was quieter, I simply took the bag down to the cliffs, added a few stones, and threw it off. It was done.'

'But Ella accused you.'

I had been drawn in now, by Sarah's story in all its manic glibness. She pounced on my observation with delight.

'Of *course* she did. I had known that she would. Being innocent herself, she was the only person who could have known – really known – the truth.'

'But you had prepared for that already,' I said slowly; and I saw the sweep of Sarah's plan with sickening clarity.

'Clever, wasn't it?'

I said nothing.

'That little monograph in the *Athenaeum*. Then my book. Everything paved the way. When Ella was weak and stupid enough to use insanity as her excuse for ending with Charlie, the game was as good as won. You should never underestimate the power of the press. Those jurors' minds were made up before ever they walked into the courtroom, and she had lied to the family for so long that no one was really surprised by what she *seemed* to have done. Shocked, of course, but not surprised. She had been seeing psychiatrists for years by the time I killed Alexander. Her hysteria did her no favours at all. Even when she tried to tell the truth – and she told the court doctors all about me, for instance – she wasn't believed. She was trapped by her own lies.'

There was silence.

'I don't believe it,' I said hoarsely.

'Yes, you do.'

But it was still with something like disbelief that I looked at her, silhouetted against the fiery last rays of the sun, and it was then that I knew that I was the last thing she had taken from Ella.

'Losing Charlie taught me something,' said Sarah softly, calmer now. 'It taught me to observe, to understand people. For the first time in my life I learned to please.'

I looked at her steadily.

'Ella had always been the charming one. I had never been able to compete. But when she took Charlie I set myself to learn her ways. And I learned how easily men are swayed by women . . .'

In the silence I remembered our lunch on the day of Ella's conviction and the ease with which I had fallen.

Without looking at my wife again I left the room.

33

The corridor was gloomy in the dusk. I sat alone in the window seat at its furthest end, watching the last of the day-trippers catch the last of the boats, just as Ella and I, years ago, had caught the last of the boats on my first visit to this place. Perhaps I half expected Sarah to follow me, to offer some word or gesture of regret. At the last moment I almost lost my nerve. I nearly retreated in the hopes of being able to forgive.

But forgiveness was not asked, as I had known that it would not be. And listening to the breaking of the waves, I sat alone, staring at the door to my wife's sitting room, wondering what right I would have had to grant it in any case. None.

I sat, watching, as the corridor sank into darkness and filled with the first of the images I have since come to know so well again. Ella in the park, with her bitten nails: the beginning of it all. Her crumpled limbs in the sunshine of my attic. Her red eyes later, in that crowded courtroom, when she was lost to me and I thought her mad and would not smile at her.

I tried not to think of her body, years after, hanging from the ceiling of her room in an asylum; I tried not to think of how I had failed to mourn her.

Slowly I got up and in the dark I walked towards the crack of light under Sarah's door. She was reading when I opened it, or at least sitting with a book on her lap, calm and unseeing. She did not say anything. She did not seem even to notice me. She was lost in her own thoughts and did not look up as I opened the bureau drawer and put on the gloves and picked up the gun. It was only as I crossed the room towards her that I saw the signs of fear on her face. It was only at the last that she lost her sense of mastery, her certainty in her own success. She had no time to struggle.

I shot her above her right ear, at something close to point-blank range.

Very deliberately, calm almost, I stepped over her body and clasped the gun in her limp right hand. Then I left the room and returned to my own, where I washed and dressed with slow deliberation. Sarah had taught me the value of detail.

The house was dark as I let myself out; only the light in my wife's window burned. Guided by its glow I took the bag that held my clothes and gloves to the edge of the cliff, to the spot – for I am sentimental, even now – where Sarah had told me of Ella's death on that blustery afternoon years ago.

The wind was calm last night; there was a full moon. I am fairly sure I found the right place.

The Drowning People

READING GROUP NOTES

In Brief

It wasn't that James and Sarah Farrell had had an unhappy marriage. For more than fifty-seven years they'd rubbed along quite nicely. The police were happy in their assumption that Sarah had shot herself, and had no reason to suspect otherwise. Why would they think that James had shot her? But he had – and with good reason he felt.

He'd never have found out the truth but for Sarah's strong sense of wifely duty. James's birthday was coming up and Sarah, like a good wife, was organising a surprise party. But James didn't like the tenants invited to such things, so he decided to have a surreptitious look at the proposed guest list. This involved searching Sarah's desk when she wasn't around. And that was when he found it – and he knew immediately that she must be punished for the dreadful thing she had done so many years before . . .

James's world slowed. The coroner's inquest was set for the next day, and he knew that soon his life would be full of distractions. If he was going to order fully the events of his life he had to do it now. But it was hard to look back on his twenty-two-year-old self and understand him. That was when it had all started. James had been accepted by the Guildhall to further his study of the violin. He felt that a future in the world of music was a real possibility – but his parents were unimpressed. His father was all for merchant banking, and even his mother – who could usually be relied upon to side with James – had visions of impoverished musicians starving in garrets. James had gone for a run to get out of the house and away from the tense conversations with his parents.

It was in the park, as he ran, that he first saw Ella. In the early morning light she cut a dramatic figure. She had clearly been up all night, and James contrived to run past her three times before the desired result was achieved and she became aware of him. After an awkward exchange of pleasantries, Ella noticed James's socks. It was odd, how the smallest thing, like what socks you happened to put on, could alter the course of your life. James's socks were in the colours of his old college rowing club and Ella identified them as Oriel, Oxford. It seemed that she knew someone who had been there.

It transpired that Ella had been on the bench the whole night – wrestling with some inner turmoil that she wouldn't share with James. She did say her life seemed to be turning out rather differently than she'd expected. As she walked away, he learned her name was Ella Harcourt. He watched her walk away for a long time but she didn't turn.

James's life moved on, and his musical career developed. His star seemed in the ascendant and he began to be talked about as a real talent. He also became entangled in the life of Ella Harcourt as she struggled to extricate herself from the situation that had kept her up all night on that bench in the park. James developed a glowing reputation as he worked with his new friend and accompanist Eric de Vaugirard, although he was convinced that Ella's burning place in his heart produced the best playing he ever managed.

Ella's family was troubled, with a history of suicide and insanity hanging over them. Their island home in Cornwall had been the location of a terrible tragedy, and would be the setting for the awful events that would lead, so many years later, to the death of James's wife Sarah. For Sarah was Ella's cousin, and bore a striking likeness to her . . .

About the Author

Richard Mason was born in South Africa in 1978 to activist parents who settled in England when he was ten. Brought up and educated here, he wrote his first novel, *The Drowning People*, before going to Oxford. In the intervening years, Richard finished his degree, then set up an educational charity in memory of his sister Kay. Under Desmond Tutu's patronage, the Kay Mason Foundation provides scholarships to disadvantaged South African children, paying for them to attend some of the country's best schools.

For Discussion

* How does the opening of *The Drowning People* set the tone, do you think?

* 'Society is like an ocean.' What does Ella mean, and do you agree with her?

* To what extent is Ella's life controlled by the generations who went before her?

* What is the significance of Ella's smoking?

* 'You need to admit to yourself that you're drowning before you can be rescued and I couldn't do that.' How far is this the root of Ella's problems?

* 'When we sin we pay in a multitude of ways.' How is this theme examined in *The Drowning People*?

* Why has the author chosen to structure the novel in the way he has?

* How does the author treat the relationship
  between old James and young James?

* How far is *The Drowning People* a novel about
  consequences?

* 'But what I do know is that there are certain
  doors in one's mind which are better left closed.'
  True?

* Have a look at how the author treats the
  following themes – punishment/confession/
  blame.

* 'But then life owes more to Chance than we
  often admit.' Does it?

Suggested Further Reading

Rebecca by Daphne du Maurier

The Edwardians by Vita Sackville-West

Brideshead Revisited by Evelyn Waugh

The Secret History by Donna Tartt

Wuthering Heights by Emily Bronte

Turn over for an extract from
Richard Mason's new novel,

History of a Pleasure-Seeker

Published in hardback by
Weidenfeld & Nicolson in May 2011

The Gilded Curve

Amsterdam, 1907

~

The adventures of adolescence had taught Piet Barol that he was extremely attractive to most women and to many men. He was old enough to be pragmatic about this advantage, young enough to be immodest, and experienced enough to suspect that it might be decisive in this, as in other instances.

As he stepped from the Leiden train into the whirling hustle of the Central Station, several passers-by turned discreetly to look at him. He had an open face with amused blue eyes, a confident nose and thick black hair that curled around his ears. He was not much above middling height but he was muscular and well fashioned, with enormous gentle hands that made people wonder how it would feel to be caressed by them.

In one of these hands on this cold February morning was an envelope too large for the pockets of his English suit. It contained a copy of his degree certificate and a letter of recommendation from a professor who owed his father a favour. As he crossed the traffic on the Prins Hendrikkade, Piet reaffirmed the decision he had made immediately on receiving Jacobina Vermeulen-Sickerts' invitation to interview: that he would knock at the front door of the house, like an equal, and not at the servants' entrance.

The family lived on the grandest stretch of the grandest canal in Amsterdam. Piet knew from the newspapers that Maarten Vermeulen-Sickerts dispensed bread to the slum-dwellers and had been instrumental in bringing clean drinking water to the city's poorest districts. He knew he owned the country's most lavish hotel and a number of similar establishments across Europe. His daughters Constance and Louisa were familiar to Piet, too, as was their leadership of the 'smart young set' and the fact they were thought to alarm their mother, Jacobina. Taken together, the family had a reputation for being colourful and modern and very rich: three qualities Piet felt sure would ease the tedium of teaching a spoiled little boy.

He sauntered down the Blauwburgwal and crossed on to the Herengracht canal. On both sides of the water, houses built for the magnates of the seventeenth century surveyed the world with the serenity that comes from surviving the upheavals of three hundred years unscathed. They were tall but slender, with none of the grandiloquence of the rich men's houses his mother had shown him in Paris; and yet the fact that they *were* rich men's houses was indisputable, and subtly advertised by the profusion of their windows.

Piet turned left, and in his head he was walking away from Leiden, from Herman Barol's dark little house on the Pieterskerkhof and the life of the university clerk that went with it. For four years Piet had been assisting his father in sanctioning undergraduates who had omitted to pay their library fines, or cheated in their exams, or been caught in the company of women of ill repute. From these young men he had learned to affect the nonchalant swagger of the rich, but he had no intention of chasing them up for ever.

He put a freshly laundered handkerchief over his mouth and inhaled deeply. The canal stank with a virulence for which life in the comparative simplicity of a country town had not prepared him. Within the odour's complex depths lurked cheese rinds, rotting shoes, rats' urine, human defecations, oil, tar, and a consignment of industrial chemicals that had leaked from a ship in the harbour. The combined effect was choking, but the people who passed him paid no attention to it. He was sure that he, too, would get used to it in time. He continued more briskly. As the house numbers increased, so did the emphasis of the architecture's whispered message: that people of wealth and distinction lived here. The narrower dwellings, two or three windows across, that dominated the earlier stretches of the canal grew rarer. As he crossed the Nieuwe Spiegelstraat, they all but disappeared. Soon the narrowest house was four windows wide. Which one was theirs? He looked at his watch. He was still twenty minutes early. To avoid being seen he crossed the canal and continued his walk up the far side.

The appearance of a house with six windows on its ground floor signalled a further elevation of status and the beginning of the Gilded Curve. He felt a pricking of panic. He had not always been a diligent student and there was little sincerity in the recommendation his professor had given him, a fact that would reveal itself to a sensitive reader. Piet was far cleverer than many who had more to show for their cleverness, but this was hardly an argument he could advance. He did speak perfect French – his mother Nina had been a Parisienne – and his English and German were adequate; but his piano playing was only competent, and the advertisement had stressed Egbert Vermeulen-Sickerts' musical genius and the desirability of a tutor who could match and extend it.

He sat down on a wrought-iron bench between two trees and collected himself. He did not have the best credentials but was wise enough to understand – even at twenty-four – that symbols on paper are not the only grounds on which people make up their minds. A tutor, after all, was more than a servant. The successful candidate would dine with the family, not wait on them; and though the Vermeulen-Sickerts had not specified this requirement, he was sure that people so *à la mode* would prize amusing conversation. This he was very good at making, having learned the arts of charm at his mother's knee.

He took out Jacobina's letter and began to sketch on the back of the envelope the austere, imposing façade of a house opposite him. When he had captured the tricky perspective of water and bricks, he felt calmer and more optimistic. He stood up and walked on; and as the canal curved again he saw the house at number 605.

The possibility that he might soon sleep in one of the rooms on its upper storeys made Piet Barol shiver beneath his cashmere coat with its velvet collar, bought second hand from a well-off student with urgent debts. The house was five windows wide and five storeys high, with hundreds of panes of glass that glittered with reflections of canal and sky. The front door was on the first floor, achieved by a handsome double staircase of grey stone, and the façade of small rectangular bricks was relieved of sternness by pretty white stucco scrolls. Despite its size there was nothing showy about it, nothing over-ornamented or insecure.

Piet approved wholeheartedly.

He was crossing the bridge towards it when a man in his late twenties emerged from the servants' entrance beneath the staircase. He was not well dressed and his suit, which had been bought in slimmer days, was too obviously 'Sunday best.' He looked a little like a young man who had pursued Piet doggedly the summer before: dark and slouched, with a drooping chin and an oily nose. Piet had not let that chap have his way, and he did not intend to let this one prevail either. As his competitor made off in the direction of the station, Piet saw he was slightly out of breath by the time he had gone a hundred yards. The spectacle cheered him.

He straightened his tie. As he prepared to mount the steps to the front door, the servants' door opened and a woman with a severe chin said: 'Mr Barol? We are expecting you. If you'd be so good as to step inside.'

The stink of the canals vanished at once and was replaced by the sweetness of an apple cake browning to perfection, which underscored the scents of polish and clean hair and the fragrance of a large bucket of orange roses that stood on a table by the butler's pantry. 'I am Mrs de Leeuw, the housekeeper. Please follow me.' The lady led him into a large kitchen devoted to quiet, choreographed efficiency. An enormous ice box stood in one corner, its oak door lined with white glass and held open by a handsome blond fellow of about Piet's age, to facilitate the entry of a polished jelly mould. 'Careful, Hilde!' Piet's guide spoke without tenderness. 'May I take your coat, Mr Barol? Mr Blok will show you upstairs.'

Mr Blok now appeared at the door in a dark tailcoat: a waxy man in his late fifties with a scrupulously shaven chin. Something in his glance suggested an awareness of Piet's charms – which Piet thought problematic, since he felt no answering inclination. On the rare occasions Piet Barol went with men, he preferred them athletic and close to his own age. The butler was neither. 'This way, Mr Barol,' he said.

Mr Blok left the room and went up a narrow staircase to the entrance hall. Piet did not wish to appear provincial, and his face gave no sign of the impression the entrance hall made. Panels with quotations from the Romantic painters surmounted a wainscot of marble shot with pink and grey. On a half-moon table was a silver bowl filled with visiting cards. Mr Blok turned right beneath a gilt lantern and led Piet towards an open door at the head of the passage, through which tall French windows were visible.

As he passed the dining room Piet glimpsed olive-green-and-gold wallpaper and a table set for five – a family dinner, which meant that Constance and Louisa would be dining in. He knew from the newspapers that they did so rarely and read this, quite correctly, as a sign of their interest in their brother's new tutor.

He longed to meet them and be their friend.

The staircase to the upper floors was carpeted in soft red wool and overlooked by a trio of statues beneath a glass dome. Mr Blok led Piet past it and ushered him into the room with the French windows, which was nothing but a tiny octagon, constructed of glass and stone and furnished with two sofas of extreme rigidity. It told him plainly that the splendours of the drawing room were reserved for men better and grander than he; and because Piet Barol had a strong sense of his innate value, he took exception to this judgement and resolved to conquer the person in whose gift the freedom of the house lay.

The butler retreated. Piet placed the envelope containing his references on a table so slender it barely bore this burden, and settled to wait. Above him, a chandelier of five gilt griffins observed him disdainfully, as if each of its winged lions could see into his soul and disapproved of what they found there. Mrs Vermeulen-Sickerts' first name conjured images of hairy patriarchs and he hoped she wouldn't be too ugly. It was harder to flirt with an ugly woman.

He was pleasantly surprised when a light step sounded on the tiles and Jacobina appeared. Although approaching forty-six, the legacy of an athletic youth was evident in her neat waist and quick, fashionable movements. She was wearing a day dress of apple-green wool with a high lace collar and a small train: an impractical garment in many respects, but Jacobina Vermeulen-Sickerts had no pressing need to be practical. 'Good afternoon, Mr Barol.' She extended a hand and shook his firmly. 'Please don't get up.' But Piet was already standing, and he smiled shyly as Jacobina sank onto one of the sofas and said: 'Do excuse the uncomfortable furniture. My husband is very fond of *Louis Quinze* and the fabric is too delicate to have the seats resprung. Would you drink some tea with me?'

'Gladly.'

Jacobina ordered refreshments on an extravagantly ornamental telephone. 'And now, may I see your references?'

It was as well to get these out of the way at the beginning. As Piet handed them to her, his eye caught Jacobina's and he understood that he had made a favourable first impression. Indeed Piet's smell, which was the smell of a gentleman, and his clothes, which were a gentleman's clothes, reassured Jacobina in ways of which she was not at all conscious. She glanced at the pages in her hand, saw that Piet had the university degree the position required, and said, 'Tell me about your family. Your father is a clerk in the university at Leiden, I believe?'

'He is, ma'am.' Herman Barol had a respectable position in the administration of Holland's oldest university. Piet conveyed this without mentioning that such posts are generally held by petty autocrats unable to achieve influence elsewhere.

'And your mother?'

'She died when I was seventeen. She was a singing teacher.'

'I'm so sorry. Do you sing?'

'I do, ma'am.'

'Excellent. So does my husband.'

It was, in fact, thanks to his mother the singing teacher that Piet was able to read in Jacobina Vermeulen-Sickerts the subtle traces of an interest that was not wholly professional, long before she became aware of it herself. Since her son could walk, Nina Barol had spoken to Piet as though he were a cultivated and delightful intimate of her own age. She had discussed the personal situations of her students with a candour that would have horrified them and later, as a boy accompanist, Piet had had ample opportunity to look for evidence of what his mother had told him. He was now unusually sensitive to indications of private emotion. As he answered Jacobina's questions, he absorbed a wealth of detail about the woman who might be persuaded to change his life. She had a strong sense of propriety, that was clear. But it did not seem to be stronger in her than in other respectable women Piet knew, who had happily abandoned it for him. 'And what of Master Egbert?' he said.

Tea was brought in and Jacobina poured. 'My son is extremely intelligent, but sometimes intelligence of that sort can be a burden. He has always had a vivid imagination. Indeed, I have encouraged it. But perhaps I have been overly lenient with him. My husband believes he needs sterner treatment, though I am looking for a tutor who can combine authority with gentleness.'

Jacobina had made this speech to each of the sixteen people she had so far interviewed; but as she spoke the word *gentleness* to Piet Barol her eyes flicked to his hands, as if they were the perfect expression of what she sought. 'Egbert completes his schoolwork very well. He speaks English and German and French and dedicates himself to the practice of his music with commendable discipline. Indeed, he has long outgrown any music teacher I have been able to find. But—'

'He is shy, perhaps?'

'Not unusually so, Mr Barol. If you met him you would not think anything amiss. The problem is— He will not leave the house.'

'Will not?'

'Perhaps cannot. We have had to obtain a special permit to educate him at home. He last went into the garden a year and a half ago, but has refused absolutely to go into the street since he was eight years old. We tried to coax him at first and then to force him; but I am afraid the tantrums were so affecting I put a stop to my husband's efforts. Perhaps that was wrong, but it is very hard for a mother to see her child so afraid and do nothing.'

'Of course.'

'So there you have it. We need a tutor who is capable of— of finding Egbert, wherever he has lost himself, and bringing him back to us.'

It was the fourth time that day, and the twelfth that week, that Jacobina had been obliged to debase herself before a stranger with this frank rendition of her maternal failings. It was not an experience she enjoyed. But Piet's expression was one of such thoughtful concern, and contrasted so well with the embarrassment of the other candidates, that she was inspired to further revelation. 'I cosseted him too much when he was little, Mr Barol. I should have made him be braver, but I did not and now he lacks the courage even to venture on to the steps outside. Have you experience of difficult children?'

Piet had no experience of any children whatsoever. 'Life in a university town acquaints one with many brilliant eccentrics,' he said judiciously.

Jacobina smiled, to disguise the fact that she might also have burst into tears. She loved each of her children fiercely, but Egbert most fiercely of all because he had greatest need of her. She took a sip of tea. 'It is essential that any tutor is able to communicate with him musically. He is devoted to music.'

'I was répétiteur for my mother and her students from the time I was nine.'

'Excellent. Perhaps you would play for me now?'

'With pleasure.'

Jacobina rose. 'Let me take you to the schoolroom. Egbert's sisters, my daughters Constance and Louisa, have banished him to the house next door. Fortunately it belongs to my aunt, who now spends most of the year at Baden-Baden. We have had a door specially constructed so that Egbert needn't use the street. I suppose it was the wrong thing to do, but he can be— obsessive, at times, about his playing, and Louisa in particular has a sensitive ear. In my aunt's drawing room he can make as much noise as he likes without disturbing anyone.' She led Piet into the dining room and he saw that on one side of the fireplace the shape of a door was cleverly hidden in the wallpaper. Jacobina opened it to reveal an entrance hall tiled in white and black and rather smaller than the one at Herengracht 605.

He held it for her as she passed through.

Jacobina Vermeulen-Sickerts had taken many men to her aunt's house to hear them play the heavy Bösendorfer that was Egbert's closest confidant. She had taken them alone and never felt at all awkward; but when the secret door clicked behind the handsome Piet Barol she felt suddenly that she was doing something improper. She crossed the hall and opened the drawing-room door. 'Egbert's in bed today. He catches colds easily – that's why we keep it so hot in here.' It was, indeed, very hot. Heavy gilt radiators burbled beneath windows hung with midnight-blue velvet. 'Do remove your jacket if you're too warm.'

Piet did so and sat at the piano, wondering what he should play. He was no virtuoso, and the possibility that an oily-nosed overachiever would snatch this chance from him made his stomach clench. He opened the instrument, waiting for inspiration, and the memory that came to him was of his mother telling him that the only key for love is E flat major. He glanced at Jacobina. She did not look like a woman whose sensual appetites were well catered for, and the room was certainly the temperature for tenderness.

What would she permit?

The idea of finding out reignited old temptations, for this was not the first flirtation Piet Barol had conducted from a piano stool. He hesitated, weighing the dangers. But already the adrenalin of risk was pumping through him and would not be disobeyed. Mrs Vermeulen-Sickerts wanted a tutor with authority and gentleness. He should play her something slow and sentimental and not too difficult, preferably in E flat major. But what? Jacobina moved past the piano and turned to face him, just as his mother's students had done. As she passed he caught her scent – of rosewater and musk and hand-laundered undergarments – and it came to him that the second nocturne of Chopin fulfilled all his criteria.

Nina Barol's edition marked this piece *espressivo dolce* – to be played sweetly and expressively – and Piet began to play it softly from memory, at a slow *andante*. The piano was first rate and recently tuned, and it lent his performance a finesse he did not often achieve on his mother's upright.

He was correct: it was many years since anyone had touched Mrs Vermeulen-Sickerts with the aim of giving her pleasure. Jacobina had almost ceased to mourn this sad fact, but in the presence of such a beautiful young man it struck her forcefully. She stepped closer, to see him better. Piet's face was manly but graceful, with succulent red lips that prompted thoughts of her husband's dry little kisses.

Jacobina looked away.

Piet tripped in a run of semiquavers but the piano forgave him and hid all trace of the jarring note in folds of rich harmony. As he played he sensed the atmosphere responding to the music's enchantments. Indeed Jacobina's nostalgia for the lost opportunities of her youth increased with every note. Watching Piet, she was not unaware of the muscles of his shoulders nor of the way his perfectly laundered shirt clung to his back as he leaned over the keys. It was a long time since she had heard any music but her son's relentless exercises, and the gentleness with which Piet's huge fingers elicited these hushed sounds from the piano was bewitching.

It was a secret she no longer shared with anyone, but Jacobina Vermeulen-Sickerts was very different from the woman her family and closest friends thought they knew. In her deepest self she was more like Louisa than Constance and had spent her girlhood imagining a life not at all like the one she now enjoyed. A change in her breathing made Piet's pulse quicken. He looked up, caught her watching him, and held her gaze until she looked away. He was used to enlivening the lessons of Nina Barol's prettiest pupils in this fashion and since his seventeenth birthday had grown steadily bolder – though he had never yet employed his stratagems on a lady of rank, or in a situation so laden with potential disaster.

~

Piet played the last bars of the nocturne very delicately and the piano's ringing made the air between them tingle. He did not silence it by lifting his foot from the pedal. When Jacobina said, 'Play me something more modern, Mr Barol,' he was ready for her. His choice was the entr'acte to the third act of *Carmen*, also in E flat major, which had been useful in similar situations before. Its pure, beguiling melody rose from the embers of the nocturne and the rumbling arpeggios of the bass line showed his hands to advantage. As he played, he thought of the smugglers who appear on stage at its close, whispering that fortune awaits if only they will tread carefully. This was exactly how he felt as he drenched his quarry in sweet, permissive magic.

Jacobina Vermeulen-Sickerts' social position protected her from the lascivious stares of men. The possibility that she had encountered one now left her flustered, but not disagreeably so. She looked away, deciding that she had been mistaken; but when her eyes flicked again to Piet Barol's she found that his were ready to meet them, and this was joltingly erotic. Jacobina rode twice a week but otherwise took very little exercise. She had recently begun to worry that this showed, and to feel rather let down by her once sylph-like body. To receive an admiring glance from a young man was exhilarating.

She stared out of the window as Piet finished playing.

'What a touch, Mr Barol.' She spoke the compliment

to the street outside and when she turned to face Piet he was smiling at her, and did not stop.

Piet Barol's smile often got him what he wanted. On this occasion it was full of charming hopefulness, and under its influence Jacobina made a decision. 'You are welcome to take your meals with us, or dine out as you wish. You will find us an easy-going family. My daughters delight everyone they meet. And Egbert …' But she left this sentence unfinished. 'Mrs de Leeuw will show you to your room.'

'I will give of my best, Mevrouw.'

'I am sure my husband will wish to see you before dinner. I'll have some shirts and socks of his sent up. We can arrange for your bags to come tomorrow.'

'Thank you, Mrs Vermeulen-Sickerts.'

'*Je vous en prie.*'

Naomi de Leeuw did not approve of tutors as a breed, nor of their ill-defined place in the household hierarchy – neither servant, nor guest. One or two of Piet's predecessors had used this blurred distinction to their advantage and she had no intention of allowing this cocky young man to do the same.

'You will share the attic floor and a bathroom with Mr Blok and Mr Loubat,' she said stiffly as she led him to his room. 'I thank you not to visit the basement, where the maids' rooms are, after five p.m. We have high standards of cleanliness. You are permitted to take two baths a week and will have shaving water every day. Shirts are to be worn three times at a maximum. Hilde Wilken will do your laundry.' She opened a door and ushered Piet into a small, comfortably furnished bedroom with a window that looked over the garden. 'There is no smoking in the house, and no drinking unless you are offered refreshment by a member of the family. The bathroom is two doors along. You are required to attend church on Sunday mornings, but may spend Sunday afternoons at your leisure. Do you have any questions, Mr Barol?'

'I don't think so, Mrs de Leeuw.'

'Very well. I do hope you'll be comfortable here.'

When she had gone, Piet sat on his bed and loosened his tie. He was half alarmed by the suddenness of the change he had wrought in his fortunes. Gone at a stroke was the tiny alcove, separated by a curtain from his father's room, in which he had slept since leaving his cradle. Gone was the outside toilet, the rusting plumbing, the vile university food to which he and Herman had become accustomed since his mother's death. The ambitions he had nursed so privately – of travel and comfort and elegance; of escaping for ever the straitened gentility of his youth – were plausible now, seized from the realm of fantasy by his own determination to act on his instincts. To have a room of his own at last! To be able to bathe without laying a fire and boiling the water; to shit without shivering in the little wooden hut beside the back door! He started to laugh as the nervous energy of the afternoon drained from him. He felt light and triumphant, capable of anything.

There was a knock at the door. It was Didier Loubat, the footman, with a pile of shirts and collars and a little box of studs. He was taller than Piet and blond, with a strong jaw and sharp sea-green eyes. 'The old man wants to see you in forty-five minutes. His office is at the front of the house, on the first floor. D'you want me to come and get you, or will you find it on your own?'

'I'll find it.'

'Good man. The whole family's gathering to vet you at dinner. *Bonne chance.*' Didier's friendliness was a relief after Mrs De Leeuw's chilly formality. 'My room's next door if you need anything, and the bathroom's down the hall. A little tip: don't let Blok see you in a towel. He's a terrible old lecher.'

'I thought he might be.'

Didier grinned. 'You need your wits about you in this house, but you'll get used to it. There's a towel in the cupboard.'

The towel in the cupboard was of vast size and fresh-smelling fluffiness. Piet took it with him to the bathroom, which was tiled in white porcelain and deliciously clean. In the corner was an eight-foot bath, and when he turned the tap the suddenness with which boiling water gushed from it took Piet by surprise and scalded his hand. The fact that such quantities of hot water could be obtained so effortlessly was miraculous to him. He filled the tub very full and undressed and got in, and stretched back at full length, baptising himself in his new life. He would cable to his father tomorrow; but Herman had never shown much concern for his whereabouts and Piet doubted that his absence tonight would alarm him. He lay in the hot water, feeling very pleased with himself, but as it cooled so did his triumph, and the complexities of his new situation stole in and replaced it.

Piet had sufficient experience of female unpredictability to know the risks of forming a liaison with his new employer's wife. As he washed, he decided that he would never again allude to the unspoken communications of the afternoon. Emigration to America and the making of a considerable fortune were the next stages of his plan. He would take no chances until he had saved the money to fund them. He submerged himself again and it came to him that his efforts with Mrs Vermeulen-Sickerts had left him in a powerful negotiating position with regard to her husband. The salary advertised was sixty guilders a month. It was clear from the establishment at Herengracht 605 that the man who owned it could afford considerably more. Piet got out of the bath and began to dry himself. Unless he was very much mistaken, Jacobina would make sure he was employed whatever the salary. His experience of wealthy undergraduates had shown him that many rich men prefer to pay more, rather than less, on the grounds that quality is closely correlated to expense.

He dressed slowly and carefully, and by the time he was finished he had decided to add a further challenge to the many he had risen to that day.

He had decided to ask for more.